Friend of Mankind

Friend of Mankind
and Other Stories

by Julian Mazor

PAUL DRY BOOKS

Philadelphia

2004

First Paul Dry Books Edition, 2004

Paul Dry Books, Inc.
Philadelphia, Pennsylvania
www.pauldrybooks.com

Text type: Joanna
Display type: Koch Antiqua Family
Designed by Adrianne Onderdonk Dudden

1 3 5 7 9 8 6 4 2
Printed in the United States of America

"Gray Skies" was previously published in the New Yorker;
"The Munster Final" was previously published in Leopard II;
"The Lone Star Kid" and "Storm" were previously published in Shenandoah;
"Skylark" was previously published in Shenandoah and Prize Stories of 1971:
The O'Henry Awards; "The Lost Cause" was previously published in Leopard IV.

The author offers his special thanks and appreciation to his agent, Sandra Levy.

Library of Congress Cataloging-in-Publication Data
Mazor, Julian, 1929-
Friend of mankind and other stories /
by Julian Mazor.— 1st Paul Dry Books ed.
p. cm.
ISBN 1-58988-016-1 (hardcover : alk. paper)
1. United States—Social life and customs—Fiction. I. Title.

PS3563.A9855F75 2004
813'.54—dc22
2003026634

ISBN 1-58988-016-1

In memory of my parents

For my sons, William and John

For Elizabeth

In memory of Joseph Guilfoyle, Jr.
1947–2004

Contents

Harry in Ireland

Gray Skies

"**O**h, the living hell with it!" I said, slumped over the rail, looking into the Irish Sea.

Wanda's face came pink out of the mist. She said, "Yes, and don't start telling me about the girl from Texas, Harry. It's too boring for words. Don't tell me about how great she was and how you should have married her. God, she sounds stupid. Like some awful, pathetic little hick. You really deserved one another."

She was talking about a girl from El Paso whom I knew when I was stationed at Fort Bliss, in the late fifties. She was a wonderful girl, sensitive and kind and very pretty, with brown hair and green eyes that really had a light in them. I would have married her, but I felt we were from two different worlds, and I was only twenty-one and didn't feel I'd seen enough of life. Years after I got out of the Army, I got involved with Wanda, and we were married in the spring of the year. We were from the same world, and almost from the start we didn't get along. As I often said, she made me feel a certain way—not too well.

It was a gray Sunday morning. The ferry sailed slowly into Cork, and the city looked altogether beautiful and mysterious— so calm and quiet and a little poor. Wanda, a red shawl around her head, smoked a Player's cigarette. She had a hurt expression on her face. Our son, Edward, wore a gray coat with a hood that was pulled up over his head. He was two and a half years old. The three of us huddled together on the deck. It was damp and cold.

Later, in our blue Volkswagen, a used car we had bought in London, we traveled along the southern coast through Kinsale and Skibbereen, and then moved north through Bantry and Glengariff. On the same day, we went around the Ring of Kerry, and we stayed the night in Killarney. On the following day, we saw some of the Dingle Peninsula and reached the River Shannon. We spent the night in a Limerick hotel. It inspired Wanda to recite a little jingle of her girlhood in Providence. "Did you know this one, Harry?" she asked. "'The Irish are so dirty/They never wash their clothes/There are no Chinese laundries/Where the River Shannon flows.'"

"No, Wanda, I hadn't heard that one," I said.

During the early time in Ireland, we got along fairly well. There were, of course, the pained expressions, the sarcasm, and the withholding of support. Perhaps we were fundamentally incompatible. For example, I liked to take life slowly, and she preferred it quick and frantic. She was always telling me to hurry up, and my favorite advice to her was "Take it easy, Wanda. Relax, if you can."

It was in the west of Ireland, in County Galway, that we finally settled down. We lived in a whitewashed cottage with a sloping corrugated roof and modern conveniences—good plumbing, electricity, and a stove that worked on a cylinder of gas. Through our bedroom window we could see pastureland and gentle hills and, far off on a rise, the tower and battlement of a ruined castle. Pink and blue flowers grew along the base of the cottage walls. It was quite a tranquil setting, and different from anything I had ever known. When we were under clouds, there were nights of pitch-black darkness, with no distraction of city lights or signs of habitation. On some evenings, we could see the moon drifting through the mist as we stood outside our cottage door, or there might be the rich, deep-blue surprise of a starry night. And there was this great quiet, with only the pastoral sounds and the wind and rain and our own voices to break the silence. Once in a while, you could hear a motorcar—usually an old black Austin—moving slowly in the distance, or our own car starting out on a trip to Galway for groceries or up to the lay-by on the Limerick road to dispose of our garbage.

We burned turf in our grate to take the chill off in the morning and at night. It was a simple country life; we took little trips and got to know the Irish. If Wanda and I had got along, it would have been a Celtic idyll; but even with things as they were—and they got worse—it was for me quite wonderful.

We had said "so long" to the U.S.A., had bade farewell to the discourtesy and peevishness, the want of dignity, the lack of kindness, the absence of brotherhood, to the nervous hysteria and mental unbalance, to the hostility, to the growing strain of insanity and the war—in short, to the obscenity of American life in our time.

Still, it was not that easy to say goodbye. I had a lot of friends back there, and there were our families to consider. We were rather fond of our own, though not of each other's. Our time abroad was made possible by a bequest I'd received from an aunt in Philadelphia.

We went over in the winter of 1969 and lived in London for a while before going to Ireland, in the early spring. I was thirty-four, not at my physical peak.

A year passed.

"I had another Yank come in here a few days ago, and I still have not got over it," the gas-station man said, taking out the gas-pump nozzle and placing the cap on my tank. He was a thin man in his fifties, with blue, watery eyes and a ruddy complexion. I offered him several pound notes, but he did not seem interested in concluding the sale.

There was a light, misty rain. I looked toward the station office and saw Wanda standing inside. She had just lit a cigarette and was trying to compose herself. We'd had a terrible argument before we'd pulled in for gas. When I stopped the car, she had said that she felt "a great need" to get away from me.

"May I fall over dead if I'm a liar, but I put ninety gallons of gas in his car," the man said. "He had a big car, a Cadillac, but God knows it was not an airplane. I thought there was something wrong with the gauge or pump. When it said thirty-seven gallons, I remember looking under the car to see if a leak was spreading out on the ground, but it was dry. And finally, when the gauge said sixty-four gallons, I said to him, 'I think there's something wrong, sir,' and he said, 'No, everything's fine.' I remember the chill went up me. I kept pumping the gas until I'd put in ninety gallons, and the tank overflowed. It was fantastic. The price of the sale was thirty-four pounds nineteen shillings and seven pence. I said to the Yank, 'I've never seen anything like this,' and it was then that he told me that he'd had a custom-made tank put in his car. He explained how he'd been living up in the American state of Michigan, in the northern part, where it's so wild and lonely, and there are only a few gas stations, and he wanted to be able to drive for weeks on end without worrying about running low and finding himself stuck in the wilderness. So he had this special tank built by an engineer in Detroit. It held a hundred gallons. If I hadn't seen it with my own eyes, I would have called the man who told me this a dirty liar. The car appeared normal in every way, except it was low-slung and heavy in the middle; but it was not something you noticed right away. It came with knowing about the tank. You see, it was welded onto the bottom and covered the entire underside of the car. When I took the money into the office and told the manager that it came from the sale of gas to an American with a Cadillac, he started to laugh so loud that I thought he was going to keel over, but when I took him out and showed him the car and the gauge, with the numbers still showing, he became very sober, very quiet, and he said very little for the rest of the day."

I looked at the man without quite knowing what to say, though I'd enjoyed the story very much; and then I said, finally, "Well, that's very interesting. Thanks for telling me about it."

I gave him the pound notes, and then signaled to Wanda that we were ready. She opened up her raincoat and drew it over her head, then stepped out of the office and ran quickly to the car. It was raining hard again.

"There's one more thing," he said, as he handed me my change through the window. "The gas tank was a failure. The American was inclined to get overconfident, and he ran out of gas up in Michigan, just as he feared he would before he went to all the trouble. You can't escape your destiny. Well, don't get too wet, now."

I said goodbye to him and pulled out on the road.

"What was that all about?" Wanda said.

"Just a little story."

"You certainly took your time."

"I didn't want to be rude and cut him short," I said.

"Not you, certainly not. You probably dragged it out."

"No, I was just listening, Wanda. He only wanted to tell me something, and I listened to him."

"God, you're really perfect for this country," she said.

The rain stopped when we were a few miles out of Galway, and I turned off the windshield wipers. There were light streaks in the gray sky, and it appeared that the sun was about to break through.

"It's clearing up," I said.

"I think you're the most selfish and irresponsible person I've ever known."

"Oh, come on, Wanda."

"Why do you force me to be a nag! Harry, I want to turn around right now. I mean it. I'm getting very worried. Will you please turn around?"

I kept going straight ahead. We were on our way to the Galway Meeting.

She was close to tears again. "I ask you, will you please turn around?"

"Relax. Everything's all right," I said.

"It's not all right. Nothing's all right. If anything happens to Edward, if he gets hurt, or worse, if—"

"That's enough. Now, for the hundredth time, Edward's in good hands. Nancy's a greathearted person, and there's nothing to worry about," I said.

"Oh, please shut up. You know she's just a negligent Irish girl. My god, Harry, she lets her own little boy run out on the road. I don't know why I ever let you talk me into it, but you put so much pressure on me—and God help me if I were to thwart you in any way, if I interfered with your day at the races. It's no great pleasure to listen to you go on about how I ruin your life with my joyless temperament. The problem is that you have no respect for me."

"I do respect you. I only said that sometimes you get so nervous where Edward is concerned that it makes you a little joyless, and that's practically all I said."

She wiped the corners of her eyes with a handkerchief.

"You know, it's very depressing to have another person always make you feel that you're a little sickening," she said.

"I'm sorry I make you feel that way."

"Oh, you're not sorry. It's the pleasure of your life."

I took a deep breath and let it out slowly. "Look, Wanda, let's start over. Say, did I tell you what Nancy said to me when I told her I was going to pay her for her trouble? She said, 'Harry, we're friends, and that's all that matters, so don't be thinking of giving me any money. I wouldn't take it if you held a gun to me.'"

"God, Harry, all that banter goes to your head. But I'm telling you one thing. If anything happens to Edward, I'll never talk to you again. Never, never, never—"

"Will you please shut up," I said.

"I will not shut up!"

A light rain began to fall again. The wipers went back and forth. They made a pleasant sound and along with the rain helped create in the car a feeling of warm coziness. I turned on the radio and listened to a program of old Gaelic songs. Wanda was slouched low in her seat, her arms folded across her chest. After a while, I turned off the radio. It occurred to me that I might cheer her up by telling her the story that I had heard in the gas station. I should have merely reported it as it was told, but I made the mistake of saying that it sounded plausible.

She leaned forward in her seat and laughed. "Oh, they must be laughing at you now, and no wonder, you're so incredibly naïve. Do you really think it would fit under a car? One thing's for sure, Harry, your strong point never was a sense of reality. It falls apart at the slightest provocation. I watched your face as he talked to you, and it was so rapt and respectful. Do you realize that he made a complete fool out of you, Harry? He'll be telling his friends about this tonight in the local pub, about this naïve American, and they'll be laughing themselves sick."

"Jesus, but you're irritating," I said.

"Irish fancy—that's what they call it, Harry."

"No, you're wrong. I talked to the man. I watched him, sensed his sincerity. He seemed truly mystified himself," I said.

She broke into laughter again, and I went on. "Look, maybe the tank took up all the trunk space as well as the underside. You see, it was welded onto the bottom. I don't know if I told you that."

"I'm going to write my father this little story," she said. "It merely confirms everything he ever felt about you. I'm going to write him tonight."

"You do that. And while you're at it, would you tell him for me to take a flying leap?" I said.

She took a pained, spasmodic breath. "Oh, God, I hate you, Harry. I hate your dirty guts."

I slowed at a curve and shifted down into third. The gear stick collided with her leg.

"Move your bloody knee," I said. I gave a slapping push to her thigh, and then heard her groan and whimper, and before I knew what was happening, she threw herself on me and started hitting me on the shoulders and the top of my head. The car lurched to the right, and I managed to push her against the opposite side, while quickly turning the wheel with my free hand, and I applied the brakes. I pulled over to the soft shoulder of the road, near a fence of piled stones. Beyond the fence was a green and rocky field.

She slumped against the car door and began to cry.

I was out of breath and angry, and I lit a cigarette and tried to calm down.

"Oh, I'm so unhappy. I can't stand it anymore," she said.

She rose and leaned out the window, as though she were about to be sick, and then she fell back in her seat.

When we arrived at the Galway Meeting, the first race was over. The rain had stopped and the sky had partially cleared. Broken dark clouds were moving eastward. I parked the car on a grassy field, and we walked toward the grandstand. Wanda remained a little to the rear. We had not spoken for twenty minutes.

I had looked forward to seeing the Meeting, and I started to feel good again. The horses had not yet come out for the second race. We went through a gate and crossed the grass track, then passed through another gate to the grandstand section. I felt this tremendous happiness. I liked the track in its pastoral setting, the Irish crowd, and the changing sky, and the air, which was a little cold and wet.

Wanda looked despondent and halfheartedly regarded her program. She finally spoke. "Where are the betting windows?" she asked.

I tried to explain it to her—how there were no betting windows, no pari-mutuel system, that you placed your bet with the bookmaker who gave you the most attractive odds, and that the bookmakers were in a special area.

"I don't need a lecture, Harry. I'll figure it out for myself," she said. "Look, I think I'd like to watch the races alone, so why don't you go somewhere?"

"What do you mean by that?" I said.

"I think I made it very clear," she said, looking remote and tired. She turned and walked away toward the grandstand.

"You'll find me on the rail," I yelled after her, and then I walked across the track again, just as the horses were coming out from the paddock. I entered the infield and took up a position beside the rail. The second race was coming up, and I thought of going across again and placing a bet with a bookmaker on the other side, but I didn't want to take a chance of running into Wanda. I was disappointed not to see the betting area. The bookmakers were a colorful and dedicated lot. I'd seen them in Kildare at the Curragh, one afternoon, while Wanda stayed with Edward at the hotel. Each bookmaker seemed to have his own following of loyal patrons. It was an interesting profession, the way it was practiced in Ireland, and it appealed to me. I wouldn't have minded being a member of their little fraternity. It was a healthy life in the out-of-doors.

The sun came out briefly, and the lovely colors of the jockey silks took me by surprise. Then the sun went behind gray clouds again. The horses moved in a tightly reined trot, and then the jockeys, up a little in their saddles, broke them into a gallop that took them past the grandstand and around the turn.

A couple of Irish boys climbed up on the rail. I judged them to be about fifteen. One was small, slight, and dark-haired, with green-blue eyes. The other boy was of a larger, more husky build, with broad sloping shoulders and red hair. They began talking about the horses with great cheerfulness. The dark-haired boy spoke rapidly, rubbing the knuckles of his hand along his cheek.

Then the race started. It was a handicap for three-year-olds, at six furlongs.

The boys began screaming at one of the riders as the horses moved around the turn, and then the smaller boy said to his friend, "He's going to make it, Martin, and remember that I said it." Shortly, a great roar went up, and then the race was over.

"Was I right now, Martin? Can you say it clearly now?" the smaller boy said.

"Oh, you were right, Jerry. I can't deny it."

I couldn't help smiling at the exchange, and almost immediately got into conversation with them. The slight boy, called Jerry, looked down at me from the rail.

"The jockey Curran on Destiny's Child, he takes out my sister," he said.

"He rode a good race," I said. Destiny's Child had won by three lengths.

"Oh, he isn't bad for an apprentice rider," he said, and then he paused. "You're an American, aren't you?"

I said that I was.

"I have an uncle in Boston and another in Chicago," he said. "And they've sent us no money in five years."

His friend laughed. "Jerry's an awful person. He's worse than a Belfast Protestant on a holiday in Rome."

"Oh, God, Martin, that's good, that's very good, but you said it yesterday as well," Jerry said.

"Did I, now!"

"And I expect it tomorrow, too—if I happen to see you then," he said. He looked at me. "My name's Jerry O'Neill, and this sad person is Martin Leary."

I introduced myself, and we shook hands all around.

"Do you like the horses?" Jerry asked.

I said that I did.

"I plan to be a trainer someday, after my career as a jockey is over," he said.

Martin shook his head. "It's over already, Jerry. I'm afraid it was over before it started."

Jerry laughed. He pulled out a pack of cigarettes from his shirt pocket and offered one to me, and then he took one for himself.

"None for you, Martin," he said.

"I don't want another today. You're just stunting your growth, Jerry, which is a poor thing as it is."

"Well, that's good. There'll be no trouble making the weight."

"Oh, you'll be lucky to get a horse, unless an owner has lost his mind. Now give me a fag, will you?" Martin said.

Jerry handed him the pack, and Martin took out two cigarettes. "I'll keep one for later," he said.

The horses for the next race came out on the track. We smoked and looked them over. The race coming up was for three-year-old fillies at a mile and a quarter.

"Harry, put a few pounds on Broken Heart, and I think you'll do well," Jerry said.

I said that I was thinking of Gray Lady, that she had placed second in her last two races and Curran was riding her.

"Oh, don't think of him. He may fall off his horse this race," Jerry said. Martin agreed.

While we were talking it over, I noticed Wanda coming toward us. It did not appear that she had been having a pleasant time.

"Now, she is good-looking," Martin said.

And then Jerry said, "She's a little haughty and angry. Do I like her? I'm not sure that I do."

"She's coming this way. She seems to be looking at us," Martin said.

I felt that it had gone far enough, and I told them that she was my wife. They broke into a wild laughter and had scarcely suppressed it as Wanda walked up to us. I introduced them to her. They could not quite look at her, out of embarrassment, and remained seated up on the rail.

"Thank you. I'm glad I provided a good laugh," she said.

Jerry, who wore the trace of a smile, got down from the rail. "It was not at you we were laughing but ourselves," he said. He held his cigarette cupped in his hand, as though this were somehow an act of respect. His face took on a look of sobriety. "It was only our natural surprise at finding you were Harry's wife, after our saying, 'Now, there's an attractive woman.'"

"That's true," Martin said, only half looking at her.

Wanda ignored them.

"How long do you intend to stay?" she asked.

"Until it's over," I said. I looked up at the cloudy sky.

"I'm wondering about Edward," she said.

"He's all right," I said.

"How do you know?"

"Well, why shouldn't he be?" I said, feeling helpless before a rising anger.

I looked out at the track. Jerry pointed to the No. 4 horse, Gray Lady, who was galloping in front of us.

"There goes Curran," he said. Curran, leaning forward and slightly up in the saddle, had a long face with a wide mouth, and there was dark hair coming out from under his cap.

"Wanda, that jockey takes out Jerry's sister," I said.

"Oh, how good for her."

"I'm not sure it is," Jerry said.

Martin laughed. "She's daft anyway. It runs in the family," he said.

Wanda sighed. "Harry, I want to leave right now," she said.

I gripped the rail and said nothing for a few moments, and then I said, "Go down that road and turn left. It's about fifteen miles."

I should never have said it. Wanda's lower lip trembled and tears welled up in her eyes. The boys regarded her with a kind of wonder.

"Oh, how could you, Harry?" she said, turning her back on them.

"Well, boys, I guess I'll have to leave," I said. I shook hands with them and gave them what was left of a pack of cigarettes.

"Thank you, Harry, and good luck," Martin said.

"We hope to see you before it's all over," Jerry said. He climbed back up on the rail and smiled. "Goodbye. And goodbye to your wife, Harry," he said.

"Yes, goodbye to her, too," Martin said.

I could hardly look at Wanda. We walked without speaking to the parking lot and got into the car. As soon as she sat down, she began to cry. "I'll never forget how you humiliated me before those boys," she said. "I hope you're happy now."

I felt that it was getting hard to breathe, that the oxygen was leaving the air. As I put the key in the ignition, I thought that I had been a kinder, more compassionate person in my twenties, when I seemed to have more hope as a human being. In all fairness, though, I'd also been happier then.

In a drizzling rain, Edward was running across a field with Nancy's four-year-old son, Jack. Several brown-and-white cows and a horse were grazing there. A large dog ran between them and the boys, who ran and screamed with their arms stretched out. Nancy sat on the steps of her cottage, nursing her infant daughter. When she saw us, she rose slowly and covered her breast. "You're back early. Who won the Guinness Hurdle?" she said.

"We did not stay for it," I said. "We thought we'd go on a picnic out in Connemara." This had just occurred to me.

She laughed. She was a slim, attractive, and cheerful girl of about twenty-eight. "Oh, Harry, you're going out there again, are you?" she said. "I'm sure you'll end up herding sheep." She looked out at the field. "Edward was lovely. He is great company for Jack." The boys came over. They were flushed and sweaty with excitement. Edward grasped me around my legs and then ran to his mother, who picked him up.

"I no' 'fraid of cows," he said excitedly. He had large brown eyes and brown hair and wore a blue sweater. Young Jack, with his open, ruddy face, was big and husky for his age. He wore only a thin yellow polo shirt.

I tried to give Nancy some money, and she refused me again.

"Please don't think of it, Harry," she said. "Have yourselves a lovely time, now. Are you going as far as Clifden?"

"I don't know," I said.

Nancy laughed. "What a terrible man you are," she said. Edward came over, and she knelt down and put a hand on his shoulder. "The sooner you're leaving me, the sooner I'll see you again." He put his arms around her neck. "Oh, you're a great man, Edward," she said.

She stood up and turned to me. "Matt's out in the river. I think he'll be bringing in some salmon. Do you want a fish?"

"That would be fine," I said.

"Good, I'll send him over tonight. Well, goodbye now, Harry—goodbye, Wanda."

"Goodbye," Wanda said, getting into the car. "And thank you."

Jack ran out on the road and waved to us as we pulled away.

It was hard to tell about the weather. Overhead, the sky was gray, and a light rain was falling, but farther west it was brighter, with blue openings in the clouds.

"I think it's clearing out in Connemara," I said. "I've got all the gear in the trunk, the stove and some canned goods in the knapsack, and we can pick up some other things in Galway."

Wanda lit a cigarette and said nothing for a few moments, and then she said, "It's a shame you can't take Nancy. She's so much fun, isn't she?"

"What are you talking about now, Wanda?" I said.

"You're both so chummy, that's all. It's always Harry this and Harry that, and she hardly even looks my way. I think she hates me for some Irish reason of her own."

"She doesn't hate you, Wanda. I'm sure she feels that you don't like her much. That's all there is to it. I genuinely like her, and she knows it, and she responds to me."

"Please shut up, Harry," she said. "You're so pompous and smug. I mean, smugness is really a secret disease with you."

After we drove into Galway, Wanda went into the Five Star Market with a cloth shopping bag that we always kept in the car, and she came out with some bread and milk. At another place, we picked up four bottles of Guinness. We put it all in a Styrofoam box in the trunk.

I drove down to the waterfront and maneuvered the car for

the sheer joy of it through the Spanish Arch, an old and beautifully weathered archway of stone, and then I turned the car around and drove through it again and started off for Connemara.

As we passed through Salthill, we stopped to look out at the nearly deserted beach. Three young girls, having been not long out of the water, stood smiling and shivering in their towels, with their wet hair matted to their foreheads, their lips blue with cold. Then one shouted gaily, "It's now or never, Kathleen!" They dropped their towels and went running toward the water again just as we pulled away.

Wanda shook her head. "What idiots."

The sky was darker, and it began to rain harder again. I told Wanda not to get disheartened, as it was obviously clearing in the west.

I turned on the radio. A theatre group was doing "The Shadow of a Gunman," and I felt wonderful listening to it.

I looked at Edward through the rearview mirror. He was strapped in his elevated safety seat, looking out at the passing country. He looked so honest and openhearted. I felt a fresh surge of love for him.

Wanda opened her window slightly and flipped her cigarette out on the road. "This country makes me nervous," she said. "The weather's so changeable. It makes me changeable."

"Don't blame your moods on the weather," I said. "The truth is, you're always the same. Impossible." I laughed.

"You're so witty, Harry. May I thank you for everything?" she said.

We were on the road to Clifden. On the outskirts of Moycullen, the rain was pouring against the windshield so hard that we couldn't see out. I had to pull over to the side of the road.

"Only you could pick a day like this for a picnic," Wanda said, shaking her head.

"It will definitely let up. You can see that it's clearing in the west," I said. "And besides, Wanda, try to be a little accepting.

Why don't you try to enjoy the rain instead of resenting the fact that the sun isn't shining?"

"Please don't lecture me on how to behave, and don't patronize me, Harry. I'm not one of those stupid girls who think you're so marvelous."

"No, but you're lovely all the same," I said.

"You're so pompous. You're so sickening."

"Thank you very much."

"I hate you. God, I hate you."

I looked back at Edward to see how he was taking it, to see the expression on his face. It was unsmiling and inscrutable. "I don't think we're doing him any good, Wanda. I've told you that before."

She began to scream at me. "You bastard, I'm going to express myself, so don't use Edward as an excuse to stifle me!" She took a halting breath, and then started breathing rapidly and blinking. "And besides, you're the one who goes berserk and has tantrums and says all the hateful things, and then afterward has the gall to pretend he's so balanced and fair, when all the time—" She began to cry into her hands. Edward misunderstood. Thinking that his mother was laughing, he commenced in a high, screechy monotone to laugh as well.

We continued westward, passing through Oughterard, and drove along the edge of some small lakes. It was very beautiful. The rain had let up, and fog and mist lay over the water.

I pulled to the side of the road and turned off the engine. I wanted to experience it all in the quiet. I persuaded Wanda to get out of the car, and then I unstrapped Edward from his seat and lifted him up on my shoulders.

There was a deep stillness. It made all the difference in the world without the distraction of the motor. I tried to catch Wanda's eye, to get her to look my way and smile and forgive me and forgive herself. She stood there in her British raincoat as though she were enduring a punishment, her arms folded across her chest, her eyes slightly squinting at the fine mist. If it had not been for the unhappiness around her mouth, accented by a faint vertical line dropping from one corner, she would have been one of those girls I fell in love with at first sight. She was quite good-looking for thirty—for any age, really—with her faintly rosy face and auburn hair and blue, unhappy eyes.

I walked slowly around the car with Edward on my back. A breeze came up, and the clouds and fog started to drift away. Some mountains could be seen vaguely in the distance. "Can you see those hills?" I said to Edward.

Wanda opened the car door. "Let's get back inside. We're all going to get the flu," she said.

I strapped Edward back in his seat, then dried his face and hair with a handkerchief. His sweater was a little damp. I made a mental note to get him a poncho at the first opportunity. We started out again.

"You're incredibly inconsiderate," Wanda said. "Just plain selfish. For your aesthetic pleasure, everyone has to get soaked through."

"You'll live," I said.

"No thanks to you, Harry. I want you to know that I still remember how you treated me at the racetrack—"

"Racecourse," I amended.

"Don't think I've forgotten how you and those Irish boys humiliated me—"

"I know you have perfect recall, Wanda, but the thing is, you get everything wrong, because you have no judgment," I said.

An expression of utter disgust came over her face. "Oh, I wish you'd shut up. I'm sick to death of how you go on in that smug, critical way of yours, killing me a little bit at a time. Why don't you just come out and say you hate me, Harry? I did a terrible thing. I took away a little of your precious freedom and forced you to accept some responsibility. I married you and gave you a child. I committed an awful crime. Poor Harry! You hate me constantly and with a passion. God, why don't you be a man and admit it?"

"I don't hate you, Wanda," I said. I turned around, looking back at Edward. "How are you, Ed? Here, give me a shake," I said, extending my hand. Edward smiled and took a few fingers and shook them.

"Can you honestly say you love me, Harry?" she said.

I didn't say anything, as at that moment I really despised her.

"It's a simple question. I ask you now," she said.

I kept my eyes on the road and did not reply.

"Oh, God, I've really had it with you, Harry."

"Well, there's always a way out."

"Yes, and I'll get Edward," she said.

"Like hell you will," I said.

We were approaching Recess. The small mountain ranges, the Maamturks and the Twelve Bens, came into view, looking gray in the mist. The rain was letting up again, and there were seams of light in the sky overhead. Farther west there were great splits in the clouds.

Near Ballynahinch, an old deserted castle rose up from a small island in the middle of a lake. It was an ancient fortress of the O'Flaherty family. I pulled over to the side of the road and got out of the car by myself. It was lovely there, with the lake and the ruined castle and the mountains and the wooded hills on the far side of the lake, and nearby there were purple wild flowers growing in the rocks. The rain was light and a little cold. In the west, rays of sunlight appeared between the clouds, and there was some pale-blue sky.

It wasn't long before we could see the spires of Clifden. We had reached the western coast, and I felt suddenly elated at being near the North Atlantic.

"Shall we stop for some tea?" I asked.

Wanda rubbed her eyes. "Yes, I guess so."

I parked the car. I picked up Edward, who had fallen asleep. He woke up as I carried him through the rain to an old hotel on the main street. We entered a small room off the lobby and sat down in a couple of soft chairs near a small, round tea table. It was cozy and warm in the room, with a dismal gray light coming in through the windows. We ordered tea, some milk and cookies for Edward, and some bread-and-butter sandwiches. We ate all the sandwiches and finished off the pot of tea and the milk. Then I took Edward to the bathroom. When we got back to the table, Edward climbed up on his mother's lap and fell asleep. Wanda had put on her dark glasses and was smoking a cigarette. I put an empty teacup to my lips from time to time.

"What do you think, Harry?" she finally said.

"About what?"

"Us."

"Not very much," I said.

"You don't even think it's worth the effort, do you?" she said.

"Well, it certainly has been an effort, hasn't it?"

She took off her glasses and wiped her eyes with her napkin, and then she put them back on. "That's what I mean. I'm making an effort, taking certain emotional risks, and you respond with sarcasm. It's very cheap, Harry." She took a shaky breath and absently rubbed Edward's shoulder. "I'm sure now we're going to divorce. Oh, God, you've told me often enough how you need your freedom. May I tell you something? What you're craving is a little license to go berserk. You want the freedom to wreck your life. I guess you need to be adored by some boring, stupid little English girl. Like that awful Cynthia in London, who pretended she was my friend."

"Leave her out of it," I said.

"Do you miss her, Harry? She was nothing much, just young and pretty, and she knew how to flatter you. Harry, I've never known anyone more vulnerable and less gracious about compliments than you. And do you know why? Because you *believe* them. Oh, Jesus, you deserve a girl like her. I can still hear her clapping her hands and saying, 'Oh, well done!' after you had made some perfectly banal observation. It was sickening. And do you remember her awful habit of saying 'super' at least forty times an hour? I know you felt that indicated she had enthusiasm for life. You're so blind and undiscriminating when it comes to women. Why don't you live in the real world? You're always somewhere over there, over the rainbow someplace. Why don't you grow up! It's about time, don't you think?"

I said nothing.

"I'm asking you, Harry. Isn't it about time?"

"Wanda, you're an intelligent girl, but you have a lot of problems."

"You won't intimidate me, Harry. You're in such sad, awful, pathetic shape. I mean, I'd feel sorry for you if you weren't such a bastard."

"Yeah, I'm pretty terrible," I said.

"Did you ever once care about my needs? Or show me any kindness? No, I'm just a bit player in your life that you can neglect and look down on. That's all you think I'm good for. Do you know the warmest response you ever show me? Sad resignation. That's right, Harry. And, oh, yes, I don't want to leave out cold formality. You know how to do your duty, Harry. You're good at that, but you always let me know how much it costs you. You make it plain how bravely you're restraining your true feelings."

"What in the hell are you talking about?" I said.

"Are you ever affectionate? Do you ever put your arms around me anymore? I need affection, Harry. There's more to love than lovemaking, than sex in bed—"

"Oh, Jesus."

"Well, it's true."

"I'm not affectionate. That's true. But you don't make me feel affectionate."

"You're always angry," she said.

"No, that's not it. I often wake up feeling fine, and *then* you make me angry. You get on my nerves, Wanda."

She shook her head and sighed. "Do you know what's wrong with you? You're having a middle-age crisis. And you've got it bad, Harry."

"Wanda, let's end this comedy."

"Yes, it's a comedy, all right, living over here, playing the role of an expatriate. I find it amusing myself. Do you know the only true pleasure you get out of life? It's going into Galway and buying *Time* magazine. I see the feverish look in your eyes when you read the news of America. I tell you, Harry, when you read the *Irish Times*, it's a pose. Your heart isn't in it."

"No, you're quite wrong. It's true I'm curious about life back there, but I love it in Ireland."

"Oh yes, you love it here. That's true enough," she said. She took a deep breath. "You know, I've just figured out your fascination with Ireland. It's behind the times, like you. Over here, the déjà vu gives you a sense of security, and you don't have all the terrible anxiety of social change, women's liberation—of contemporary life in general."

"Wanda," I said, "I'm a little sick of this."

"Well, I'm sick of you, Harry."

I felt quite exhausted. My mind wandered to the time we were in Dublin and stayed at the Shelbourne Hotel, across from St. Stephen's Green. I had taken Edward to Trinity College to see the Book of Kells. It was a lovely, cool sunny day. Afterward, we were standing on Grafton Street, and I was admiring the great Palladian façade of Trinity, when a lovely young Irish girl of about nineteen stopped and began to admire Edward. "Oh, he's gorgeous. He's the playboy of the western world," she said.

We exchanged a few pleasantries, and then Edward suddenly hugged her around the legs. "Oh, I'm so flattered," she said. We all laughed, and then she went on her way.

Back at the hotel, I told Wanda of our little encounter. "I can imagine how it really was," she said. "She thought *you* were the playboy. Did you get her phone number? Oh, I bet you tried so hard to please her, and she thought you were wonderful. Of course, she doesn't know you like I do, Harry."

"You're absolutely wrong. She didn't notice me at all. It was Edward she was interested in," I said.

"But I imagine you were quite interested in her," Wanda said. "You're not terribly observant, Harry, but one thing you do notice is a pretty girl, unless she happens to be your wife. Well, I'm very attractive, Harry, and I'm damned sexy, and there are plenty of men who think so."

I left the room, feeling nauseated and hollow inside. I felt like throwing myself in the River Liffey, but I merely took a walk down Lower Baggott Street. When I returned to the hotel, a few hours later, the door was locked, and Wanda refused to let me inside. As I saw it, I had no alternative but to stay out all night. It was far less unseemly than begging someone to open a door. I went to various pubs, and really enjoyed myself talking to the people there. When the pubs closed, I wandered around, waiting for morning. I walked along the river, as far west as the Kilmainham Jail; and then I strolled across the Island Bridge to Phoenix Park. It was a beautiful night, sort of balmy for Dublin, and the stars were out. I slowly walked east again, just taking my time, drawing clear, free breaths. Outside the Customs House, I saw the sun rise. It had been one of the happiest experiences of my life.

When I saw Wanda later that morning, she was in tears; she probably thought I'd met with a bad accident or, worse, deserted her, but when she finally realized I was standing before her in one piece, intact, with all my faults, both real and imagined, she began to accuse me of infidelity. It was so pathetic and sad that I felt no anger at all.

Other women were always a sore point with Wanda, for despite all her flash and sparkle and genuine quality, she basically had no confidence in herself. Or perhaps she had none in me.

"Shall we order another pot of tea?" I asked, watching the rain fall in Clifden.

"If you want, Harry. It's up to you."

I ordered the tea.

"I guess we're through," I said, finally.

"I did my best. I honestly did," she said.

I lit a cigarette. I wasn't quite ready to call it a day with Wanda. The thought of floating around without responsibility gave me a pleasant but uneasy feeling, and leaving Edward was out of the question. I would try to stick it out a little longer—at least, until the fall of the year.

A group of Americans, consisting of two married couples in their mid or late fifties, entered the room and sat down. By their general demeanor, they appeared to be Midwestern, and they seemed to be having an awful time. One of them, a stout man in a brown suit, was complaining about the weather. He said that he was disappointed in Ireland—in the entire British Isles, for that matter. His wife said that they should definitely have gone to a Mediterranean country and had some fun, for this was definitely a waste of money and time.

"It's so gloomy, and I'm sick of it," she said. She was a large-boned, hefty woman, and wore white powder on her face.

The other man, a thin figure in a red plaid coat, said, "They can all go to hell, as far as I'm concerned."

I supposed that he meant the Irish.

Shortly after a young girl brought in a tray with four glasses of whiskey, the heavier man shook his head and said, "This is the damn last straw. Did she put Irish whiskey in your glass, that Paddy junk? We asked for Scotch."

The others tasted their whiskey. It wasn't what they had ordered.

"And where's the ice, Frank? She didn't bring the ice," his wife said. "Will you get her over here and change the order right now?"

The waitress came into the room, carrying an empty tray. She was a pale, slight girl of about sixteen, with a pleasant face and a distracted manner. When she appeared, the heavier man took the initiative.

"What did we order?" he said to her.

"Whiskey, sir," she said, reddening slightly.

"You're God-damned right we ordered whiskey, but not this Irish stuff. We asked for Scotch," he said.

"I'll speak to the barman, sir," she said, putting their glasses on the tray. "It's my mistake."

"And the ice, Frank," his wife said.

"Bring some ice. Do you think you can remember all that?" he said.

"Yes, sir."

I was surprised he didn't order her to bring them some sunny weather and an interesting life.

"Maybe he'll send in the Strategic Air Command and bomb her back to the Stone Age," Wanda said. "God, they're ridiculous, Harry. They're why we left America."

"Sure, that and a thousand other things," I said.

She shook her head.

"I hate that sort of brutality," she said.

"Yeah, it wasn't too pleasant," I said.

"Look at the little fat man. He's just so contemptuous of everything—and so stupid and vile—and why must he come over here and ruin it for everybody else? Oh, I loathe them."

"It's a sad little spectacle," I observed.

"I hate it when you get so detached. It's just an affectation," she said. "It's more than a 'sad little spectacle.'"

"You're right, I'm terribly affected," I said.

"You hate them as much as I do, but you have to be above it all. I feel what I feel, and that's that."

"That's not that, Wanda. You said that they 'come over here and ruin it for everybody else,' but let me remind you of one thing. We've ruined it for each other."

"I'm not talking about that, Harry, and you know what I mean," she said. "I just hate them, and I know you hate them. So why don't you admit it?"

"I refuse to hate them, Wanda. I'm sorry to disappoint you."

"You're such a bloody fraud," she said. "But I know to what

lengths you'll go just to turn the knife in me a little and play the saint."

Edward woke up. He lay there for some time, breathing evenly, with his eyes open. Then he sat up and yawned. Wanda leaned over and kissed him on the cheek, and he suddenly hugged her. I looked at the Americans across the room, and I saw that they were looking at us. I gave Wanda a slight nudge. The thin man's wife, a gaunt-faced woman wearing a blue satin turban and a dress of the same material, suddenly exclaimed, in a loud, confident voice, "Why do the Irish raise such fat children?" And then the other woman said, "He's not very cute, either. He's bloated-looking."

"A little beer belly!" said the main in the red plaid coat.

General laughter followed. We were stunned. I never saw Wanda look so stricken. "Did you hear that, Harry?" she said in a heavy whisper. "Those filthy peasants don't even think we can understand English. Oh, those stupid bastards! Edward is a lovely, beautiful, robust boy, and they called him fat and bloated."

"Forget it, Wanda. They just can't see very well," I said.

"What is it with them? Do they think we speak only in Gaelic? They won't get away with this," she said.

She was at a high pitch, even for her, and I knew we would not get out without an incident. Her one great talent was telling people off. I called for the check and left the young waitress, as a form of consolation, a sizable tip.

As we rose to leave, the Americans regarded us with a kind of dumb hostility. On the way out, Edward took my hand, and Wanda said, "Excuse me for one moment."

She walked over to their table, with a vague, frozen smile on her face, and she said, "I want you to know that my mother tongue is English and I think you're disgusting and a disgrace, and I hate you. I hate everything about you. I hate the clothes you wear and the things you talk about and the stupid expressions on your faces. I hate the sounds of your voices and your dirty mean little souls, and most of all I hate that you're Americans and that we share the same country, and that you can make me feel so mortified."

As we walked out to the small lobby, we could hear fragments of conversation.

"Did you ever!"

"What the hell's the matter with her?"

Then the stout man's voice came through clearly. "I'll tell you what's wrong. That crazy bitch has got more nerve than brains."

"They ought to lock her up—"

"And throw away the key."

In a little while, we were driving south along the western coast toward Ballinaboy. The sea was on our right, and on the left were low walls of piled stones and grassland strewn with large boulders. In the fields, sheep were grazing. The sun broke through and the fields brightened into greenness. White gulls flew over the water, which was blue in the sunlight. It was turning out to be a fine day.

"We can still have our picnic, Wanda. It's seven o'clock, but there'll be light for another two hours, and it should be great to get out on the beach—or on the strand, as we say in London. That is, if it's all right with you. I don't want to selfishly impose my will on our little party."

She laughed, "You're so thoughtful, Harry."

We passed through Ballyconneely and continued southeast down the western coast. Then we left the water and moved southeastward on the way to Roundstone. I remembered a wonderful beach in Dog's Bay from a previous trip. We'd looked down on it from high up on the road, and there'd been no one there.

Our blue Volkswagen appeared on the southern coast just as the sky clouded over again, and a light rain began to fall.

I turned right on a bumpy dirt road, drove a little way, then stopped by a huge boulder. We were up on a small hill, and down below, in the shape of a crescent, was a beautiful white beach. It was deserted.

We sat there for a while, looking out. I thought of the Spanish Armada. Many of their ships had cracked up off the western coast of Ireland in a terrible storm nearly four hundred years before, and I wondered if it was in those very waters that the ships went down. The rain had let up to a drizzling mist. I suggested that we go down the hill and set up our campsite behind some large rocks, as shelter against the breeze.

We unloaded the car. I handed Wanda the knapsack filled with canned goods—tins of beef stew, tuna fish, and kidney beans. I picked up the folded ground cloth, the camper's stove, and the Styrofoam box that contained the bottles of Guinness, the milk, and the loaf of white bread. With Edward holding on to my pants leg, we walked to the edge of the hill overlooking the beach. Then I stooped down and Edward climbed up on my back. In this way, we slowly walked down a sandy path to the shore.

I turned on the gas cylinder of the camp stove, lighting it with a match. After I opened a can of beans, I poured the contents into a tin pot, which I put on the stove.

"Daddy cook," Edward said, getting to his feet and looking down at the beans.

I made some tuna-fish sandwiches, and then I put the pot of beans on the lid of the Styrofoam box that rested on the ground cloth. After the beans cooled, we dipped our spoons in the pot and ate communally.

Wanda sat cross-legged on the ground cloth and smoked. "Harry, when are we going back?" she asked.

"It's hardly raining, and it's early enough," I said.

"Oh, I don't mean to the cottage. I mean back to America," she said.

I poured some Guinness into a tin cup and drank a little. "I'm having a grand time," I said, at last.

She put her head in her hands and rubbed her eyes with the

heels of her palms, and then she regarded me with a look of urgency.

"Harry, I know it's terrible, but I want to go home. At least, I understand it there. I don't want to go to the Aran Islands anymore, or to County Donegal. I'm tired of all this pastoral beauty. I want to get on with my life. It's passing fast enough. I know it's terrible back there. God knows, I remember what it was like, but we're Americans, aren't we? I mean, apart from everything else, don't we have an obligation to return, to improve the situation, instead of turning our backs? I'm awfully homesick, Harry."

I drank and looked out at the water and the sky. Westward, below the dark clouds, the sky was pale orange, with a line of red at the horizon. The sea was gray, and small frothy waves were coming into shore. Edward kept holding his sandwich up to the rain. He enjoyed making the bread soggy before he ate it.

Wanda drank from a bottle of Guinness. Though our marriage was quite shaky, possibly doomed, and my hopes had more or less collapsed, I felt a sudden rush of warmth for her and a terrible remorse for the way I'd treated her, for having been so critical and intolerant of her faults. I felt a great sympathy for the sincerity of her unhappiness. I walked over to her and put an arm around her shoulders and kissed her on the side of the face. She responded with a look of pleasant surprise and gratefully took my hand. "We're going back to the States, Wanda," I said.

She looked startled, and pulled Edward to her.

"It was just a matter of time," I said. "We're running out of money. I guess I'll have to get a job, you know."

We had enough money left over from the inheritance for a few months' rent on an apartment in Boston, with something left for food and necessities.

"Harry, I wasn't going to force you to return. I know you like it here, but if we have to go, then please don't worry about anything. It could be wonderful. We'll go back and start a new life. It could be the making of us."

The thing is, my favorite way of being an American was at a distance of three thousand miles.

While Wanda wrapped the trash in a copy of the *Irish Times*, I took Edward for a walk down the beach on the smooth, wet part of the sand near the water. I picked up some broken shells and seaweed, and I gave the shells to Edward. He regarded them with interest, then dropped them on the sand.

We drove home by way of Roundstone and Toombeola and Ballinafad, and then, a few miles from Recess, we entered on the main road to Galway. Wanda was asleep, slumped against the side of the door, with her arms covering her head, as though she were protecting herself.

Edward was awake in the back seat. "All dark out. I can't see no sheeps, Daddy," he said.

I started saying farewell to Ireland.

In a week's time, we drove down to Cork in the evening, and on the following day boarded the ferry to Swansea.

It was a beautiful morning, crystal clear, with the sky deep blue and a sparkling sunlight on the little houses on the banks of the hills of Cobh Harbor. We stood on the deck as the ship pulled out. I smoked and watched the Irish coast grow smaller until it was a fading line.

All the way to Swansea, I thought about entering the mainstream of American life.

And I considered the matter during our brief stay in London, where we saw friends and sold our car.

And when the plane touched down at Kennedy Airport, with Edward on my lap, and Wanda smiling and saying, "Oh, God, we're home!" I was feeling fairly apprehensive about it all.

The Munster Final

While a light rain fell, a forty-one-year-old American sat behind the wheel of a white Ford Escort parked on the main street of Ennistymon, a town in the west of Ireland. He was listening to the radio. A voice announced that there would be a reunion of the Tenth Infantry Battalion that had served in the Emergency. The weather forecast followed, rain and occasional sunny spells over the entire nation.

As he lit a cigarette, a slight tremor played about his mouth and the corner of his left eye. Inhaling deeply, he let out a fine stream of smoke which passed out the car window and faded into a background of low, somber buildings and cloudy sky. Then he leaned forward and rested his head against the steering wheel. "Cheer up, Harry," he said, but he was a depressed personality, serving in an emergency of his own.

He was waiting for a woman with whom he had been living for two years. Her name was Ardis, and she was buying provisions in a local market for their rented cottage farther north in County Clare. Having come over only the day before on the ferry from Swansea to Cork, they were on their way to the cottage for the first time.

A month before, Ardis had given him a warning. After their

week in Ireland, he either married her or they went their separate ways.

Pressing two bags of groceries against the car with her body, she used her free hand to open the rear door, then placed the bags in the back seat. Then she stood up and raised her face to the light rain, rubbing her eyes with the backs of her fingers. She was an attractive woman, pink and ruddy in the moist air, but she appeared vulnerable and uncertain, with small lines at the corners of her eyes. She was thirty-two.

Standing for some time by the rear fender, she avoided looking at him, pulling aimlessly at a stray wisp of auburn hair. Finally, she took a deep breath and walked over to him, turning up the collar of her raincoat.

"Why don't we take a walk, Harry. It might do us good," she said. She had hoped to sound cheerful but felt embarrassed by a slight stridency in her voice. Humiliated by her helpless desire to please him and by what she saw in herself as dishonesty and emotional confusion, she hated him at that moment as much as she hated herself.

He let out a small groan and got out of the car.

As they walked along the main street, Ardis observed that she had never seen so many bars in one little town.

"We might as well have a drink," Harry said. It was about four o'clock in the afternoon.

They descended a narrow iron stairway and entered a dim room. An elderly bird-like woman was seated at a table near the door, talking to a man whose hands were folded by his glass.

"Well, come right in," the woman said, smiling and rising from the table. She led them to a dark wooden bar on the other side of the room.

Harry had a little trouble getting up on the stool.

"He has a back problem," Ardis said.

"Oh, the poor man. Would you care to sit at a table then?"

"No, this is fine," Harry said.

He had a shot of Jamieson's and a glass of water on the side. The old woman put down a draft Guinness for Ardis.

"May health and joy go with you," the woman said.

"Thank you," Ardis said. "May it go with all here."

Harry raised his glass in a salutary gesture and drank some whiskey, then water as a chaser.

"I can't get over all the bars in Ennistymon. It's amazing," Ardis said.

The old woman smiled.

"Yes, there are twenty-three here now. But in my father's time, there were forty-three. And there were coopers, five black-smiths—a different place altogether," she said, without regret. "Well, may all change be for the better."

"God bless you," Harry said, and he had another drink before they started on the road again.

"Are you all right?" Ardis said, as they drove along.

Harry nodded, but he was so numb with exhaustion that he could scarcely keep awake, and he wondered if it was the whiskey that had made him tired, though it never had before. It might be hypoglycemia, he thought, the low blood sugar syndrome that he had read about recently. At times he seemed to have all the symptoms, the hunger and nervousness, profuse sweating, alternate pallor and flushing of the face, and vertigo. He thought he was having a little vertigo at that very moment.

They began the final leg of their drive through the gray lime-stone hills of the Burren. Meandering through the twisting turns of Corkscrew Hill, they descended with a view of the bay into Ballyvaughan.

It was about seven in the evening, but there was still plenty of summer light, though the sky had clouded up again.

"How lovely," Ardis said, genuinely moved.

It was her first time in Ireland, but Harry had been there seven years before with his wife and young son. They had lived for a year in County Galway on a small inheritance from his aunt. His marriage had ended in divorce a few years after their return to America. He had been resigned to its ending, but leaving his son was the saddest experience he had ever known, and he had not gotten over it, nor did he think he ever would.

As for his future with Ardis, or without her, he was unable to clear up the doubts in his own mind. It wasn't that he didn't care for her. He was very fond of her, but the idea of settling down and starting over with a new wife unnerved him and oppressed him almost to the point of illness. After all he had been through, he no longer believed in the possibility of conjugal happiness; and the last thing he wanted at this time of his life was to get involved in a doomed marriage. He really liked her. He knew that she was a good person, and that she loved him more than he deserved. But he felt depressed, and he often told himself that it was Ardis and her sorrowful nature that depressed him, though he knew the painful truth: that he, not her nature, was the cause of her sadness, and what made him unhappy was his awareness of what he had done to her. If she could only smile occasionally from the heart; if she could only manage, even after all he had put her through, to show a little gaiety and lightheartedness and cheer him up somehow, then perhaps he might feel more inclined to marry her; but as it was she stood before him as a living accusation. When he was with her, he often felt the urge to get away for good, but no sooner had he decided to leave than he would begin to miss her, and he would remain, tentative and double-minded and on the verge of leaving again. He was confused. He knew it. What he needed was more time to work things out.

"But you've had two years," she had told him.

It was true. He felt that he was ruining her life. And in spite of his recent talent for flight and evasion and self-apology and tricky rationalization, he was obsessed with his own guilt.

In her desire to please him and make him happy, and to have him love her, she had lived at first in a state of hope and exhilaration. It was only later, after things had gone wrong between them, after Harry, through panic and guilt over the question of marriage, had become unreasonable, hostile, and critical of her slightest fault; it was only then that she had become a discouraged and unhappy person. Though she knew what a poor impression her unhappiness made on him, and tried in spite of everything to be cheerful and pleasant, her heart wasn't in it; she was shaken by the seriousness of her predicament, that time was passing, that she was getting older with nothing to show for her life. She hated to lose him, and loved him still; but the strain had become too much for her, and she had given him, sorrowfully and with regret, her ultimatum.

Did he love her? God, what was love? he thought. It was an illness from which you always recovered in time. Did he love her? He really couldn't say. Perhaps he did. But then, was it good for the duration? Perhaps he loved her today but he wouldn't tomorrow. Yet, whatever the truth, he didn't want to entirely lose her. It would be nice to see her regularly, to see her happy and pleasant, the way she used to be when they were just living together without talk of marriage and commitment. If she could only be reasonable and kind and large-hearted about his difficulty, and not obsessed with security, which was only an illusion; for he felt that life was brief and uncertain and that you had to take it on the wing. And how much time did he have left, anyway? He thought. Not much. He wasn't that well. No, he didn't have time for that sad convention called marriage. But the thing is, he was very fond of her, he thought, and he wanted to get close to her, though not too close. He wished to be her friend and lover but at the same time not get too involved with her in ordinary life, not at least until he had worked things out in his own mind. Yes, he had to make up his mind, he thought. He had to make up his mind. In truth, he did not know what he wanted, saw no solution, and he hoped for a miracle.

"She lives on the main street," Ardis said, as they passed a small hotel. "There, Harry, the house with the red shutters." Ardis got out of the car and knocked on the door of the house where the caretaker lived. A thin woman in her fifties opened the door and peered out.

"Who is it you want now?"

"Deirdre O'Callahan, please."

"About the cottage, is it?"

"That's right," Ardis said.

"Deirdre, it's the Americans," the woman yelled inside the house.

"I'm coming now," a voice rang out, and then a small pretty woman with reddish hair came to the door.

"How do you do?" she said, fastening the belt of her rain-coat and holding out her hand. "The McNeills wrote that you were coming, but I expected you yesterday."

"We moved slowly," Ardis said. "I hope it didn't inconvenience you."

"Not at all, but when you weren't here at half-eleven, I began to wonder," she said. She was about twenty-five, lightly freckled and with blue eyes. Harry admired her at once, thinking that she had a gravity and calmness seldom found in American women of her age.

"Well, if you'll follow me out, I'll take you to the cottage. It's just a few miles from here," she said.

She started up the engine of her car, a small brown Morris Minor, and they followed her farther east along the coast road.

In a little while, they turned off into a side lane that went part way up a hill. A white cottage with a red slate roof was built on its slope, and it looked out on Galway Bay.

Deirdre pointed to the hills behind them.

"You're on the Burren. All the hills along the coast here are part of the Burren. You can climb up and find lovely wildflowers, but you mustn't uproot them. They were brought here by the glacier," she said. She nodded toward the cottage.

"Well, please make yourselves at home while I prepare the tea. Scones I made earlier, and they need only to be warmed."

They sat down at an oval table by a window that looked out

on a mist over the water. The scones were on the table with a plate of butter and a jar of rhubarb preserves. A turf fire burned in the grate.

"It was so nice of you to do this," Ardis said, smiling.

"Oh, it was nothing at all," Deirdre said. "Well, what are your plans now? Do you plan to tour about?"

"Harry has been to Ireland before. He's going to show me some of it."

"Ah, that's good. There are Norman castles nearby and an old stone fort, and there are the megalithic tombs and the Cave of Allwee, and the Burren itself. But there's one other thing that you might enjoy while you're here, and that's the Munster Final. It's for the hurling championship of the province, and County Clare is in it this year, against Cork. Clare has not won in my lifetime, not since 1932, not in forty-five years, so you might be interested in seeing that. But I ought to tell you, it's a long drive to Thurles. It's in County Tipperary."

"When is it?" Ardis said.

"On Sunday."

"Do you think we could go, Harry?"

"Sure, why not," he said. He had always loved the sporting life.

After the tea, they looked about the cottage. There were four rooms in all, two small bedrooms and a large sitting room with a fireplace that burned turf, since there was no wood available. Located near the front door was a small kitchen which included a metal sink, a refrigerator that had one compartment and was built low to the floor, and a gas stove. The cottage was without a telephone or a television, but there was a radio in good condition in the main bedroom.

As they walked Deirdre to her car, she stopped on the porch and raised the lid of a wooden box. "Your turf's in here, for burning in the grate," she said. "If you need me for anything, please come by the house. Somebody's usually there, and I'll get your message. Well, goodbye then. I'll bring you lettuce from time to time, and tomatoes. My uncle has a vegetable garden."

"Was that your mother at the door?" Ardis said.

"Oh, no, it was the mother of my husband."

"We hope to meet him and have you both to dinner while we're here."

"That's kind of you, but my husband and I are separated. He lives in Dublin now."

Later, in the dusk, Harry and Ardis sat on the porch and watched the sky and water. The mist had cleared away, and the lights of Galway sparkled on the far shore. About a half mile toward the water, there was a farm that bordered an inlet. The farm buildings and a Martello tower on a small peninsula beyond were in silhouette.

"It's so peaceful and lovely," Ardis said.

"It is," he said, feeling oppressed.

In the morning, they went down to the farm near the water to buy some fresh eggs. Walking down from their cottage, they crossed a field, then climbed a low stone wall, following a path through another field until they came to a stone farmhouse. Ardis knocked on the door, and a small woman with gray hair and wearing wire-rimmed glasses looked out the window. Harry said that they were Americans living in the McNeill house, and that if possible they would like to buy some eggs from her.

"So it's eggs you want," she said.

She invited them inside and put fresh eggs in a paper bag for them. When Harry tried to pay her, she said, "It's all right. I don't want any money today. You can pay me next time." The kitchen had white rough plaster walls, and there was an open hearth with a hanging black pot above an iron grate. On the far wall was a picture of Jesus of the Sacred Heart.

It was the O'Ryan farm.

They walked outside with Mrs. O'Ryan. Several sheep were in the pasture. Mr. O'Ryan waved his cap at them from a distant field as they walked to the barn. Inside, the O'Ryan's son, a twelve-year-old boy, was milking a cow. Ardis asked him if he was going to fill the bucket with milk.

"Oh, no, it takes two milkings to fill a pail," the boy said, smiling. "But I'll fill it in the evening."

"God bless you," Harry said.

That afternoon, they drove along the coast road until they came to a ruin by the water. It was from there that Ardis wished to climb one of the hills of the Burren, and Harry had agreed to try. It was the least he could do for her, he thought. Parking the car near the ruin, they walked across the road to the hill called Cappanwalla. It was slightly over a thousand feet high.

With Ardis leading the way, they began to climb. It was cool and cloudy, with the threat of rain.

The lower part of the hill was primarily underbrush, briars, grass, and lichen. Farther up, they climbed two stone walls and made their way over rocky limestone with large fissures. Harry found that the physical exertion was making him out of breath and irritable. He watched her far ahead of him, moving through a slope of wildflowers, yellow and purple ones, thyme and blue-bells. She turned and waved and shouted encouragement.

Harry climbed slowly to the area of wildflowers, and then stopped and rested, breathing in the fragrance.

Near the top, she held out her hand for him and pulled him up. Stepping on cracked, flaking limestone slabs that were full of erosion holes, they climbed higher to a summit of green vegetation.

From there they could see the Aran Islands, Galway, the twelve bens of Connemara, and stone walls on green land.

Harry was still out of breath, and his heart rate seemed abnormally rapid to him.

She saw that he was tired, and she put her arms round him. "Harry, maybe this was too much for you. I'm sorry."

"No, I'm fine. I'm really all right," he said. He sat down on the ground and lit a cigarette.

She knelt beside him.

"Harry, please listen to me now. I can't just let the days pass without saying what's on my mind. This is our last chance. If we don't get married, I think it will be a tragic mistake. Years from now you'll regret it very much." He groaned and shook his head, not so much out of disagreement but that he found the whole subject distasteful. "Harry, I love you, and I know that deep down you really love me, too. I know that or I wouldn't still be here. But this is our last time together, and I find it very sad, very poignant. You're a very intelligent person, but you're so troubled by this that your mind isn't even working. I think if we got married, you'd find that we'd be good for each other. And we'd be happy. I honestly believe that. I'm quite convinced of it, Harry. But you have to show a little courage."

"Ardis, I haven't resolved it yet," he said.

"You haven't resolved it yet? What does that mean?" she said. "What do you mean, you haven't resolved it?"

"I have doubts. I need more time."

"Harry, you've had worlds of time, you know that. We have only a few days left. And more time wouldn't resolve your doubts. It would just deepen your confusion. Everyone has doubts. In the final analysis, you just have to take a chance." Some white gulls flew low over the water. He could see some men in the small fishing boat. "I'm not pleading my case, Harry. Not exactly. I'm just trying to appeal to your intelligence."

"Ardis—" he said, unable to say more, and he shook his head and made a small wave of his hand.

Looking stricken, she stood up and walked away from him.

He took a deep breath and shook his head. He knew that he had been a lot braver the first time he considered marriage, but then he had been ignorant of all the things that could go wrong, even between two people with the best will in the world.

"Well, I'm going," she said, and she began to go down the side of the hill with great single-mindedness.

She was going to leave him, she was really going to leave him this time, he thought, as he rose to his feet; and he felt heartsick already at the prospect of separation; but there was nothing he could do about it.

The descent was hard on his knees. He tore his pants on the briars, and his legs began to bleed. He felt sort of an aura, a prelude to a spasm in his lower back. It was a relief to get down on the road and back in the car again. The physical comfort that he felt more than compensated for her silence and his mental anguish.

When they got back to the cottage at about five in the afternoon, Harry went right to bed and didn't leave it until the next day.

On the following morning as they entered County Galway and Harry saw the familiar terrain he remembered from seven years before, he thought of his former wife and his son and of all the changes that had taken place. He was so moved that he could hardly speak.

He and Ardis were on their way to Galway city to play tennis and do the laundry. Not too far past Oranmore, Harry slowed down and parked outside a grocery store.

"I knew the owners," he said.

It was the store that he and Wanda had patronized, and the proprietors, John and Kate McBride, had become friends of theirs.

Harry saw Kate in the rear of the store. She was behind the counter, reading the paper and drinking a cup of tea. Aside from having gained a little weight, he did not think she had changed much.

Ardis remained up front while he walked back.

"Hello, Kate," he said.

She looked mystified, frowned, then her face broke into a wide grin.

"Oh, no, it can't be. It's Harry," she said, coming out from behind the counter. She put an arm round him and squeezed his shoulder. "Well, I never thought I'd see you again. The other day John remarked how people you're fond of disappear and you don't see them until the next world. He'll be sorry he missed you. He went to Roscommon to see his sick mother. Young Jack went with him." She looked up front and saw Ardis and said in a low voice, "Oh, you've got a new one."

Harry explained that he and Wanda had been divorced for almost four years.

"Divorced? You and Wanda? Well, I hope you're happy now," she said, with a note of reproach in her voice. "And how is Wanda—and dear little Edward?"

"I think Wanda's all right. She married again. As for Edward, he's not so little anymore. He's nine years old."

She looked toward a back room.

"Megan, come here," she said. A willowy girl with brown hair and green eyes came out. She was about ten.

"Look who's here. It's Harry—the American. Do you remember him? It's little Edward's da. You remember Edward, don't you?"

"I think I remember him," she said, smiling shyly.

"I can't believe it. The kids have changed, and we've remained exactly the same," Harry said.

Kate laughed.

"Of course, you look younger. Are you back for long, Harry?"

"Only for a week. We're at a cottage near Ballyvaughan."

Harry waved to Ardis. She came back, and he introduced them.

"So, you married Harry. Well, good luck to you. You'll need it," Kate said. "Tell her I'm only joking, Harry."

Harry smiled. He thought of explaining to Kate that they weren't married, that they only lived together, but he felt the news would have been a shock to her moral system, as Ireland had not yet caught up with much of the western world.

"It's good being back in Galway," he said.

"It's here you should stay, not Clare. Down there all they think of is the Munster Final. Well, good for them, but Cork's going to win," she said. "Are you going to it, Harry?"

"We might."

"And do you know about hurling then?"

"Very little," he said.

She looked at Ardis.

"Well, ignorance never stood in his way," she said. "One thing about Harry is that he always enjoys himself."

He had to smile. The Harry she described had long since departed.

"It's been very nice meeting you," Ardis said, as they were leaving.

"Take good care of him. He needs all the help he can get," she said, smiling. "Goodbye, Harry, come back and see us before you leave."

"God bless you," Harry said, as he put his arms around her. He felt very moved at seeing her again.

They passed the greyhound track and continued on into Eyre Square. After showing Ardis the square and the cathedral and the River Corib, he drove along the beachfront and turned right on the road to the Galway Tennis Club.

With its brown wall and wooden gate, it was the way he had remembered it when he had last walked through with Wanda and young Edward. The grass courts appeared on the right, but instead of being deserted as they usually were at that late morning hour, there were players on all of them. A tournament was in progress.

Harry and Ardis stood outside the small clubhouse, where a number of players speaking German and French were sitting round a few small tables, drinking Coca-Cola.

"It was an entirely different atmosphere seven years ago," Harry said. "All the players in the tournament were Irish, and mainly from this part of Ireland. A Dublin player was considered exotic. And the tournament itself was not played in the morning or afternoon, but, as I recall, in the twilight."

"A Celtic twilight," Ardis said. "You sound so disappointed, Harry."

"Do I?" he said.

He ordinarily liked an international flavor but not there. The truth was that he regretted all the changes that he saw. He had grown conservative and preferred to live in the past that he knew and remembered, in that time when he was lighthearted and alert and winning, not leaden with fear and confusion. He embarrassed himself now, and the past was very appealing to him.

Harry had hoped to get a guest membership, as he had done when he was last in Ireland, so that they might play for an hour or two. But the club was not available for private play until the end of the tournament. They decided to leave.

On the way out, he saw one of the old men he remembered who had maintained the courts.

"Hello, Frank, do you remember me?" he said, extending his hand. "I'm Harry, the American who came here seven years ago. I gave you a lift to Salthill a few times. We had a drink together before your kidney surgery."

The man's eyes strained for recognition.

"Oh, yes, I remember you," he said, polite and bewildered; and Harry knew that he had been forgotten.

"Well, it's good seeing you, Frank," he said.

The man nodded earnestly.

"And it's good seeing you, and may you have a good day now."

They drove back to Eyre Square and parked the car. Harry took the bag of laundry from the back seat.

"I'll take care of this. Why don't you look around, Ardis," he said.

He pointed out the streets he thought she would find interesting and mentioned some old bookstores that she might enjoy.

They arranged to meet in an hour and a half at the square, by the statue of the storyteller, Padraic O'Connaire.

"This is awful for you," she said.

"I've seen Galway many times. I don't mind," he said. Actually, he preferred it, he was so depressed.

Carrying the bag of laundry, he walked to a washeteria on the top of Prospect Hill. From a nearby construction site came noise of generators and jackhammers. A mist of fine dust hovered over the street. He found it hard to breathe.

He went inside and put the clothes into a machine and, after adding soap from a dispenser, started it up. He sat down on a chair against the wall and picked up a day-old newspaper from the floor and began reading the front-page stories of violence and death in the north, of bombings and assassination, of murder, of random and accidental killing, of the death of innocent bystanders. Wanting to be cheered up, he turned to the sporting news. He was about to read a story on the Munster Final when he felt suddenly tired; he put the paper down and looked at a blue wall on the far side of the street, and though he tried not to think of anything, he began to think of Ardis. It occurred to him that no matter what decision he arrived at concerning marriage, it would be the wrong one. It was true that he didn't want to marry her, but at the same time he feared the loneliness of their separation. As he sat there with a vision of himself growing old alone, sitting in bars for the sake of conversation and human warmth, he tried as he had often done in the past to imagine himself married to Ardis, settling down in the small routines of domestic life. He imagined himself, for example, going regularly to Schenectady, New York, to visit her family. The thought depressed and frightened him, and he became light-headed and faint. He was too old, too nervous, he told himself, to go through all that again.

An old woman came through the door with her laundry in a plastic bag. She was in no hurry to get on with the wash, and she sat down and smoked a cigarette before putting her clothes in a machine.

Harry put his wet clothes in a Loadstar dryer, and then he sat down beside her.

"How are you?" he said.

"Not well at all, but I'm not complaining."

Harry nodded sympathetically.

"Well, who's going to win the Munster Final?" he said.

"Cork. Clare doesn't deserve to win. The people there are daft, and I won't be sad when they lose at Thurles. I'll raise my glass to the side from Cork."

She stood up and sighed, and put her clothes in a washer.

Harry looked through the window of his dryer and watched the clothes go limp as the cycle ended. He folded the laundry on a table and then placed it in his bag.

"Well, goodbye and good luck," he said, waving to the woman.

"We all get what we deserve. Luck doesn't enter into it," she said.

Outside, it was warm for Ireland, and the air in the narrow street was heavy with fumes and dust.

He had about half an hour before meeting Ardis again, and after he walked back to the square and put the laundry in the trunk of the car, he sat down on a bench near the O'Connaire statue.

Feeling tired, his back bothering him, he watched the traffic move around the center of the city. Exhaust fumes irritated his throat and nasal passages. He went into a paroxysm of coughing, which lasted for nearly a minute. A feeling of weakness came over him. He wiped his face with a handkerchief, and he thought that he felt worse than he had in a long time.

A man and woman in their twenties walked by, laughing.

"I don't believe you, Conor. You're too outrageous," the young woman said.

"I don't care. What do I care?" he said, and he began to laugh

harder than before. She took his arm and pressed it affection-
ately to her side.

Harry found the contrast between them and himself
unspeakably painful. God, to be young again, he thought, and
he continued to envy them long after he couldn't see them anymore.

A little later, Ardis arrived, with a few small parcels. He was
not glad to see her.

"I found some sailing prints and some wonderful maps of
the region," she said, smiling. "I had a lovely time, Harry. But I
missed you." He nodded. It seemed to him that she was only
pretending to be happy in order to please him, that she was
being insincere. He would have preferred an open declaration
on her part of sorrow or blame, not this false good humor with
its depressing unreality. It was genuine feeling that he needed,
and he only wished that she was capable of it. Was that too much
to ask? he wondered. And he felt a lingering suspicion, always
with him, that he was being unfair to her again.

During lunch at the Great Northern Hotel, Harry was reti-
cent and shamefacedly polite. Afterwards, during a long silence,
he watched her write postcards to her parents and sister and a
favorite aunt, and he was touched by her real affection for her
family.

Later they drove to the waterfront and strolled along it, passing through the Spanish Arch, and looking at the ships and small
boats in the harbor.

"Harry, thanks for showing me Galway," she said, with a
remoteness and formality that nearly broke his heart. It was as
though she were already fading from his life, and he had a feeling of grief.

On the way home, a man in the road shouted something
unintelligible, and then he shouted again. "Clare will win!" He
smiled and waved, and Harry waved back and drove on.

Back at the cottage, they ate a supper of poached eggs, potatoes, salad, and wine; and then, feeling tired, with the sky filled

with orange light, they turned in early, as they were going to the Munster Final in the morning.

Ardis went right to sleep, but Harry couldn't fall asleep for some time. He lay in bed and listened to the radio, to a program called *Across the Water*. It was dedicated to staying in touch with the Irish who had gone to England. These transplanted Irish men and women living in Irish enclaves across the Irish Sea spoke of their present life in London or Liverpool or in some other English city, with an air of homesickness for the towns they had left behind. It seemed, Harry thought, that life everywhere was longing and regret.

He heard a program about prison life in Ireland, about the deprivations experienced in prison, the loss of privacy of the prisoner, the disappearance of identity, the loss of power over his own life, the loss of hope. The speaker said that there were many ramifications of the loss of freedom, but the main one was the effect on the personality of the prisoner. Freedom was necessary for personal development. A man must make mistakes in order to learn. And this was also to be considered. The prisoner was deprived of sensory life. All the stimuli needed to feed his identity and personality were denied him. Total deprivation occurred in solitary confinement. It was almost impossible under those conditions to retain the personality intact, for we needed continuous stimulation to remain ourselves. Problems served to identify us. Prison life was an anesthetic. There was an awareness that one was less than a person, less than a human being. A prisoner is forced into a routine, and he ends up in a numbed condition, out of touch with his deepest feelings, his spontaneity gone. A former prisoner told of his experience after his release. "I couldn't bring myself to go back to the prison, though I had promised to bring things to my friends still inside, to do errands for them, and to stay in touch. I felt guilty of a kind of betrayal, but I couldn't go back for the place had such a terrible effect on me."

They left for the Munster Final in the morning. It was Sunday. After the rain of the previous night, the sky was a clear rich blue, the air was fresh with the smell of grass and hay and wildflowers. Wet fields sparkled in the sunlight.

At Ennis they filled the car with gasoline and then followed the main road to Limerick. They came upon a great procession of cars filled with Clare fans on the way to Thurles. Blue and yellow streamers were flying from many of the cars. On the slow ride to County Tipperary, they passed children on walls and by the road waving Clare colors. In the towns, people stood in doorways and leaned out windows, shouting, "Up Clare" and "Beat Cork."

"Up Clare," Ardis yelled out of the car window. She was genuinely excited. "I love it, Harry. I love it."

He felt a pleasant excitement himself, the false spring of the sporting life.

They parked the car on a grass field about a mile from Semple Stadium and walked along the road with the crowd. On the way, some celebrants from Cork carrying a red and white banner and raucously singing surged past them.

Semple Stadium was brownish and old. At the ticket window, Harry purchased two general admission tickets. The reserved seating had been sold out for hours.

Inside the stadium, a preliminary match was in progress between two junior teams from Cork and Limerick. Finding no vacant seats in the unreserved sections, they looked for the standing room area. They were pushed along with the crowd, amidst much jostling, laughter, shouting, and confusion.

A young man put his hand on the shoulder of an old priest and said, "If you're on your own, Father, you might come along with us."

Over the public address system, there was an announcement, "A little girl four years old by the name of Jane Hayes has been lost."

Harry and Ardis finally ended up standing behind a barrier

at ground level in back of one of the goals. Large men pushed in from all sides, and the crowd roared as the teams came on the field.

"What a crush," Ardis said, ducking her head slightly.

They struggled for a position behind the barrier. Harry received an elbow in his ribs and Ardis was knocked sideways. He put his arm round her and led her away.

"Rough country lads," he said.

A deep masculine roar rose into the air, as they made their way to a small ground just outside the stadium, still within the main enclosure. People were picnicking there, sitting on lightweight folding chairs or half sprawling upon blankets on the grass. The excited voice of the commentator, reporting the introduction of the teams, came over a number of portable radios. When the game commenced, the crowd noise came over the radio and from the stadium itself, and at times the cheering nearly drowned out the voice on the radio.

It was sunny and pleasantly warm. They sat down on the grass. Harry read the program and listened to the radio, and Ardis turned her face to the sun.

After a while, Harry went back inside the stadium with the hope of seeing some of the match. Returning to the barrier behind the goal, he managed to wedge his way in among the crowd of men. He stood on his toes and caught fleeting glimpses of the players swinging their hurling sticks, sending the small hard ball with a sharp crack in long high arcs through the air. He had no knowledge of hurling. He only knew that if the ball went under the horizontal bar of the goal it was one point; and if it went above the bar and between the uprights, it was three.

He stayed there for a good part of the first half.

When he rejoined Ardis outside, she was seated cross-legged on the grass, reading the program.

"Listen to this, Harry. It says that the hurling stick is called a hurley. It's made of ash—that's the only wood suitable," she said. "I quote, 'No other timber has the same strength and elasticity to withstand the most severe strain and sudden shock which the hurley is subjected to on our fields of play.' " She smiled up at him. He genuinely hoped that she was having a nice time. For a few minutes, he imagined again the sorrow of their coming separation, and he hoped that she would remember some day how they had enjoyed themselves at the Munster Final, and think of him with affection.

They stayed out on the grounds, listening to the radio and taking the sun. Harry went inside the stadium a few more times to get the feeling of the crowd.

The match was nearly over, with Cork leading Clare by a small margin, when they came out onto the road. They hoped to avoid the traffic and get an early start home. As they started up the road, a huge cheer rose from the stadium, and shortly after the cheers died down, people came through the gates and onto the road.

A thin, angular man, with the blue and yellow colors of Clare hanging from his coat pocket, moved quickly past them.

"Who won?" Ardis said, smiling at him.

He stopped and glared at her.

"Go to bloody hell," he said, and then he turned and walked rapidly away.

"What's wrong with him?" Ardis said, her feelings hurt. "I thought it was only a game."

Harry shook his head.

"No, that's the whole point. It's more than a game to him. Much more than that," he said.

"He was rude to me—and for no reason."

"It's true that he was rude but not without a reason," Harry said. "I think it was the way you asked the question that upset him. You weren't deeply involved. He picked that up right away. You came at him from an unserious level, and it bothered him."

"Oh, I see. It was my fault that he was rude."

"I didn't say it was your fault," he said, feeling guilty. "It wasn't anybody's fault." Why was he so helplessly critical? he thought. Why did he hurt her at every opportunity? Was it simply because she had a talent for irritating him? Or did he have some special problem of his own? As they walked along, he wondered if he was a difficult person, or simply a person with difficulties; and the more he thought about it, the more confused, uncertain, and hopeless he became.

They moved slowly with the crowd. Cork partisans waving red and white colors and shouting, "Up Cork," moved with wild hilarity up the road. The Clare flags and streamers were put away, or carried at some angle of defeat.

On the road to Limerick, Harry turned on the radio just in time for a special bulletin. "The ticket office of Semple Stadium at Thurles was robbed during the second half of the Munster Final by three armed men. The men were judged between eighteen and twenty-one years old. They warned the officials not to move. The sum taken was estimated to be about 24,000 punt." The weather forecast followed. Long spells of sunshine.

"And we never knew it," Harry said.

He looked over at her. She was slumped sideways in her seat, leaning against the door. Her mouth was slightly open, and she appeared drained and remote. It wasn't his fault, he thought. God knows, he had never promised to marry her.

Harry made a wrong turn in Limerick, and it took him twenty minutes to find his way again.

They were on their way to Doolin in County Clare. Earlier he'd promised Ardis that he'd take her to hear folk singing at one of the pubs there. The folk singing was a local tradition, a woman from Kinvarra had told them, that took place every Sunday and was "particularly attractive to Americans." He had never been to Doolin and, until recently, had known it only as a place where a boat could be taken to the Aran Islands.

At about seven in the evening, they went into McGann's Pub and sat down at a small table and ordered draft Guinness. The room was crowded. A young man with a guitar was singing an

Irish folk song. Some older men at a table across the room nois-ily interrupted him by singing a song of their own.

"Will you not show me the courtesy? Is that too much to ask of you?" he said.

After he finished, another man sang and played the guitar. His voice was thin and sincere, and his song was in Gaelic. There was relative quiet for a time, and some of the older patrons appeared contemplative. Then the room became noisy again. A man stood up and played an accordion and danced a jig. The waiters passed back and forth with large glasses of dark stout and lighter shades of ale. The young man with the guitar who had sung first played and sang again, and he was once more interrupted by the group of older men at the table across the room.

"For God's sake, be quiet now," he shouted.

A few of the older men laughed, and he resumed his singing, with a quaver in his voice that had not been there earlier.

Harry got up and went to the lavatory. On the way back to his table, he passed by the table of the older men, and they looked up at him.

"And who are you then?" one of them said, with a touch of belligerence. The man's face was ruddy, and he was missing some of his upper front teeth.

Harry nodded and smiled at him and was about to walk on, when the man said, "Where did you get that cap now? It looks like an old one."

"It was my father's. He gave it to me years ago," Harry said.

"Oh, it was your father's. Do you know the song, 'Me Father's Hat'?" He began to sing it, and though it was in English, Harry couldn't understand all of the words.

"That's an old cap," one of the other men said. "There were caps like that during the Easter Rising."

"Sit down and join us in a pint," the man missing the front teeth said.

"I should probably get back," he said, nodding toward his table across the room.

"Oh, she'll wait for you. Sit down, lad."

Some of the men made room for Harry, and he pulled up a chair and sat down at the table.

"What would you have?" the ruddy man said.

Harry hesitated, thinking of his glass of Guinness.

"Give him a pint of Smithwick light," the man said to the waiter. "And the same all round."

A man at another table stood up and began to dance to the sounds of a fiddle, and then he stopped abruptly, as though he had pulled a muscle in his side, and sat down again.

Filled glasses were put down.

"My name's Thomas," the ruddy-faced man said. "All at this table are from Corofin or nearby. This is Matt and Colum and Martin—and this is Joe. Joe has been living in New York." The man called Joe nodded. He was a thin, gaunt, elderly man. "Joe has come back to live for good in Ireland, not just for visits in the summer," Thomas said.

"New York is no longer a good place for an Irishman," Joe said. "I've come to live on my brother's farm. The social security will come each month."

Harry introduced himself.

"And you're an American yourself, by your accent," Thomas said.

"Yes, I am."

Harry finished the pint of Smithwick, and before he could leave, another pint was put down in its place; and though he said that he had to be going, the men insisted that he remain.

"You must show us the courtesy and finish your pint," Thomas said.

Harry looked over at Ardis. She regarded him with a look of suffering, and he felt that he was neglecting her.

After he finished his pint, he said, "Let me buy this round."

"Oh, you can't do that. It isn't right. Not in McGann's," Thomas said. He ordered the same all round, and then said, "And what have you been doing in Ireland?"

Harry said that he had not been doing much of anything, but on that day they had been to the Munster Final.

"The man was there. He was at Thurles," Thomas announced to the others. He looked at Harry and shook his head. "It's a bloody shame how the referee threw the Clare lad out of the game—and he had got eight stitches in his face, and yet *he* was called guilty!"

"And did you hear about the robbery? They got away with the whole bloody take," Colum said.

"No doubt they were Clare men," Matt said.

"If it was one, I'd say it was a Clare man, but since it took three, they are from Galway," Colum said.

"And the game itself, that was a robbery!" Thomas said.

"We don't want to talk about the bloody game," Martin said. "To hell with County Cork."

"Speaking of Cork, here comes Desmond," Thomas said. "He's from Cork but is here visiting his wife's family. Of course, he's glad of the result."

"Oh, I don't care at all," Desmond said. He was a slightly built, affable man, and he carried a small dog.

Harry made room for him, and Desmond sat down. Thomas introduced them.

"Jesus, he brought the mutt again," Colum said. "That dog can't get enough to drink."

Desmond laughed, and he ordered a pint of ale.

He told Harry that he was a coach driver, and that his profession took him all over Ireland.

"What I like most about all of the traveling is observing the differences in people," he said. "The people in Cork, for example, are more homely than the people in Dublin, who are more cosmopolitan. Of course, it's only my opinion."

"And what about the people here?" Thomas said.

"Oh, the people here are very odd, particularly the ones from Corofin," Desmond said.

The men laughed.

After he finished his ale, he said that he had to get back to his wife and her family. He shook hands with Harry, then stood up with his puppy.

"Goodbye to all here and good luck. Wave your paw at them, Sonny," Desmond said, and then he left.

Harry looked across the room at Ardis. She appeared embarrassed and confused, and she seemed to question him with her eyes, which seemed to say, "How can you go to such lengths to be unpleasant to me?" Although he felt guilty, he was unable to move.

"Have another one, Harry," Thomas said, and a glass of Smithwick was placed next to an empty glass which was then removed.

A man sang "Spencer Hill." Then he said something in Gaelic and slumped down in his chair.

"Did you hear this one?" Thomas said, nodding at Harry. "A priest was giving a sermon about whiskey. 'Drink kills,' he said, and he illustrated the point by taking a live worm out of a small box he was carrying in his pocket, and then he drowned the worm in a glass of whiskey. Then the priest poured some whiskey in another glass and drank it down, and a man who was watching this said, 'But, Father, if drink kills, then why are you drinking that whisky?' and the priest said, 'I've got worms, man, and I've already demonstrated that whiskey kills them.' " Thomas slammed a hand down on the table and threw his head back and laughed.

"He had worms, you see," he said.

"What I want to know, is drink more dangerous than music?" Colum said. "This priest said to me that it was music that makes the first assault, for it breaks down the nervous system, and then any craziness can enter."

Thomas shook his head.

"Craziness doesn't enter in such a case. It was there all the time. The music is just an innocent bystander." He turned to Harry. "And speaking of music, I played a tin whistle long ago, but now the lads get paid for it, and it isn't the same. A man from here recently came home with a packet of money for playing Irish music. It wasn't like that in my day, when it was played for fun and played for nothing." He paused. "Well, Harry, you're not quite done, and here's another." A pint of Smithwick was put down before him.

"Oh, no, I couldn't," Harry said.

"Did you hear that, Colum? Harry said he couldn't," Matt said.

"Drink it or you'll get sick," Colum said. He laughed and put a hand on Joe's shoulder. Joe looked pale and old, and his eyes were tired.

"Well, you'll not see New York again," Colum said.

"He'll not miss it," Martin said. "It's not a good place for an Irishman."

"Was it ever?" Colum said.

"Oh, yes, a long time ago," Joe said.

"What I want to know, is Ireland a good place for an Irishman?" Thomas said. "The north is a bloody disaster, and in Dublin there are gang rapes in Phoenix Park, and Galway City, well, that's become a poor sad place. The courtesy's gone. The people don't even say 'sorry' when they jostle you on the street but push you aside without a word. It's money on their brains, not kindness."

"It's the Common Market," Colum said.

"Well, here's to prosperity, at least," Martin said, raising his glass.

"The saddest thing of all is the younger generation," Thomas said. "They show no respect for anything."

"And what about you, Thomas?" Colum said. "What do you show respect for?"

"I'm a courteous man," Thomas said.

Colum smiled and turned to Harry.

"He was a wild boy, and now he envies the younger lads, that he can't be wild like them."

"He's still wild, but he's slow and can't keep up with them," Martin said.

Thomas laughed.

"Oh, God, what lies they say about me," he said.

Harry finished his ale as Ardis walked over. He was surprised to see her. He stood up and introduced her to the other men.

"You thought Harry had run away, but he had just gone across the room," Thomas said. "Some go across the water, and you never hear from them again."

Ardis smiled.

"She has a beautiful smile, Harry," Thomas said. "You had better not go far from her."

"I won't," Harry said. He shook hands with all the men at the table. "I wish I could repay your kindness," he said.

"Oh, we'll meet again," Thomas said.

"Yes, in heaven," Colum said.

It was late twilight, and a breeze with the smell of the sea passed through the town.

They got in the car, and Harry started up the engine. The car began to move down the road.

"Harry, the car is weaving."

"Don't worry," he said, but he felt light-headed and drowsy, and he had a hard time judging the road.

He pulled over and slumped forward with his head on the wheel. "I'll be all right in a minute," he said. "I know a good restaurant in Kinvarra."

"You'd better rest first, or we'll never get there," she said. She shook her head and sighed. Her feelings were still hurt from the way he had abandoned her in the pub.

Harry slumped down in the seat and half dozed, with the radio playing. A commentator was speaking of Gaelic football, of the time when Galway won the Connacht Final by beating Mayo, who had won in 1931. Galway and Mayo had met in nine Connacht Finals. Bobby Baker was one of the great heroes of Gaelic football. And Montclair and Jerry O'Malley were other Connacht players worthy of remembering.

He fell asleep to the sound of their names and slept for half an hour. He was all right when he woke up, except for a feeling of melancholy and a stiffness in his lower back.

The twilight was turning to dusk.

After they came round a curve, Harry saw in the distance, on the slope of a hill, an old trailer and a dilapidated car. In front of the trailer, a big pot was sitting over some dead coals. Suddenly, as the car approached, a man began to run down the side of the hill, frantically waving his arms. A teenaged boy was with him.

"You better not stop. They're tinkers," Ardis said.

"Maybe they're in real trouble," he said. He went past them, then stopped and backed up the car.

He had always felt a little sorry for the tinkers, Ireland's itinerant population; but he felt uneasy in their presence.

The man wore a shabby pinstriped coat over a white T-shirt. He was smiling abjectly and carrying a piece of hose. Beside him stood a husky, slightly-stooped boy of about fourteen with a large metal bucket.

"My wife is sick. Can you spare some petrol?" the tinker said.

"What's wrong with your wife?"

"An ailment."

"I'll take her to the hospital," Harry said.

"No, the doctor is coming."

"If he's coming, then why do you need the gas?"

"To give to him for having used up his own. It's the least I can do since I have no money to pay."

"Well," Harry said.

"Harry, this is absurd," Ardis whispered.

He got out of the car.

"All right, I can give you a little," he said.

"May God keep you," the tinker said. "My boy will siphon some of your petrol." He made a sign to his son who walked over with the bucket, quickly removed the cap, and then blew into the hose, dropping one end into the tank and the other into the bucket. Harry could hear the gas begin to flow onto the bot tom.

He tried to watch the siphoning, but the man moved between him and the boy.

"Would you have fags then? For my nerves," the tinker said.

Harry gave him what was left of a pack of cigarettes.

The tinker's son removed the hose from the gas tank and started to walk away with the bucket. Harry noticed that it was filled to the brim.

"Good lord, he filled the whole bucket!" he said.

"No, the bucket was partly filled when he started," the tinker said, backing away and smiling.

"Then why didn't you give *that* gas to the doctor?"

"Oh, it wasn't nearly enough. He's coming a great distance."

"Look, the bucket wasn't filled when he started. I heard the gas hit the metal bottom."

"Did you hear that then?"

The boy hesitated. His father shouted at him and struck him hard on the shoulder. Looking frightened and tilting to one side, he carried the bucket up the hill.

The tinker slowly backed up the slope.

"You have plenty left in your tank. May God bless you for your kindness," he said.

Harry stood by the car, feeling sick and light-headed; and then he got in and started up the engine and began driving down the road.

"What was that all about?" Ardis said.

He didn't say anything.

"I'll tell you what it was all about. You let him take advantage of you, to punish yourself."

He felt warm with anger, but he tried to be measured.

"Look, I know I was a bit of a fool. But my basic impulse was to be fair, to do the right thing," he said.

She laughed with sudden hysteria.

"The right thing? You don't know anything about that. Look what you're doing to me."

He excitedly raised one hand from the steering wheel.

"God, can't you ever be pleasant? You're so damned depressing," he said.

"I'm depressing? And what about you, Harry? You're the depressed personality of our time."

Harry raised a hand and waved it wildly.

"Well, you've depressed me," he said. "You never let up from morning to night, with your sighs and sadness and your litany of complaints. I'm really sick of you, Ardis."

Her eyes began to blink rapidly, then her mouth trembled.

"I can think of plenty that's wrong with you, too, Harry," she said. She shook her head, and her breath caught in her throat, and she gasped. Then she took a deep shuddering breath and tried to let the air out slowly. She wanted to be calm and retain what was left of her dignity. "You're selfish and arrogant and blind," she said in a tremulous voice. "You're an emotional invalid, a hypochondriac. I don't know why I ever loved you, Harry. But I really hate you now."

"I'm glad," he said.

She began to sob.

It was all over, he thought, feeling suddenly weary. It was finally obvious to him that there was not even a glimmer of hope for them, that they would separate, and the sooner the better. It was a relief, in a way, he thought.

Then the car lost power and the engine died. As he got out to look under the hood, he realized what was wrong.

"We're out of gas," he said.

Ardis leaned forward against the dashboard and continued sobbing.

He looked at her through the car window.

"I'm going to Kinvarra for gas," he said. She looked up briefly, her face distorted and wet with tears, and then buried her face in her arms again.

Kinvarra was nearly two miles away. In the dusky light, Harry walked past fields with small herds of grazing sheep. What was wrong with him? he thought. He was getting old, nothing pleased him, and he displeased everyone. It was a hopeless situation.

A car passed, the first car he had seen. He forgot to hail the driver, then decided to walk all the way to Kinvarra.

The sky was filled with stars. It was one of the clearest nights he had ever known in Ireland, and one of the more beautiful days. He thought he would always remember it as the day he finally finished with Ardis, on the day of the Munster Final.

A breeze came out of the fields and chilled him. He had a headache and began to feel sick. After he had walked about half a mile, he decided to stop and rest. Feeling dizzy and slightly nauseous, he sat down on a stone wall. She was making him ill, he thought. It was bad to live in such an atmosphere, and it was making him sick and tired and old before his time, and he couldn't take it anymore. It wasn't right that he should feel such guilt and distress, he thought. He wasn't a bad person, not compared to all the really bad people in the world. He didn't deserve to be the target of her rancor and bitterness and her disappointment in life, and of his own tormenting conscience. He began to feel sicker, more nauseous; and there was now a mild pressure in his chest.

He looked beyond the wall to a field with a haycock. The gray light seemed to waver and bend, and he thought there was something wrong with his eyes. Some crows flew up in the sky. Part of him seemed to rise with them, and the sense of motion increased his nausea and vertigo. As he rose to his feet, he felt a sharp pain in his chest and a heavy pressure on his shoulders which forced him to sit down by a ditch on the side of the road.

He broke into a sweat. His chest began to tighten, and the ground seemed to rise and then drop away from him. Holding on to the side of the ditch, he tried to smile and relax. "Cheer up, Harry," he said, but he was badly frightened, for it occurred to him that he was dying. 'Oh, no, I've got to get gas. Ardis is waiting for me,' he thought.

In order to calm himself, he lay down on his back and attempted to meditate. At first, he tried to concentrate on his uneven breathing, and then he closed his eyes and imagined a vacant white screen from which he tried to remove, as they appeared, all unpleasant impressions.

His breathing became labored and his heartbeat rapid and irregular. Along with fear and intense disappointment, he experienced hurt feelings. It wasn't fair, he thought. It wasn't right. He rose to all fours, then collapsed on his side, sliding down the bank of the ditch. The ditch appeared like an open grave to him. Frightened, he staggered to his feet and climbed the stone wall, then went reeling into the pasture, ran for twenty yards, and fell.

He lay face downward on his arm, his cap beside him, and lost consciousness.

He dreamed that he was leaving his body and that he began to rise slowly into the air. Looking down he saw himself in the field, his head resting on his arm. As he continued rising, the details of the landscape grew smaller, and the whole region stretched out before him. He could see their white Ford Escort to the west and the town of Kinvarra farther to the east and small moonlit lakes and fields and little houses and the winding road. Rising higher, he felt an unbelievable gladness that he was in a new realm, that his suffering was over. He could see the western coast of Ireland and the Atlantic Ocean, and then he found himself suspended above pale clouds, no longer rising. He reached upwards to go higher, but he began to go down, descending slowly to the west of Ireland, to County Clare, to the small field by the road to Kinvarra, until, hovering over his body, he said, "Oh, no," for he wanted to rise again, and he entered into himself.

Harry opened his eyes and looked helplessly around him. He got to his knees as another wave of pain and nausea swept over him, and he threw up in the field all the ale he had drunk in the pub at Doolin, and everything else.

He lay back and looked up at the night sky. The stars shone down in a vast profusion of benevolent light. A breeze passed over his face and body. He felt better. The nausea and pain were gone, and he could breathe easily again. He was very moved that he was still alive. He sat up and laughed. A flock of birds flew over him. Sheep bleated in the pasture. "I'm all right. It was indigestion," he shouted in the direction of the haycock.

It was then that he realized that he had decided to marry her. The more he thought about it, the more his conscience felt at peace; and this produced in him a sensation of light-headedness. Yes, he loved her, he thought. He had always loved her, and he would be kind to her now. He wouldn't have to leave her and never see her again and add that mistake to all the others he had made, and it would have been the worst mistake of all, he thought.

He looked forward to her happy surprise when he asked her to marry him over the wine at dinner. It made him glad to think that for once he would be the bearer of good news. In his mind's eye, he saw her looking nervous and confused at the change that had come over him, and then he asked her to marry him. 'I don't believe you, Harry. Are you serious?' she said, and began to cry and asked through tears if it was true. 'Yes, it's true, Ardis,' he said, and he put his arms round her.

Harry rose to his feet and walked to the stone wall and climbed over it to the road, and then he began walking toward Kinvarra. The tightness and contractions of his body had eased; the stoop had gone from his shoulders. He swung his arms and moved with a confident and easy gait, his head erect. He was not himself. But after he had walked a mile, he became hesitant and uncertain, and he slowed down and stopped. "What do I think I'm doing? Am I out of my mind? I'm not ready. I need more time," he said. It seemed for a moment that he would not begin walking again.

But he continued on through moonlight and shadow, feeling a troubled happiness and wishing life were clearer; and as he approached the outskirts of Kinvarra and walked on into the town, where he discovered that its lone gas station was closed, he knew in his joyous and fearful heart that he would become again a married man.

Jack Atherton in Texas

The Lone Star Kid

The other day I was standing on the courthouse square, leaning against the memorial to the Confederate dead, when Sheriff
Holcombe came up to me, and he said, "You ain't carrying no
stuff on you, are you, Jack?" and I said, "You mean I'm looking
that happy?" and he said, "Well, I hope you ain't taking LSD or
smoking that marijuana just to pass the time," and I said, "No,
sir, I'm just high on fresh air." And he laughed and slapped me
on the back and said, "Jack, you're some dude. Hey, you boys
ready for the Denison game?"

If you are a Texas boy and can't play football, people tend to
look down on you some no matter what else you can do. But if
you are a great player, that's a different story. I guess you could
be in Wichita Falls, Denison, Fort Worth, Abilene or El Paso or
any other place in the Lone Star State, and if you happened to
say, "What do you think of Jack Atherton of Lacyville?" there
would be a lot of excited talk, and a few girls might feel a little
faint for no other reason than they just heard my name. I guess I
am one famous schoolboy player.

I sure am lucky to live in Texas. It makes me feel good just to
walk around under this sky. It's so big and grand, and on certain
days in the winter the air gets so crisp and clear that you can see

for miles in the distance, and all the barns and fences and trac-
tors and cars and railroad tracks and white houses and small red
buildings, they all look so sharp and bright and shiny, like a lot
of new toys; and you feel so good and happy. On such days, I
feel I'm hardly walking on the ground but am part of the sky
itself, just floating through the world and loving everything I
see. And when the sun goes down in Texas and night comes and
the bright stars come swarming out, well, you couldn't see a
better sight, even if you were in the middle of the Gulf of Mexico and there was nothing but the water below and the sky
above. You know the expression, 'I'm up in the clouds'? Well, I
bet some old Texas boy who was just walking down the road
was the first to say that. All you have to do is cross the Red River
and go into Oklahoma and you'll see the sky change. I don't
know why, but it's just plain sky up there and you don't feel like
you're in the heavens as when you're down in Texas.

So here I am walking along wearing my light gray Stetson
and flared blue jeans and the boots my daddy bought me four
years ago in Nogales, Mexico (I'm just now growing into them);
and I'm wearing my green Lacyville varsity jacket with the tan
leather sleeves and a white 'L' on the front and number 7 on my
left arm, just below the shoulder. Coach Dixon says they are
going to retire my number after I graduate in June. It's all right
with me. According to my Granddaddy Jim, the only thing really
wrong with me is that I need a haircut. I guess my hair is getting longer, and the other day Jim said, "Jack, you're getting to
look like a hippie." He said that my hair was so long that I could
be a rodeo clown and pick up some extra money jumping in
the barrel. He acts like my hair is hanging over my shoulders
when it's just over my shirt collar some. I wear some fancy side-
burns too but only because my girlfriends like the way it looks.
Where they're concerned, I aim to please.

I live in Lacyville, which is in northeast Texas, in a little old
wood house in a field off the side of a road, with my mother,
Granddaddy Jim, and my brother, Davey, who is twelve years

old. My daddy died three years ago, and he was the greatest man I'll ever know. His name was Jack Atherton, Sr., and you might have heard of him. He was one of the greatest saddle bronc riders of the late forties and fifties. He was something out there. To please my mother he gave it all up and became a salesman for farm equipment. He died in an automobile accident. It was the worst thing that ever happened to me. Daddy was a wonderful man, and he always looked out for us. I never met anyone who knew him who didn't think an awful lot of him. When I was ten he whipped me for talking back to him, and he said, "Jack, you don't want to have a big smart mouth so that no one will listen to you or like you. Now before you answer a person, think about what he has said, and then you answer kindly." He sure was right about that. Afterwards my mouth slowed down so much for a while that you could have called me Silent Night. Oh, we all miss daddy. When his sister Ramona comes over from Odessa, we often sit around and talk about him. It's wonderful to hear great stories about your father, and it eases the hurt that he is gone. When Ramona comes over, she'll say to Davey and me, "Come here, honey, let me hug your neck." I used to wipe off her kisses, and she'd pretend to be angry and say, "Now, Jack, don't you wipe off my sugar."

As Jim says, "We are poor but I can't say we are wretched." He is my mother's daddy, and he has been living with us for five years, ever since he retired from the MKT Railroad. He is seventy-one years old, and every month he gets a pension check from the railroad and another one from social security. Mother works as a teller in the Harlow County Savings and Loan Bank, and two nights a week she works in Miss Millard's Ladywear until nine o'clock at night. It's a hard life for her, and we all help out doing chores around the place. Mother doesn't do any cooking except on Sundays when she may bake some corn bread and make a pie. It's Jim and me and Davey who take turns at the stove. Jim is a great cook, and he makes chile con carne better than the Mexicans. He grows vegetables on about an acre of ground, and we go out there in the summertime and pick our meal right from the earth—tomatoes, okra, black-eyed peas, onions, corn, and green beans.

Who were the greatest players in the history of Texas football? Well, I'd say John Kimbrough and Dick Todd of Texas A & M; Sam Baugh and Davey O'Brien of Texas Christian; Bobby Layne of the University of Texas; Doak Walker, Kyle Rote, Don Meredith, and Raymond Berry of Southern Methodist; and Dickie Moegle of Rice Institute. Will I ever be as good as those boys? Only time will tell. But I'll say this right now. I'll never have the edge on Sammy Baugh. There was never a boy who put on pads who could play with him.

Oh, I'm just singing along today. Good morning, Mr. Zip, Zip, Zip, I'm just feeling fine. Good morning, Mr. Zippety Zip Zip, I'm zipping the ball on a line. Oh, I love to throw that ball, and I guess I'm one great forward passer. I can throw short, medium or long. I can throw any kind of a pass. I got some receivers who can't handle a perfect spiral, so I put a little wobble on the ball to make it easy for them. I can throw it with the front of the ball tilted up or down or dead level with the ground. I can pop, zing, zip, float, whip, fling, and sling that football. I can send it forty yards on a flat trajectory or seventy-five yards in the air with a friendly loop on it. Yes, sir, yes, ma'am, I can throw at any speed, and I got such a quick release that I amaze even myself. And when I'm not passing the ball, I'm running with it, and I can fake them out of their shoes or run over them if necessary. It don't matter, I just do what the situation calls for. I'm Jumping Jack Atherton, the Lone Star Kid. It's the sportswriters that gave me the names. I think it was some boy from Fort Worth who started it. I'm Texas born and Texas bred, and when I'm on that field there is no way we are going to lose. I'm just a mild-mannered dude until I take over in the huddle. That's where I let them know that I'm calling the plays and don't appreciate mistakes. When some boy messes up and he comes back to the huddle, I don't say, "Thank you, friend," but I let him know that he'd better concentrate or he sure is in some trouble with me. Those boys don't sulk when I chastise them. They play for Old Jack. I tell them we are going to get the ball and move smart and quick. We're just going to move like hell and take it to them. I may take them strong side, weak side. I may call pass or run on the option plays, or send Junior Eberlee on the sweep or Tom Folds up the middle. And we're just going to keep going down the field until we go in for a score. Oh, there ain't nothing like being a quarterback and moving up to the line.

I don't know where I'm going to play my college ball. There are at least twenty-five schools wanting me to sign a letter of intention. I'm leaning toward playing for Coach Darrel Royal down at U.T. But they don't have a passing offense down there and mostly run the ball off the wishbone T formation. Of course they've never had no great passer like me and that includes Bobby Layne, the all-time great. Coach Royal is always talking about how he has got three options off the wishbone T. Well at Lacyville, I put in a formation where we've got four options off one play. It's what I call the 'Jump' play, and that's why the writers call me 'Jumping Jack.' It starts out from the pro set formation, with two wide receivers, on the left and right, and two running backs. I line up over center and take the ball and fake a handoff or give the ball to a back going into the line between guard and center, and if I keep the ball, I move around toward right end and then suddenly I stop and fake a lateral or send one to my other back going around left end. If I fake the lateral, I spin around and continue toward the right, and if I see a clear lane, I'll run the ball, or—and this is what I usually do—just before I reach the line of scrimmage, I jump, going way up in the air, and throw the seventy-yard bomb to Lew Carlton who's running the fly pattern down the left side, or to Bobby Maxwell who's streaking the same pattern down the right. Oh, we pulled it last year on Gainesville and Paris, and it was perfect each time, Lew taking the ball in full stride over his right shoulder. Coach says I'm going to get killed some day doing the 'Jump,' with some big lineman hitting me in midair and then crashing down on me, and then it will be, So long, Jack. Well you can't live forever no way.

Do I know everything? I sure don't. There's one question I can't answer. Am I better at football or baseball? There are some big league scouts telling me I could be on a major league roster tomorrow, or the day after.

There has been a lot of hell-raising lately. Larry Carlton, Lew's brother, threw a brick through the window of Franklin's Clothing Store on North Travis Street. The police said he was either drunk on beer or 'drugged up.' There have been some armed robberies. Last Thursday the Texaco station out on the highway south of town was held up at two in the morning, and the day after, the Big Tex supermarket got robbed in broad daylight by four boys wearing masks. The sheriff thinks they were from Oklahoma. Some of the boys have been caught for drunken driving both in cars and on motorcycles. On Saturday night Joe Lee Moore started firing a .38 caliber handgun up into the sky while sitting in his car at the Dairy Queen.

Yesterday we were all sent to the high school auditorium to hear a talk by a prisoner from the Huntsville Prison. He was a big, long-legged, red-faced old boy, about thirty-five years old. He was from El Paso, and he was in for armed robbery. I thought he had a real pleasant personality. He said, "Boys, when you walk out of here this afternoon, you can go home to your families, but when I leave they are going to put the cuffs on me and drive me back to the Huntsville Prison." He told us to consider carefully what we were doing and not to go astray of the law and end up like him. As we sat there listening, Lew Carlton told me that he saw that boy as a bronc rider at the Huntsville Prison Rodeo. Anyway, he made a real good talk, and then I guess they put the cuffs on him like he said and took him home to prison.

Denison game. Friday night. We were eighty yards away from a score with only forty seconds showing on the clock, and we were behind, 13-7. I threw a bomb to Junior Eberlee, our colored halfback, and he went all the way to the Denison six, and then I faked a pass and ran in for the score. Bobby Maxwell kicked the point. Lacyville, 14; Denison, 13. Hooooooweeeee! It sure saved the weekend.

On Saturday I went odd jobbing. I mended fence, planted three trees, repaired a broken door, cleared off most of the rock from Hazel Grayson's backyard, and helped put up a tool shed. I was one tired boy at four in the afternoon. I'd made me nineteen dollars, and I drove into town and walked into the Franklin Clothing Store and bought me a pair of flared blue Levis with thin white stripes and a red shirt. Heeeeeeeehaaaaa! I was taking out Sally Ambrose. Her daddy's got the biggest used car lot in northeast Texas. You can see him on television saying, "Hello, folks, this is Jimmy Ambrose. You want a '69 Thunderbird that ain't got no more than ten thousand miles? You want a Maverick or a Dodge Dart? It don't matter what you want in the used car line, Jimmy Ambrose got it, friends. And remember this, Jimmy don't send no lemons on the road. So come on out and see me, hear? We'll work it out." During the season, he's letting me use a year-old Camaro for nothing. It's good advertising for him to have Jack Atherton driving one of his cars. At least this year. I sure give those eight cylinders one good workout. Aside from taking out his daughter, who is one pretty girl, I got a girlfriend in Honey Grove, the Sweetest Town in Texas. Her name is Teresa Blankenship, and she is just the pride of Syrup City. I met her in Lacyville about three weeks ago when she was visiting her aunt, Doris Holman, who lives about a quarter of a mile from us. I happened to run into them at the 7-11 Store on Lamar Street, and I never saw such a pretty girl. I went up to her Aunt Doris, and I said, "Why, hello, ma'am, it's sure been a long time." She smiled, for I had just seen her the day before in Ted's Cafe, and she said, "Teresa, this is the Jack Atherton."

"How are you?" I said, breaking into a smile.

"I think I'm surviving," she said. I nearly fell in love with her right then.

I try to get over to Honey Grove at least twice a week to see Teresa. Weekends I date Sally, and so far she is a lot of fun. I can't say which one I like the best, and naturally I don't tell neither girl about the other. If one of them asks me if I'm a 'little serious' about somebody else, I just smile and change the subject. Like I heard some country singer on the radio, "Just don't ask me no questions and I'll tell you no lies, and we'll get along just fine, fine, fine." In other words, don't crowd me, hon.

We went to the Big Star drive-in movie and saw *Rio Lobo* with John Wayne. I was on a double date with Lew Carlton and his girl, and we were all in Lew's daddy's car, a 1965 Oldsmobile. I was sitting in the back seat, watching the movie with Sally. Lew was up front with Doreen 'The Screamer' Halsey, and he said, "Hey, I hear some heavy breathing back there. You sure are fogging up the windows." I said, "Hey, close that big mouth, boy, so I can hear this thing." Then Lew started to laugh like a horse— it's his natural laugh—and Doreen began to scream. Boy, they are a pair.

Lew came to Lacyville two years ago from a town called Happy, which is in the panhandle. He was so country that all he could talk about was the weather—rain, sleet, dust storms, tornadoes, and 'blue northers' coming down from Canada. Lew is some old boy. He wants to play his college ball for Texas A & M. That's right, he wants to be an Aggie. He is just right for them.

After the movie, on the way to Oklahoma to get some 3.2 beer, I told a few Aggie jokes. "Hey, Lew," I said, "Did you hear about the Aggie who stayed up all night studying for his urine test?" I thought he'd drive off the road he laughed so hard, and Doreen was really screaming. And then I said, "Do you know what you get when you cross an Aggie with a chimp? A three foot janitor." I stopped telling them after that, as I wanted us to get to Oklahoma in one piece.

We ended up in a real raunchy place. It was called the 'Smokey Okie.' They had an entertainer and guitar player named 'Woo Woo' Harris, and he would say things like, "If you all happy, say 'Woo Woo'" and a lot of people yelled, "Woo Woo," and he said, "If anybody here from Texas, say 'Woo Woo'" and he kept on like that and later on this old colored waiter, he said, "If anybody tired, say 'Woo Woo'" and then he said "Woo Woo." Boy, that really broke us up. We stayed out until three in the morning.

When Lew dropped me off, he said, "Say, Jack, where are you going to end up, no kidding?" and I said, "Same place you are."

"No stuff? A & M?" Lew said, and I said, "No, sir, the Mekong Delta."

Lew would like me to end up at A & M with him. That'll be the day.

"Well, you take it easy," I said, getting out of the car at the gate to our field. "All you lovers need your rest." Lew shook his head and smiled, then gunned the engine and pulled away.

Oh, he is some old boy, six feet four and two hundred and five and hasn't finished his natural growth. He is a typical wide receiver—hungry for glory and touchdowns. Sometimes I think he wants to stay my friend so I'll throw to him during the games. But friendship don't enter into it. I just hit the open man.

This year we have a fine chance for winning the district. We could easily go on to the bi-district and regional if we don't get bad injuries, and from there we only have to make it through the quarters and semis to be playing in the final for the Texas schoolboy AAAA championship. It's a wonderful team. I've played with most of these boys from way back in grammar school and junior high. We are all playing like demons out there. What is the big difference this year? Junior Eberlee, our colored halfback. Boy, that dude can outrun me. He can go inside and outside and has great hands and fine moves as a receiver. So I'm throwing to some good boys—Lew Carlton, Bobby Maxwell, Joe Clyde Hooker, and Junior. It's the first year we've had a colored boy on the team. Actually, we have two Negro players. The other colored boy is a tackle named Walter Cunningham. They are both fine, intelligent, kind-hearted boys, and I feel lucky to know them. The morale on our team is perfect, and we don't have no trouble on account of race. I can't say that about the rest of the school.

Lacyville High School has been integrated for over a year now. A few days after the federal court passed down the integration order, the ministers started coming to our school. I guess they figured that the school board couldn't stop it and they had better help us get ready for it. They said that God didn't intend for us to be unkind or unfair to someone just because he happened to be colored, and we owed it to ourselves and God to try to get along. How did I feel about integration. Well, I wasn't sure I wanted to go to school with the colored. It didn't seem natural, but then I thought it over, and I thought, it can't hurt anything. It could be a new experience, like foreign travel. So in the fall, when school started, Mr. Heresford, the principal of Lacyville High School, asked me to make a little talk welcoming the Negroes. Why did he pick me? He said it was because I was a leader. So early in September I made a talk outside the school. All the white kids were standing behind me on both sides of the main entrance. The colored who had gone to Frederick Douglass High, about a hundred and fifty of them, were gathered on the steps, waiting to enter. There was a crowd of townspeople standing across the street from the school. I stepped up to this little podium. There was a little breeze that fluttered the two flags—the American and the Lone Star—that were on each side of it. It was a sunny morning. I just said, "My name is Jack Atherton, and I hope you're doing fine. We want to welcome you all coming from the Frederick Douglass school. We are glad to see you, and please just come right on in and make yourselves at home. It's going to be a fine year." Then we all sang "The Eyes of Texas." Right after the song ended—it was real quiet for a second—this old boy yelled from across the street, "Hey you goddam niggers, go back to where you belong." It cracked the air like a gunshot because everything had been so still. And then somebody else yelled, "Atherton, you damn turncoat, we'll get you." I looked to see who said it, and I saw. It was Woody Prud-homme, and he was standing with his brother, Alvin. I knew them. They are big, raw-boned old boys, and they were wearing some dirty old Stetsons and muddy boots, standing there with some other boys. The Prudhommes are in their early twenties, and they got a mean reputation. When all the kids went on into school, I told Mr. Heresford who was standing outside that I had to walk across the street for something, and he said, "Go ahead, Jack." So I walked over to the Prudhomme boys—most of the others had drifted away—and I said, "What are you boys doing in town? I figured you'd be out in the fields busting rock." I just wanted to say something smart to them. Woody just nodded and squinted his eyes—he has a moon shaped face, with a lot of brown freckles on his forehead—and he said, "Atherton, we're going to get you, boy. I ain't going to tell you where or when, but we'll get you, don't worry." Alvin, his brother, nodded. They were about six foot three and weighed over two hundred. I said, "Why don't you all get out of town? Go on back to the trough and feed the pigs, and while you're at it you might as well stay for dinner—if it don't make the pigs sick." And then I walked away, and Woody said, "You're smart to run as I'd a knocked you on your ass." I'm not scared of them, and I'd have stayed and made a few more remarks, but I had to get back to school.

The Prudhomme boys live on a little spread about ten miles north of town with their father, two sisters, about a hundred head of cattle, and some pigs, chickens, and horses. They are some bad news. The story going around is that they killed some boys up in Muscogee, Oklahoma, but they can't get no evidence on them. I'm sure they did it though. They are a couple of wild dogs.

When the Negroes came to school with us, they were a little shy and scared and eager to please. We all tried real hard to get along, and we did for a while. It was an interesting time, and even for the white kids who resented them, it was a new kind of experience. But then it all changed. Maybe the colored kids resented having to try to please everybody and just wanted to be themselves. One thing led to another. In the assembly hall in front of the whole school during a Texas History program, a colored girl named Mary Jones gave a speech on how the Lacyville courthouse was burned down in 1932 by a white mob to get at a colored prisoner who they lynched. It was the truth and everybody knew it, but the report was resented. You'd come to school and there was this tension in the hallway and in the classroom. The colored kids started letting their hair grow and wore 'Afros' and dark glasses. It rubbed a lot of people the wrong way. It was like they were saying, "Man, we don't need you, and we don't want to be like you anymore." A lot of the boys felt insulted and got upset. There are fights all the time now. Harry Lakewood has been waving the Confederate flag and singing "Dixie" whenever he can. He told me yesterday, "They just walk around and give you smart-ass looks and act like if you're white you ain't worth a damn, and I told one of them, 'Boy, you are still in Texas, and don't you never forget it.' Jack, they act like they're too superior to have any school spirit. I don't know why they ever come to the games unless it's just to flaunt that they don't care one way or the other. The only time they cheer is when Junior Eberlee carries the ball. It's enough to make you sick. If they don't like it here, why don't they stay the hell away. Nobody sent for them. I'm really tired of this crap. You know what Earlene Graves said to me? She said, 'Harry Lakewood, we're going to get the Black Panthers after you crackers down here. Our brothers are going to straighten you out.' I really wanted to puke. I said, 'Look, Earlene, you can take your brothers and sisters and get on the ship to Africa as far as I'm concerned.' You should have seen the dumb-assed look she gave me. They're all upset that I'm waving the Confederate flag. Well, that's just too damned bad. I'm surprised they can see it through their dark glasses. Boy, they are sure making me sick. Listen, you know what I did at the Longview game? I went out of my mind, Jack, that's what. I grabbed this colored boy, Randolph Smith—he was just sitting

there like he was half asleep, and I said, 'Boy, are you with us?'—
I swear, Jack, he just didn't give a damn—and I said, 'Boy, we
got to pull together, are you with us or against us?' and I was so
goddamned mad that I slapped him in the face a few times, and
he just sat there and took it. He is damn lucky he did or I would
have stomped hell out of that nigger. Jack, sometimes I feel like
stomping on all their dark glasses and shaving off their afros.
That would teach them some manners. Where do they get off
acting superior to white people? I don't need no colored people
lording it over me. Hell, this ain't Chicago, Illinois. This is Texas,
Jack."

I told Harry that he had just better put away his Confederate
flag. That wasn't the way. You've just got to try to overlook a lot
of things in this world. Hell, I'm not going to fight every time
somebody calls me a name or says something smart to me. I'd
never have time for nothing else. (My motto is never fight unless
you're cornered, and then fight to kill.) I'm a tolerant person. I
take each person as he comes down the road, and I judge him
as a person and not by the color of his skin. I'm real friendly
with Walter and Junior, the colored boys on the team. I couldn't
hate them now if I tried. I explained all this to Harry who got
more angry by the minute.

"What are you talking about, Jack?" he said, like he never
really knew me before. I didn't say nothing more to him.

Generally I'm friendly with all the colored. The dark glasses
and bush cut don't make me nervous, and so far they have been
real decent to me. Why is that? Well, who can resist Jack Atherton? That's a joke, boy.

This afternoon two colored girls from school, Minnie Morris and Nadine Robinson, forced a white woman off the side-
walk and into the street. One of the girls had said, "Clear out,
lady, the express train is coming through." I was there and saw
the whole thing. The white lady was Mae Harrell who is about
fifty-five and works in a beauty parlor on Travis Street. When
she got forced off the sidewalk, she was so shocked she couldn't

talk at first, but then she went to the sheriff. I followed her down the street, as I wondered how it would all turn out. The sheriff was sitting in his car outside his office talking to Art Jones, one of his deputies, and Mae started screaming about what these girls had done to her.

"Did they put their hands on you, Mae?" Sheriff Holcombe said.

"I *told* you they forced me into the street."

"Well, what do you want me to do?" he said.

"I want you to lock them up, that's what."

He said he couldn't do that to them for just blocking the side-walk and saying something to her.

"They talked smart to me," Mae said.

"But they didn't break no law, Mae," he said.

"They were rude and disrespectful," she said. "And I don't think a decent white man would let *that* slide." Then she really went wild. She said, "In my daddy's day, they would have been horsewhipped for just looking at you wrong, and I sure am sorry times have changed." Then she looked at me and said, "Why I can even remember the time when all the white boys weren't dopeheads and sex maniacs." I don't know why she looked at me when she said it.

At school today during lunch, Harry Lakewood started waving the Confederate flag outside the building, and a colored boy tried to take it away from him. There was a little scuffle which didn't last long. Some coaches broke it up. Then the colored and white kids started yelling at each other. Naturally I tried to calm everybody down, and I guess I was successful. I made a little talk. I said, "We aren't just white boys and colored boys. We are all Texas boys, and we have got that in common. I know we can get along." They all listen to Jack, at least this year.

Gainesville, Texas. Friday night. Our sixty-piece marching band and a thousand people from Lacyville traveled to Gaines-ville to see us play. It was a beautiful night. We came running out on the field in white helmets and green jerseys with two white stripes on the sleeves and white pants with green stripes on the sides. Gainesville wore white jerseys with red stripes on the sleeves and red pants and helmets. When we came on the field there were some loud boos from the Gainesville crowd, but we could still hear some cheers from our fans. The grass smelled fresh and was bright green under the lights.

In the fourth quarter, I called the 'Jump' play and threw a sixty-five-yard bomb to Bobby Maxwell. We won, 28-13, and we are closing in on the district championship.

This morning I heard that Alvin Prudhomme had made a remark that "somebody" was going to kill me "after the sun went down." He said it at Ted's Cafe on Cherry Street, and three people heard him.

I got two hate letters this week. One went, 'Atherton, get ready to die.' The other said, 'Nigger lover, kiss the world good-bye.' I know they were from the Prudhomme boys, though they never sign them. I wonder what they are doing this very moment, at eight o'clock in the night. They are probably sitting around with a bottle of gun blue and a can of oil cleaning their artillery. That's their recreation. Boy, they are really crazy. I guess I am a little more alert these days.

Sunday dinner. Mother fixed salmon croquettes, ham, corn bread, crowder peas, and mashed potatoes with brown gravy. It was really fine. After lunch, Jim poured himself some J. W. Dant (100 proof) bourbon and water (not very much). He started singing, "Oh, I'm going to leave old Texas now, they've got no use for the longhorn cow ..." and so forth. He has a fine, gravelly old voice, and Davey and I enjoyed the recital. Then after all that good food had settled, Davey and I went over to the junior high-school field, and I threw the football to him. He ran all the routes, square in, square out, fly pattern, post pattern, little curls and look-ins, button hooks. And I'd throw to him on a count; that is, on a count of three or four I'd throw to a certain spot, and Davey would time it so he'd be there. He wants to be a split end for Rice Institute, and he is pretty good for twelve years old.

I threw to him for half an hour, and then we quit. I didn't want to tire my arm. And then us Atherton boys walked back to the house. It was a perfect day. The sky was deep blue and the air was so clear. It was great to be walking down that sunny road. Davey sure is proud to walk with me. He is always looking to me for advice, and naturally I always have plenty for him.

Back at the house, we sat around on the porch. Davey found Mother's high-school yearbook, the Lacyville Lookout of 1939, and we had a good time reading through it. The kids looked different then, older for their age. Mother looked so sweet and innocent and serious. One girl had written in her book, "Dorothy, I certainly think a lot of you, and that's no kidding. I think you are so cute and sweet and have a darling figure. Your personality is just tops and that's no kidding. I only hope one thing—that you will always stay as sweet as you are. I hope we stay friends always. With lots of love, Mabel Lou Worthington."

We read the other inscriptions in the book, and they all had something good to say about Mother.

I got another hate letter today. It went, "Atherton, you son of a bitch, your days are numbered."

In the team bus, on the way to Paris, Texas, going through the Blackland Prairie Country. We passed through Greenville, and there was a sign outside the town. "The blackest land and the whitest people." I wondered if Junior or Walter saw it. Grand Prairie and then Celeste, and then we came out on Route 82 and drove through Bonham, and when we passed this white frame house right on the highway, Lew Carlton yelled, "Hey, hey, Mr. Sam," and then we all let out a cheer. That was Sam Rayburn's house before he died, and now it's a museum. We always give him a cheer when we come through Bonham, on the way to one game or another. I was really looking forward to playing Paris, because that's where Raymond Berry is from. He is maybe the greatest end of all time.

A reporter from some newspaper asked me what was the secret of my success, and I told him I get so happy before a game

I can't hardly stand it, and then I go out there, with this happiness building up inside me, and play as good as I feel.

We beat Paris, 35-6. I won't say what I did, as it would sound too much like bragging. But I'd like to give some special credit to Lew Carlton, Junior Eberlee, and Tom Folds.

I saw Sally Ambrose today outside of school. She said, "Jack, honey, where have you been?" Even though she was smiling, she seemed angry and hurt.

"I've been to practice," I said.

"You don't practice all the time," she said, smiling. "Have you lost my phone number?"

"Look, I've been busy," I said, starting to walk away.

"Oh, you're so busy being the Lone Star Kid and getting a big head," she said.

I kept walking. And then she ran over to me and started to plead with me. "You know how I feel about you, Jack," she said. She kept tugging at my arm, my passing arm, and I pulled it free and kept going; and I never said a word to her.

She started calling me at seven o'clock every half hour until nine thirty. I had Jim and Davey say I wasn't at home.

It rained real hard today, and there was no practice. Sally was waiting for me again, and I was almost glad to see her. She looked awfully pretty. I went for a ride with her, and we parked out on a side road near a deserted oil rig. I figured we were going to make love, but she started complaining about how I had ignored her, how I had done this and that, and then I just completely lost interest; and when she threw her arms around me and said, "Jack, aren't you going to kiss me?" I was so fed up that I just started up the engine, and we drove on back to town. She cried all the way and said I was a person that didn't have no heart and only wanted to hurt people.

The more I see of Sally the more I like that girl from Honey Grove—sweet, little Teresa.

When I came home, Jim and some of his friends, these old men from his railroad days on the MKT line were sitting on the porch. As I walked up, Joe Hillyard, a bony, bent old man with a wide mouth was saying that the people used to have more character and that the world had gone to hell and nobody had no self-respect anymore. He said it was enough to make you sick to watch what was happening, that it was like the whole country was going under. "Hell, they are even trying to get rid of the Texas Rangers," he said. Then he looked at me, and he said, "Jack, how are you, son?" I nodded. They all said I was one hell of a boy, and of course Jim was real proud.

I got another letter. "You dirty bastard you'll be dead before Christmas."

It was on Saturday afternoon when Davey brought a colored boy home for lunch. I was really surprised. It was a friend of his from junior high school, and his name was Frankie Dunes. Davey asked me if it was all right for him to have lunch with us. He seemed like a nice little old boy, and I said, "Son, you just pull up a chair." We ate out on the porch. It was very pleasant in the sunshine with the air a little cool. Jim was real nice to that colored boy, and he made sure that he had plenty to eat. We had hot dogs and sauerkraut and black-eyed peas and corn bread and some cold fried chicken. Frankie was shy at first but after a while he was talking a streak.

He said he sure liked to watch me play football, and that he had seen three games this year and that I was the best he had ever seen. "Man, you sure are the Lone Star Kid!" he said. Hoooooo-weeee! I gave that little dude a large piece of pecan pie and a giant dip of ice cream. He was skinny as a rail but he sure was smart.

After a while we finished lunch, and Frankie said he had to be going and he shook hands all around. Davey walked him to the road.

A half hour later, Jim was taking a nap upstairs in his room, and I was sitting out on the porch watching the sky. Then I saw Davey come across the field at a run. He was crying. I took him in the house and put a cold wet towel on his face and tried to calm him down. He finally was able to tell me what happened. He said that the Prudhomme boys were waiting for them out on the road. They'd been parked alongside the fence in their pickup truck and watched us having lunch on the porch. Davey said that as he and Frankie came out on the road, Woody got out of the truck and told Frankie to get moving. After Frankie ran off, Woody and Alvin grabbed Davey and Alvin put the point of a knife to his throat, and he said, "You boys going further than the Supreme Court. They integrated the schools, but you're bringing the niggers home to lunch. Boy, we're going to take care of you if you keep taking your meals with colored boys." And then Woody said, "Tell your brother that he's nothing but a son of a bitch, and we're going to get him." After that Davey said Woody Prudhomme kicked him sprawling down the road, and then they got in their truck and drove away.

I told Davey not to say anything to Jim or Mother about what had happened as they would only worry. "It's going to be all right," I said, and then I got in my car and drove into town. I was going looking for them, and I figured they'd be in town on a Saturday afternoon.

I drove around the courthouse square looking for their truck, and I found it, opposite Marshall's Hardware store on Crockett Street. I pulled in alongside of it and then got out of my car. It was about four in the afternoon. There was orange sunlight on the old red buildings on the east side of the square. Rising up beyond the buildings was an old water tower. Some men were on a scaffold painting it silver. I walked into the hardware store, but they weren't there, so I went back outside and leaned against their truck and waited for them. About twenty minutes later they came walking down the street, passing the courthouse and the Confederate memorial. They were wearing their old spotted tan Stetsons. Woody was in overalls, but Alvin was wearing some old blue denims stuffed into boots. He walked along with his hands in his back pockets, sort of loping along with his chin stuck out. They were both chewing tobacco and looking raunchy and mean. They looked awfully big, but I told myself I wasn't exactly small. I'm six feet one and one hundred and sixty five and about the quickest old boy you ever saw. Was I scared? No, sir. I was still so mad over what they done to my brother I didn't feel any fear at all. When they saw me, they slowed up and said a few words to one another, then kept coming.

"What the hell do you want, Atherton?" Woody said, as they came up to the truck; and I said, "Boy, I just may kick your ass from here to Greenville." I told them that if I ever heard of them coming within a hundred yards of my brother or bothering him in any way, I was coming after them. Woody spit some juice at my feet. Oh, he is quite a boy. I grabbed him and threw him against the side of his truck, and then I gave Alvin a hard shove just to let him know I hadn't forgot him. I'd have swung at them, but I didn't want to hurt my passing hand. (I never like to do more than is necessary.) They were both plenty riled but I caught them by surprise and I scared them a little so they didn't do no more than just swagger around. Woody said, "What's wrong, Jack, you getting to love the niggers so much?" Alvin kept looking at me and nodding his head, and he said, "You're damn lucky you're in town, boy, but we'll get you later." They climbed up in their truck, and started to back out, and I told them I knew they were sending the notes, and they were just a bunch of crude, ignorant boys and every night before I went to bed I thought of them and laughed to think of how dumb and crude and stupid they were. Alvin's mouth dropped open and Woody sneered, but they didn't say anything more.

We got knocked out of the district by losing to Richardson, 20-14. A few days before the game, about eight boys including Lew Carlton and Bobby Maxwell came down with the flu, and Junior sprained his ankle in practice (he's out for the rest of the year). The whole season went right down the drain. It ain't no consolation that I never played better. We have just one game left on the schedule, against Abilene, and I guess we are playing that one for glory. Nothing else is riding on the game.

I saw Sally outside school today, and she said that she wanted to talk to me. So we stood there under a little pine tree, and she said that I had changed, that it was no fun anymore and that we had better just say goodbye. I said that it was all right with me. "But don't you care for me at all?" she said, suddenly taking my hand. I told her I wasn't in love with her anymore. I'm not sure I ever was, but I didn't want to hurt her feelings. She pulled her hand away and ran off in tears. Well, if some old boy gets her pregnant, she better not call me the daddy.

I'm going to spend more time with that sweet thing from Honey Grove. As far as I'm concerned, Teresa, hon, you're the ideal girl.

When I got home, Davey said to call Jimmy Ambrose, and I figured Sally must have talked to him. I called Jimmy, and he said he was sorry but he wanted the car back. "No hard feelings, Jack, but I got a buyer for it," he said.

In half an hour a boy from Jimmy's place came over for the car, and I sure was sad to give up the keys to that little Camaro.

Abilene, Texas. I broke my leg on the 'Jump' play. A tough old boy named Bobby Harsdale hit me from the blind side in midair and nearly broke me in half when we hit the ground. I broke a bone in my lower left leg and smashed some cartilage, and tore some ligaments in my knee. I don't know why I called that play. We were ahead, 26-7, with only a minute left. I guess I wanted to be Jumping Jack Atherton for one last time. That's what you get with fancy stuff.

It could have been worse. It was my left leg, and I set up on my right leg to throw.

On Saturday night, Jim and I sat around in the front room. Jim poured himself a few drinks of J. W. Dant bourbon, and I drank a few cans of Coors beer to help kill the pain in my leg. Before Jim fell asleep in the soft chair, he said, "Jack, don't get discouraged." A little later Mother walked in, and she kept saying, "Honey, I'm so glad you're home." I just lay on the floor with my leg in a cast from my toes to half way up my thigh. I tried not to feel discouraged, but it just killed my soul.

In a few days I'm going to Dallas for more x-rays. All the colleges are waiting for a medical report. They want to know one thing. Can I play again?

We went to Dallas today. My mother's brother, Harley, loaned us his Pontiac, and I drove. The right leg was all I needed. Mother got the day off from the bank, and she and Davey came along to keep me company. And guess who else made the trip with us? Teresa. She took the bus over from Honey Grove the night before and stayed with her Aunt Doris so she would be ready to leave with us at first light for Dallas. She knew what it meant to me, and she came along for moral support. She looked so pretty and fresh with her honey-colored hair and green eyes that I hardly thought about my leg. The trip took four hours. It was raining when we started out, but an hour later the sun came through the clouds and it turned out to be a fine day.

It was a real pleasant drive. I could tell that Mother liked Teresa, and Davey was so shy and full of smiles that I thought he was going to break into tears any time she talked to him. She said once, "Oh, Jack he is really cute," and that nearly finished him.

At the hospital, the doctors took off the cast and x-rayed my leg again. The fracture is healing all right, but the knee is damaged real bad. They don't think I'll ever play again, and they are going to write that in the report to the colleges. They put a new cast on my leg, and then we left.

I could tell Davey was all broke up for me, and Mother and Teresa were real sad. Nobody said a word all the way out to the hospital parking lot. What could anyone say? That was life.

We came to the outskirts of Lacyville about four in the afternoon, the brown fields looking red in the sun, and far off I could see the water tower glinting silver. And then I saw the Prudhomme boys, riding on quarter horses down the side of the highway.

"Hey, Jack, look yonder," Davey said, tapping my shoulder.

"I see them," I said.

I don't know why but I slowed the car down to a stop and looked out the window at them. When he saw me, Woody set up straight in his saddle and pulled the reins, and Alvin pulled up, too. They were smoking thin cigars. Woody leaned a little over his horse, who was tossing his head, and he said, "You busted your leg, didn't you, boy? Well, I was real glad to hear it, you nigger-loving son of a bitch," and then he looked at Teresa, who was sitting beside me, and he said, "Hey, you ain't his girl-friend, are you? Listen here, why don't you come out and see old Woody. I'll show you what a real man can do. You don't want to mess around with no one-legged boy. Hell, he ain't much good on both his legs." Alvin laughed and gave me the finger. I looked over at Teresa. Her face was red, and she was looking down at the floorboard. I just looked out the window at them, and I said, "Don't worry, boys. Your time will come." Then I drove off, feeling sick about everything.

In the back seat, my mother was real upset, and she said, "You stay away from them, Jack. Those boys are killers. Honey, you don't have to prove a thing to anybody."

Teresa kept shaking her head.

"Oh, lord, Jack. They are just so dumb and raunchy. Don't even think about them," she said.

I didn't say a word. I glanced back at Davey for a second, and he looked white as a sheet.

I've been talking to Teresa on the phone, and she keeps wondering when am I coming to Honey Grove. I told her I'd try to borrow Harley's Pontiac sometime soon. But it gets me down to think of showing up on crutches. It ruins my natural rhythm and I can't be myself—old Jack. I know some boys who would prefer to show up on crutches and play the wounded hero. Lew Carlton, for one. There is no one who likes sympathy more than him. Oh, he is some old boy.

At school today, I'm going down the hall on crutches and trying to hold my books at the same time, and I suddenly get so tired that I had to stop and lean against a wall. Then I heard this girl's voice, real mocking, "Well, if he isn't pathetic. Will you just look at the Lone Star Kid?" It was Sally, and then she and her friend Reba Kincaid began to titter and laugh. I just said, "Well, girls, you sure are looking pretty today."

The colored and white are going their separate ways. But things are quiet.

This morning, we took Jim into the Railroad Hospital. He had pains in his back and chest, and we were worried that it was his heart. It turned out he had pneumonia. The doctors can clear it up with penicillin, and Jim is not in any danger. It was sad though leaving him at the hospital and not finding him at the house when we got home.

We weren't back in the house for more than half an hour when the telephone rang, and it was a call from Amarillo for Mother. Her Aunt Bertie had died. Mother was very fond of her. I was real fond of Bertie myself. She always liked to say to me, "Jack, I can tell there's no stopping you." She was eighty-one years old, and she was originally from Odessa, Texas. I'm really sorry that she's gone.

In the afternoon, Mother took the bus for Amarillo. We promised her that we'd check on Jim every day and that we'd take good care of ourselves. She'll be gone for about five days.

It seemed that inside of four hours nearly everybody in town knew that Davey and me were alone. Some ladies called and offered to cook for us. We thanked them kindly but said we could make it all right.

Teresa called. I told her what had happened. She was sorry and hoped I was feeling all right and wasn't too lonely and downhearted. She said that she missed me and hoped that I felt the same way about her. I admitted that I missed her and said I hoped to see her real soon, after I got on my feet again.

I saw Junior Eberlee today. I'd heard the great news how he's going to Southern Methodist on a football scholarship. "Junior, there ain't nobody who deserves it more than you," I said. I really meant it. We shook hands, and he said, "You're really the Kid, Jack. I hope you come back all the way." He is a fine old boy.

We are getting a little lazy, particularly since I can't move around so good, and the last two nights we have eaten TV dinners—roast beef with mashed potatoes, peas, and a roll and a small slice of apple pie. Not bad. It's easy to prepare and no trouble afterwards. You just warm them up in the oven and then tear off the foil and you're all set to eat. If we are still hungry, we open a can of red beans and eat them cold. In the mornings before Harley comes by and takes me to school, I've been frying us some eggs and sausage and making some strong black coffee to go with some corn bread Mother made before she left. Tonight Davey said he was going to cook some red beans to go with the last of the corn bread. I told him I was getting tired of red beans. He said, "I'll get us some fresh tomatoes, Jack, and some takeout fried chicken." I told him that sounded a lot better. He is a good old brother.

I've been calling Jim on the phone, and Davey rides out on his bike to the Railroad Hospital to see him. Jim is coming along.

It's been a quiet life.

After we ate, Davey and I put on our coats and stood out in the field in front of the house. It was so quiet and all the stars were out, and there was a little wind that bent down the grass in the field. There was dew on the ground and everything was sparkly and clear. We saw a couple of shooting stars, and one went right behind the moon. Once in a while we could see the lights of a car or truck out on the road about a quarter of a mile away. I hopped around a little on the crutches, and Davey said, "How's the leg, Jack?" He looked a little shy, like he was scared to ask.

This afternoon while I was helping Davey fix the wheel of his bike, Joe Wilsford came out to see me. Joe was one of the boys who had jeered at me on the morning the high school was integrated. He looked troubled and sad, standing there in a pair of overalls with a blue bandanna around his neck. He is a thin, wiry farm boy in his thirties, and almost all he could do at first was look down at the ground. Then he said, "Jack, I don't like your views as far as the niggers is concerned, but I don't have nothing against you personally. So I came out here to tell you one thing. The Prudhomme boys are coming for you tonight."

In a way, I was kind of relieved. I was glad to have a chance to settle it one way or another.

I thanked Joe for the warning, and he just turned and walked back toward the road.

I picked up Davey's bike. It was all fixed, and I said, "Davey, you get on your bike and go over to Tommy Longford's. You're staying at his house tonight."

"No, I'm staying with you, Jack," he said.

"I'm telling you to get out," I said, but he wouldn't make a move to go. I opened the screen door and went into the house.

Davey followed me.

"I'm going to call Harley," I said. "He'll come and get you."

"Then I'll tell him everything, and he'll call the police," Davey said. "I'm staying, Jack. You ain't no match for them with your leg."

I went for him, hopping on one crutch and waving the other at him, but he ran out the door and down the steps. "Please, Jack," he yelled from outside. "Ain't I your brother? Can't I stay with you? I swear, I won't get in the way."

I thought it over and decided to let him stay. If he left, he'd just spread the word and some other boys might come over, and then I'd never be able to settle it for myself. I decided to lock Davey in his room and make sure he stayed away from the window.

A couple of hours passed.

There was still plenty light out, and I knew we had time. I told Davey we might as well eat so we'd have our strength. He went to the kitchen and started pulling down cans. He was so excited and proud that I let him stay that his face was a little flushed and his eyes were bright. We ate a large can of Irish stew and half a loaf of white bread, and then for dessert we opened two cans of peaches. After we finished the peaches, we were still hungry, and I cooked us some scrambled eggs and sausage.

"I'll help you, Jack. The both of us can take them," Davey said, as he ate the last of his eggs.

Oh, yes, he is really something.

"You're going to stay out of the way," I said. I made it plain that when I told him to go upstairs, I wanted him to obey me. I said that he could get us all killed if I was worrying more about him than thinking of the Prudhomme boys. He said that he understood and that he promised to listen to me.

After a while, I sent Davey upstairs to get my 410 shotgun and two boxes of shells out of my closet and the .38 caliber hand-gun out of the top drawer of Jim's bureau. I wondered if the Prudhommes would come on their horses or in their truck. At first I thought of going out in the field and firing on them as they came through the gate, but then, I thought, that's not the way. They might not come through the front gate anyhow. No, I'd just sit on the floor of the front room with the door open and the lights off so I'd get used to the dark, and when they came up on the porch I'd give them a surprise. Then it crossed my mind that maybe they'd come up on us from the rear, sneaking across the small dry creek bed behind our house and coming in through the back door. I told Davey to go up to Jim's room, which looked out over the back, and if they were coming that way to give me a low whistle and then go right to his room and lock the door. I'd let him know if they were coming from the road, but either way he was to go to his room and stay away from the window. He promised to listen to me and went upstairs.

I sat down a little back from the open front door, and I put the .38 in my belt in the back of my pants, and I cradled the shotgun in my lap and loaded two shells. Then I put eight shells in my belt in case I had to move around and forgot to pick up the box. Another thing I did was to prop my crutch up against a chair on my left so that if I had to move fast I could use my gun as a cane to get to my feet and then I'd put the crutch under my left arm and hop around and fire the gun at the same time if necessary. I knew I could do all these things because of my coordination. I put the gun on safety and practiced getting up and firing on the move—all the time I was ducking and weaving and reloading. I did it all pretty fast. The 410 shotgun is a natural weapon for me. I've shot down many a gray squirrel from the pine trees down in southeast Texas, so I guess I know how to use it.

I watched all the orange go out of the sky, and then the blue dusk and the gray dusk, and then it was dark out. It was a hazy night, and the stars were pale, but there was more light outside than there was in the house. My eyes were used to the dark, and I felt I had the advantage.

Every so often I'd yell up to Davey, "Nothing yet," and he'd yell back down, "Nothing here, Jack." My leg was hurting me, especially the knee. I got up and down a few times just to practice the move with the crutch and shotgun. I was getting pretty graceful at it. Once I got up and went into the kitchen and got a glass of water and brought it back to the front room and set it down on the floor beside me. My mouth was a little dry.

Looking out the door and across the field toward the road, I watched the lights of passing cars, and then I saw a car slow down and stop on the road in front of our place, and then the lights went off. I watched real close, and I saw our front gate open, and somebody came through. I yelled up to Davey that they were coming and to go to his room. I could make out just one person, and he was wearing a white shirt, and I wondered why he made himself such an easy target. I put some shells in my gun and cocked the hammers and waited. I couldn't tell if it was Woody or Alvin, but this boy was moving up the path to the house, and he was carrying something large and dark against his chest, and he was struggling a little to hold on to it. When he got closer, I could see he wasn't too big, and I knew it wasn't neither of the Prudhomme boys. I couldn't understand it. If this boy was helping them out, why would he just come right up the path almost like a sitting duck? And what was he carrying? A kerosene bomb? Halfway up the path, this person stops and yells out, "Anybody home?" It was a girl's voice, and I knew that voice all right. It was Teresa. Oh, Lord, I thought, what is going on? I called for her to come on in, and she came the rest of the way and then walked up the steps to the porch. She was wearing a white blouse and a pair of jeans, and she was carrying a big pot with a lid on it.

"Jack, why don't you turn on a light? Hey, what are you doing with that gun?" she said.

I grabbed my crutch and got to my feet.

"Honey, what are you doing here?" I said.

"I was visiting Aunt Doris, and I made you all a pot of soup. I knew there was nobody cooking for you," she said. "Why are you standing in the dark with that gun, Jack?"

"You got to get out of here," I said, looking out toward the road.

"Why do you keep looking out yonder? Who are you expecting?" she said, half smiling and uncertain, but when I didn't smile back she started to look a little scared.

Davey came down the stairs. He looked confused.

"Teresa brought us some soup, Davey. Take it to the kitchen," I said. He took the pot away, and then he came back. We all stood in the front room, and I was trying to figure out what to do. I couldn't send her back to the car, as they might be coming through the gate just when she got there, and I hated to think what they could do to her if they caught her alone. And then Teresa said, "Are they coming for you, Jack? Is that it?" I didn't say anything, but Davey blurted out, "Some old boy came out and told us this afternoon."

"Well, you got to call the sheriff," she said.

I kept looking out to see if they were coming and trying to think of what to do with her at the same time.

"Do you hear me, Jack?" she said, grabbing hold to my shoulder and shaking me.

"Honey, I can't do that," I said.

She started going for the phone, saying somebody had to show some sense. I didn't have no time to mess around, and I put down my gun and grabbed her, and told Davey to get some rope. I tied her up like a little old calf, and she started screaming for me to let hold of her and call the sheriff. "Oh, God, what are you trying to do? Get yourself killed?" she yelled. I tied a bandanna over her mouth to keep her quiet, and then me and Davey carried her upstairs and put her in a soft chair in my mother's room. I felt awful about doing that to her, but I didn't have no choice.

I eased back downstairs on my crutch, and Davey returned to the back window. I tried to put everything out of my mind but the Prudhomme boys, and I was a little worried they might have slipped on to our property while we were taking Teresa upstairs.

I sat down on the floor in the front room again, and I propped my crutch beside me. I looked out the door toward the road and drank a little water. I watched the road, and every so often a car would pass, and I looked out at the empty field. About a half hour passed, and I began to think they weren't coming, that Joe Wilsford was wrong. And then I saw a car slow down and stop and the headlights went out. Then I knew that wasn't a car but a pickup truck. I yelled up to Davey that they were coming in the front way and he'd better go to his room and lock the door and stay low and out of sight. He didn't argue with me.

And then sure enough I saw them come in through the gate. They were carrying rifles. My heart started to beat very fast, and my palms broke out into a sweat. I drank some water, and then I dipped a handkerchief in the glass and wiped my eyes. They were slowly coming toward the house, walking in the fields rather than on the path, and they were about fifteen yards apart.

I checked everything, the shells in my belt, the .38, the crutch. Then I locked my gun and pulled off the safety. I took a deep breath and let the air out slow.

They were about ten yards apart and crouching. They seemed a little uncertain. I figured they must be half scared out of their minds approaching a dark house and not knowing what to expect. I began to feel a little calmer.

When the Prudhomme boys were about twenty yards from the house, I knew what I had to do. I got to my feet and grabbed my crutch and went hopping out on the porch. I gave a blood-curdling yell and fell on my stomach, pulling the triggers and letting go both barrels right at their feet. Some dirt flew up and ripped into their pants, and I jammed in two more shells just in case, but the next thing I knew they were running for the road. I had scared the living hell out of them. I stood up and came limping down the porch steps with my crutch, and I yelled after them, "I had you in my sights, boys, but I let you go. But the next time you're gone—you hear that, damn you all?" Davey came running outside, and we stood out in the field hollering at them. Then we saw the truck lights come on, and they drove away. We continued to laugh and holler at the empty field, and then we remembered Teresa.

We went upstairs and untied her. She threw her arms around me and was shaking like a leaf, and she said, "Jack, when I heard that gunfire, I thought you were gone," but I kept telling her I was right there. I was really sorry that she had to go through that. After a while, I managed to calm her down, and we all went downstairs. I told Davey to heat up the pot of soup. I put a short candle in the bottom of a coffee can and I lit it, and I put the can on the kitchen table, and then we all sat down and waited for the soup to heat. Then I ladled it into bowls and got some spoons, and we sat there in the quiet eating the soup, with the candle throwing wavy shadows on the walls. I told Teresa it was the best soup I ever ate, and Davey agreed. Teresa's eyes were shining and teary. We didn't say too much. After we finished the soup, it was about eleven thirty, and then I walked her down the path to her car that was parked out on the road. She was feeling a little better. I kissed her goodnight and said I'd see her soon.

What I said was the truth. I missed those boys on purpose. Why didn't I kill them? I had the upper hand and could have easy. The answer is, I'm no cold-blooded killer. I don't enjoy gunning down nobody, not even a son of a bitch. I'll drop you to stay alive, but that's all, boy. I'm a sociable person.

Mother is back from Amarillo, and Jim is home from the hospital. Life is normal again. We had a fine Sunday afternoon. Jim made some chile con carne, and we had corn and sliced tomato and cucumber salad. It was good for us all to be together again. Davey and I never mentioned the 'night riders,' as it would have just upset them. We ain't worried though. It's the last we'll see of the Prudhomme boys.

There ain't one college that wants me now. Am I discouraged? I can't say I am. There is a surgeon down in Houston who said he can take out the busted cartilage and repair the ligaments in my knee. He wants to do it for nothing because he admires me, and he said, "Jack, I'm going to make you a player again." If Coach Royal don't want me down at U. T., it's all right with me. I just may go on down to College Station in the fall and join up with Lew Carlton and play for Texas A & M. It don't matter that the whole world makes fun of them.

Meanwhile I'm going to borrow Harley's Pontiac and drive to Honey Grove and see Teresa. She don't care whether I'm the Lone Star Kid, the greatest player in the southwest. All she wants is Plain Old Jack Atherton. She is in love with my personality. Well, I think we're going to get along, at least for a while.

John Lionel in Washington

Skylark

A few weeks ago, on a hot Saturday afternoon in July, I decided to go to the Army Medical Museum at the Smithsonian Institution and just wander around. I felt a little restless and strange and couldn't seem to settle down. My best friends, Ewing and Hal, had afternoon dates with the Margot sisters who were up from Richmond. I probably would have gone out with them, if I'd had a date. Ewing and Hal wanted me to come along, date or not, but I felt that four's company and five's a crowd. I had a date that night with Alice Hammershorn, but that would have been too late to meet up with them, as the Margot sisters would be on the train for Richmond by then.

I certainly didn't want to get any old date for the afternoon merely to be going out. I guess I'm rather particular for sixteen. I only like to take out girls I'm fairly much in love with, or at least infatuated with. Not that I was in love with Alice. She was merely an old friend as far as I was concerned. Though I suppose that she was in love with me, not that I ever encouraged her.

She was one of the best-liked girls in school. I mean she wasn't the cheerleader type, but she was very popular, in a way. In the high school yearbook, it said she was the "truest of the true" and "a good friend." She was very intelligent, too.

Actually, I was growing tired of Alice. What bothered me about her was that she was always so eager to please. I wish she could have been more nonchalant. She took everything so seriously that she got on my nerves. I hated myself for feeling that way, but there was nothing I could do about it. The more she looked at me with her large sad eyes, and the more she tried to please me, the more irritated and unpleasant I became. I hated it when she went out of her way to be kind and thoughtful. It was like it took all the fun out of life, though I can't say why.

I guess I was the most important person in the world to her. She even kept a scrapbook on my life—not that there was much to put in it except for a few clippings from the Washington papers about me as a baseball player in the local amateur leagues. There was even a picture of me sliding into third base in a cloud of dust in a game on the Washington Ellipse. It was a perfect fadeaway slide. It started out as an ordinary hook slide, but then I threw my leg up and over, going into a kind of roll, and went by the bag, grabbing it with my hand. I'd faked out the third baseman, and my hand went right under his glove. It was really beautiful, even though I was called out. I guess I'm a fairly good player. Ewing and Hal and I play for a team that's going to the Johnstown Tournament this year, and we should do all right.

Anyhow, Alice had these clippings in a scrapbook, and she had a section called 'Mementoes' as well. In this part, she pasted onto the page scraps and souvenirs, like the menu and a book of matches from the restaurant in the Carlton Hotel, where we had dinner with her parents one time, a postcard I'd sent her from the Luray Caverns in Virginia, ticket stubs from the National Theatre, where we saw a play, and the red ribbon that went around a flower corsage that I gave her before I took her to the junior prom, and many other things as well. If I threw the wrapper of a Baby Ruth candy bar up in the air, Alice might run and catch it and paste it in her scrapbook, and write something about me underneath. There was even a page called 'Important Dates'—like the day she first laid eyes on me, January 4, 1941; and the time I first said something to her, April 15, 1942; and when I first smiled at her, later in the same year. As far as I know, the scrapbook still exists, and the important dates probably go right up to 1946, which is the present time.

She was fairly sad lately, and I guess it got on my nerves. Of course, maybe I was the one who made her sad. I don't know. Sometimes she'd get this strange expression on her face—a far off look with a sad little smile, and I'd really get upset. I guess she was just rather 'melancholy,' as they say in English poetry. She once said to me on a rainy day, "John, I love the rain so," and I said, "Alice, you're just a melancholy girl." I just wanted to use the word, but I guess the way I said it must have hurt her feelings, and perhaps I really meant to hurt her feelings. I don't know. She's certainly easily hurt. Only last spring, sitting in the school library, I read her a poem that was assigned for English— "To a Skylark" by Shelley. I thought it was a swell poem. It starts off, "Hail to thee, Blithe Spirit, bird thou never wert." I read it through to Alice, and then I said, "Alice, you're certainly no blithe spirit," and she put her hands over her eyes and began to cry. When she wouldn't stop crying, I said to her, "You can cry all you want," and I just got up and left her sitting there. It was getting to be a terrible strain to be with Alice. I was getting a little sad myself.

Not too long ago, Alice told me that she loved me and that she hoped I felt the same way.

"Well, I like you a lot," I said, but I didn't say that I loved her, which would have been a lie. I was glad I hadn't lied to Alice. I believe in the truth, which is the most important thing in the world. It was hard not to lie to girls though. You just had to tell them what they wanted to hear, particularly where sex was concerned. A few months back, my father said that he wanted to talk to me about my relationship with girls. He said, "John, there are two things that you have to remember. Never give a girl a line, and never seduce a virgin." In a way, I agreed with my dad. I hate guys who give a girl a line and aren't honest and straightforward, though I guess I'm one of them. But I try not to say, "I love you." As for seducing a virgin, I can't see anything wrong with that—as long as the girl is willing. The fact is, I'm still a virgin myself.

The first time I went out with Alice was about four years ago, when I was twelve. It was my first date. Alice asked me to take her to the class picnic which was in Rock Creek Park. Since her parents were friends of my parents, and as I knew her brother, Jack, I felt I had to take her. I'd much rather have gone alone.

It was a warm night in June. Ewing and Hal were there. They just came by themselves and didn't bring dates. "That way," Ewing had said, "we don't have to get stuck with any one girl but can take our pick." I knew right away that I'd made a mistake getting stuck with Alice. I'd picked her up at her house at seven o'clock, and I'd said hello to her mother and father and was very polite. As we left, her mother said, "Now, Johnny, don't bring Alice home too late. I'll be waiting up." We took a bus. The bus brought us to a stop not too far from the picnic site, a little meadow near the creek. There was still some light in the sky but it was growing dusky. All the boys and girls in my class were there, sitting at picnic tables or toasting hot dogs and marshmallows over the fire, or just running around. It was very pleasant, with the crackle of burning logs and a soft breeze and the good smells of the grass and trees and the food cooking on the fire. Farther off in the meadow, there were some swings. Some girls were sitting on the swings in white summer dresses. Most of the boys were running wild, yelling, throwing paper plates—sailing them into the creek—and the teachers, Miss Craddock and Mrs. DeLong, were yelling for everyone to come and get something to eat. We'd got there just in time.

At first I was very polite and treated Alice with great courtesy, and I made sure she had enough potato salad on her paper plate and got her hot dogs from the fire, but as the evening wore on, I got impatient to leave her. I couldn't think of anything to say to Alice, or I didn't want to, and I resented that she wouldn't mingle with the other kids but just wanted to be with me. I wanted to wander off and do as I pleased. Ewing and Hal came over for a while, and we talked and kidded around, but it wasn't the same with Alice looking so sad and everything. She was like an anchor pulling me down to the bottom. But the main reason I wanted to get away from Alice was that I was very much infatuated with a pretty blonde girl named Mary Lou Turner who was sitting on a swing and laughing and kicking her feet. I was so infatuated with her that she made me a little shy and wild at the same time. While I was getting Alice some potato salad, I said to Hal, "Say, why don't you sit with Alice for a while?" Hal liked Alice, so I persuaded him to deliver the potato salad and keep her company for a while. He walked off with the plate, and I went and found Ewing, and we went over to the swings and asked Mary Lou if she wanted to hear an imitation of a sports announcer doing a broadcast of a football game. Ewing and I alternated at the mike, and we made it a very exciting game, with the Redskins winning in the last second on a long pass from Baugh to Milner. "That's the stupidest thing I ever heard," Mary Lou said, her eyes smiling. "Would you get me a vanilla Dixie cup?" We ran off and got her some ice cream. I ran right by Alice, who was looking sad and hurt, but I pretended I didn't even see her. Hal was sitting there and looking at his hands. I knew he was trying to think of something to say. He was a wonderful friend. But it wasn't my fault that Alice loved me, and I was infatuated with Mary Lou Turner. At about ten o'clock I got into a fight with Martin Denison who told Mary Lou that I was "the biggest fool in the entire class." We fought and rolled on the ground, and I finally managed to twist Denison's arm behind his back. "Now you just take that back," I said, twisting it more, but Martin said that he didn't care if I broke his arm but that he still meant what he'd said. I couldn't help but admire his courage, and I let him go, hoping that I wasn't too silly in Mary Lou's eyes. When I got to my feet, I noticed that she had moved away and was sitting at a picnic table with some other kids, just laughing and enjoying herself like she didn't even know I was alive. I was furious that she just ignored me, and I was sure that she'd done it on purpose because she knew how much it would hurt me. I was certain I really loved Mary Lou. It was so beautiful in the park, with the dark woods rising up beyond the meadow and the darting blinking lights of the fireflies. There was a pleasant breeze. The light from the campfire made little flickering shadows. In the sky, there was a slight haze and pale stars and a quarter moon. I suddenly hoped that we'd get to play Spin the Bottle or Post Office later on, so that Mary Lou would have to pay the postman—me, of course, with a whole lot of kisses. But though Ewing and I tried to organize a game, the teachers put a stop to it. Then I just started running wild, and later on Martin Denison made another remark about what a fool I was, and we had another fight, and I knocked him in the creek. Then I got knocked in the creek by somebody else, and there was a real battle royal with a lot of boys going in the water. The teachers were really mad, but there was nothing they could do. Ewing and Hal and I were laughing so hard we could hardly stand it, and it took us nearly ten minutes just to get to our feet, and then we'd all fall down and laugh some more. We sat on the bank and dried off. Mary Lou was paying a lot of attention to me now, and she kept walking along the creek bank, back and forth—like a cat who wants to be friendly—and she said, "John, I know someone who thinks you're swell." I knew she was the one who thought that, and I guess I'd never been so happy in my whole life. As I was about to talk to her some more, Alice came over and said that she wasn't feeling well and wanted to go home. I was really furious, as I knew there was nothing wrong with her except that she couldn't stand I was having fun. "Oh, what's the matter, Alice?" I said. "I don't feel well," she said. "I have a headache." She looked so sad and resentful, like she'd had a terrible time and it was all my fault. "Oh, come on, damn it all. Let's go," I said. She began to cry, and I grabbed her hand and just pulled her out of the park. I didn't even say goodbye to anyone. I didn't even nod to Ewing and Hal, or Mary Lou. We walked a quarter of a mile to the bus stop, which was a small clearing on the side of the road. We stood there, with the silent woods all around us, and we waited for the bus. Alice leaned against the bus stop pole, with her head slightly forward, her long straight hair on the puffed shoulders of her white dress, and then she looked up and tried to smile. I really hated her then. Far off I could see the trees lighted by the campfire, and I wished I was back at the picnic. Alice put her hands over her eyes, tried to smile again, and then began to cry. "I'm sorry," she said, sobbing. "But I don't feel well." Her shoulders, which were frail and narrow, began to heave. Suddenly, Alice's face got red and her mouth got very bitter, twisting into an angry little sneer—I'd never seen that expression before—and she said that I was just "too stupid to go around fighting and falling in the creek." And then Alice began to cry harder than ever. What she was really sad about was that I liked Mary Lou Turner. She was jealous. When the bus came, I was a little ashamed to get on with her, the way she looked, and I was afraid everyone'd think I'd done something to her. In the bright light of the bus, I could hardly look at her, with her eyes all red and her face all stained with tears.

As the bus moved up the hill, I noticed my own house come into view, and I don't know why but I was so surprised to see it that I got kind of dazed—it was so sudden—and I was tired, and I felt terribly strange all of a sudden, and I just got up when the bus came to a stop and said, "Well, so long," and then I got off the bus. And before I knew what happened, the door closed and the bus pulled off on the way up the hill to Alice's house, a mile farther on. It was like a dream seeing her face in the window, and I knew I had done something terribly wrong. I'd come out of my daze and realized I was letting Alice go home by herself. She looked so sad, even a little stunned, like she didn't think that even I could do something like that. I tried to catch up with the bus, breaking into a little run, but then I realized that it was no use, and that I'd really done it. I felt sick, kicking the ground; and then I covered my face with my hands for a few moments.

I wasn't even angry anymore. Actually, I'd stopped thinking of

Alice half way up the hill. And when I got up from my seat and saw her there, it was almost like I'd seen her for the first time, and after I said, "So long," I could hardly put on the brakes and keep from getting off the bus. In a way, it was like an unseen hand was pushing me.

I tried to explain all this to my dad—Alice's mother had called the next morning, and he wanted an explanation—and I never saw him so mad. He said I was no gentleman, and he called me every name you could imagine, and whipped me with his belt besides. My mother acted like I was a criminal, and she had a look of horror on her face for two days. As for my sister, Carol, who is two years older, she has always rather enjoyed seeing me in the wrong. She said that no girl in her right mind would ever go out with me, even when I got older.

I had to call up Alice and apologize, and I had to apologize to her mother and father, and then I had to write Alice a letter and another one to her parents, saying fairly much what I'd said on the phone.

I didn't see Alice much after that for about a year and a half. Then every so often I'd walk her home from school, and since she was very good in science, I'd sometimes copy her chemistry experiments or get some help for some project in physics. When I was about fourteen, I took her to the movies about two times. But I really didn't start taking her out until I was sixteen. That is, when I wasn't taking out the more exciting girls, I would spend some time with Alice.

I guess my trouble is that I'm fairly 'hard to please,' as Ewing would say. He ought to know. He's the same way. Hal is different. Everything pleases him. He's almost always polite and pleasant. Ewing and I've never heard him complain. If Hal was fixed up on a blind date with an orangutan, he'd be the perfect gentleman. I'm just the opposite of Hal. I get upset if a girls' speech or tone of voice isn't just right, or if her legs aren't perfect, or if she's not a good conversationalist. I get almost sick if her smile is false and insincere, or if she has a stupid laugh.

Anyway, it was really interesting, as I sat on the bus on the way to the Smithsonian, to think back to when I was twelve. I've changed quite a lot since then, but not necessarily for the better.

I walked into the Army Medical Museum about three o'clock in the afternoon. It was a hot, cloudy, rainy day. I'd got caught in a sudden shower on my way through the Smithsonian grounds. Inside the museum, I wiped my face and hands and hair with a handkerchief, and then I took off my khaki poncho—it was army surplus—and folded it up. Except for my sneakers, I was dry, though it wouldn't have mattered if I'd gotten soaked. The clothes I was wearing were fairly old and torn up—a pair of blue pants with a rip and a little dried white paint on one leg, and the shirt top from a baseball uniform of a team I used to play for, with the lettering 'Roger's Supply' on the front and number six on the back.

I began to wander through the museum, in the part called the Hall of Pathology. It's a strange place and quite ghastly in a way, but very interesting, too. There are diseased organs preserved in formaldehyde, and there are exhibits on how a child is born, and about yellow fever and typhoid and how these diseases were brought under control. One of the exhibits was on venereal disease. It nearly scared the living hell out of me. Then there were the various examples of battle wounds, with the preserved organ or bone still holding the bullet or piece of shrapnel. There was one exhibit on Major General Sickles's leg. His lower leg bones were preserved in a case. According to the write-up, he had been a Union general in the Civil War, and he had been wounded at the battle of Gettysburg, where his leg was amputated by an army surgeon. The amputated leg was sent to the Army Medical Museum in a little coffin, in which there was a little visiting card which said, 'With the compliments of Gen. Sickles.' I thought it was fairly interesting but rather strange.

While I was reading something about malaria, I heard someone say, "Oh, how disgusting!" in this loud, clear and incredibly confident and musical voice. I turned around, and I saw a girl staring at one of the glass cases. She was alone. She was the most attractive girl I'd ever seen in my whole life, and I was nearly struck dumb with admiration. Standing there in a tan raincoat, with a hand on her chin, staring intently with large blue-green eyes, she seemed about eighteen. There was a slight smile on her face, as though she had just had some very interesting and amusing thought. Looking at her, I was nearly turned to stone. She was lovely, about five feet four, with a full mouth you'd just love to kiss, and beautiful, soft auburn hair that was partly under a yellow kerchief. I couldn't take my eyes off of her, and the sound of her voice kept swimming around in my mind. I knew right away she was everything I had ever desired in a girl, or ever would for that matter. Fortunately, she hadn't seen me, and I put on my poncho. I didn't want her to see me in my baseball shirt, as it made me look too much like a kid.

I thought maybe she'd appreciate the careless approach, and so I tried to figure out a way to ease into conversation so it would seem as though I was just passing the time of day. I didn't want to scare her and have her call the guard. That was all I needed. I'm easily embarrassed, and I knew I'd never be able to stand that. The more I watched her walk around the Hall of Pathology, the more impressed with her I became. I hate to use the expression, but it really was 'love at first sight.'

It was fairly dim and murky in the room, but there was enough light to see that she had a truly wonderful face. There was a golden glow about her which came right through the shadows. God, I wanted to meet her very badly, and yet I was afraid of making a fool out of myself. It was obvious that she was a sophisticated girl, and this meant naturally that she wasn't from Washington, which made her even more exciting. My heart began to beat very fast, and my palms broke out in a sweat.

I took a deep breath and began to sidle over to the glass case which she happened to be then observing, until I was standing next to her. She was looking at a model of the large intestine. Watching her out of the corner of my eye, I tried to pretend that

I was interested in the model. I've got to do something right now, I thought, or she'll go over to another case, and if I follow her then, it would just seem too obvious. Of course, I thought, I wouldn't have to follow her, but could start circling around her and then pick a better time to make a move. I took another deep breath. What a fragrance! It was probably some rare perfume. I was nearly paralyzed. I couldn't say anything. If she had handed me a revolver and told me to shoot myself, I would have seriously considered it. At least I might have shot myself in the leg. I never felt so great and terrible at the same time.

She turned slightly, with this absent look on her face, and then tucked a few strands of hair under her kerchief, and then she saw me for the first time. She was startled. "Oh, pardon me, I didn't realize anyone was so *close* to me," she said.

I was terribly embarrassed, and I said, "I didn't realize I was so close," in this very strained, unnatural voice. It was a stupid thing to say as well, and I really hated myself.

She ignored me and just looked in the case again; she wasn't even aware that I was alive. I felt like an awful fool, but being rather paralyzed in my mind, I couldn't find the strength just to walk away. If I could only have said, "Look, my name is John Lionel. Why don't we have dinner tonight?" but I could no more have done that than taken a swan dive off the Washington Monument. We were the only two people in the room except for the guard. It must have seemed very strange, the way I was acting. I backed away from the case, trying to think of an approach; I was really upset.

She slowly turned around and saw me standing there. I looked up at the ceiling, as though I were really interested in something. My heart was beating very fast. It was now or never, I thought.

"Excuse me," she said. "Do you have the time?"

I'd halfway expected her to tell me to stop bothering her. I looked at my watch.

"It's quarter to four," I said, rather nonchalantly.

"Gosh, I'm late," she said, and then she started out of the museum. I don't know what was wrong with me, but I started right after her; and then I suddenly stopped, as she turned around at the door and said, "Can you tell me the way to Pennsylvania Avenue?"

"I happen to be going there myself," I said, thinking fast.

Outside it had stopped raining. There was a mist in the air, and from time to time the sun came out of the gray clouds and went back in again. We walked across the Mall toward Constitution Avenue. I walked beside her, though slightly to the rear at times, and then slightly to the front. I didn't quite know how I should walk with her—like a guide or as a friend—and so sometimes I'd walk on the grass and then I'd weave back on the sidewalk alongside of her. At first I was very quiet, afraid of ruining the good impression I might have made. But then I became a little embarrassed by the silence—I was afraid she might think I was stupid—and I said, finally, "Well, anyway it stopped raining." I didn't like the sound of my voice.

"Yes, it has," she said, without turning her head in the slightest, as we walked through this small grove of trees still dripping from the rain. Her voice was clear as a bell. She seemed to have a kind of British accent.

"I guess you're not from Washington," I said.

"Oh, no," she said, looking straight ahead. "I'm just visiting."

I nodded. She was probably visiting her boyfriend, I thought, hoping I was wrong. "Where are you from, may I ask?" I said.

"New York City," she said.

I knew that must be true.

I nodded, and then I said, "I guess you must be visiting relatives."

She looked at me rather quickly, and then looked away, not saying anything.

"I didn't mean to get personal," I said.

"I'm visiting my father," she said.

I nodded, feeling great. I hoped I hadn't been too obvious.

"How is he?" I said, not that I cared.

"Very well, thank you."

We walked along. Since she knew where Pennsylvania Avenue was by now, I wondered if she would suddenly say, "Well, thank you very much. Goodbye," and then speed up her pace. But she continued to walk along beside me, though she was rather aloof.

I tried to think of something interesting to tell her, but I knew I couldn't tell her anything she didn't already know. I took out my handkerchief and wiped my face. I was a little warm in my poncho, but I didn't dare take it off. She suddenly looked at me with this strange little smile on her face.

"Are you in college?" she said.

It really took me by surprise.

"Well, yes," I said. "I mean—"

"I'm sorry. I didn't hear you," she said rather offhandedly.

My face was burning.

"You might say—"

"Are you in high school?" she said.

"Not really."

"What do you mean, 'not really'? You're either in or you're out. Now which are you?"

"Well, I'm on my summer vacation—"

"Why can't you answer a simple question?" she said, stopping and looking at me directly in the eyes. She smoothed her hair.

"Well, I'm not in college," I said, feeling sick. I knew it was all over. I should have told her I was in my third year at Yale.

"And you're still in high school," she said, in this rather haughty way.

"Yes."

"Well, that's settled," she said, beginning to walk. "I prefer the truth, don't you?"

I nodded.

"I guess you're in college," I said.

"I'm at Bryn Mawr."

I knew that was really a great school, and I admired her quite a lot for going there. I liked the way she was so frank and open about things. She was a very honest person, I thought, and I was ashamed I wasn't the same way.

We continued to walk without saying much. The clouds were blowing away, and some birds were flying over the monument, which was gleaming in the sunlight. When we reached Constitution Avenue, she said, "Well, I know where I am now. I guess I can make it to the hotel."

"Where are you staying?" I said.

"The Willard."

"I happen to be going that way," I said. "It's not too far from here."

She didn't indicate one way or the other whether she was glad that I was going with her, and we started off for the Willard Hotel. On the way, I introduced myself, and she told me rather halfheartedly that her name was Sheilah Lorraine. It was as though she had to tell me her name, as I had told her mine. That was putting pressure on her, and I should have just let her volunteer her name. I really didn't like the way I was acting—so artificial and insincere.

"How long are you going to be in Washington?" I said.

"I'm leaving in the morning."

"Are you meeting your father now?" I said.

"I said goodbye to him this morning out at Walter Reed."

"Is he in the army?"

"He's a general," she said, a little annoyed. "He teaches at the Army War College, and he's in Walter Reed for a checkup." She pushed some stray hairs under her kerchief, then stopped and looked at me in this very cool and slightly haughty way. "Do you have any more questions?" she said. I was a little embarrassed, but I felt very bold at the same time, and I said, "Sure, what are you doing tonight?"

She stopped. There was this glazed look in her eyes.

"I don't know. Why?"

"Well, I thought we'd go out and have dinner or something," I said. I thought I sounded fairly debonair.

"I can't see the point of that," she said, very cool and reserved. Then we began to walk again.

"I could really show you around Washington," I said.

"Well, I'm not sure that's a very good idea."

"Oh, it's a pretty good idea," I said. "And you'd agree, after you got to know me."

She smiled slightly, then stopped and adjusted the collar of her raincoat. We were standing on the corner of Eighth Street and Pennsylvania Avenue.

"Well, why don't you think about it?" I said. I wiped my face with my handkerchief.

"Look, uh—what is your name again?"

"John."

"Well, John, I'm afraid I can't."

"I'll call for you at seven thirty," I said.

"Well, I can't stop you from calling," she said, smiling slightly.

We arrived at the Willard Hotel. It's a fine old building really, and my favorite hotel in Washington, not that I've stayed in any, but I've been inside of most of them, visiting friends of ours who've come to town, and I've had dinner in a lot of the hotel restaurants. I was glad she was staying at the Willard.

I certainly didn't want to say goodbye, and I just stood near the entrance waiting for her to say something about the evening, but she just said, "Well, thank you again," and she extended her hand. I nearly raised her hand and kissed it the way they do in France, but I wasn't that crazy, and we just shook hands.

"Goodbye, Sheilah," I said. "I'll call you later." And then I felt a little sick and warm. I shouldn't have used her name like that. It was hardly casual or nonchalant, but rather too eager to please. I should have just said, "See you later," or "Seven thirty then." I was a little disgusted with myself. I hate to be too nice.

I felt like calling up Ewing and Hal and telling them lightning had really struck, but I imagined they were probably still out with the Margot sisters, and I was feeling a little strange anyway.

On the way home on the bus, I felt sorry that I wouldn't be able to pick up Sheilah in my father's car. I knew how to drive and had a learner's permit, but I didn't have a license to drive alone. I was going for my test next week. Even if I'd had a regular permit, I doubt that my father would have let me drive his LaSalle. He thinks I'm the kind that takes a curve at eighty and the straightaway at a hundred and ten, and he'll say things like, "All right, Barney Oldfield, cut it down to ninety," when I'm only going sixty-five.

So, I thought, I'd have to come down to the Willard on the bus, and then I'd take her out from there in a taxi. I had fourteen dollars put away, and that was plenty for an evening in Washington. I became a little nervous. What would I talk to her about? Suppose I couldn't think of anything that made sense. I told myself not to worry, that it would work out all right. I'd just be very natural and pleasant and I wouldn't let little things embarrass me. I was rather excited to be going out with a Bryn Mawr girl. It was like I was a college man myself.

Suddenly, I thought of Alice. I was supposed to take her to a movie at Keith's Theatre. She'd been really looking forward to it. Well, I'd just have to disappoint her, I thought.

When I got home, I immediately went into my father's study and closed the door. Nobody was home but our maid, Bessie, and she was in the kitchen. I wanted privacy. I sure as hell didn't want to be overheard. I took off my poncho and laid it across a leather couch, then took off my sneakers and sat down in a chair and placed my feet on my father's desk. I looked at the green backs of a set of *Encyclopedia Britannica* on the top bookshelf, and I thought for a few minutes about what I was going to say to Alice. Then I called her up.

When she answered the phone and I heard her sweet little voice, I felt a kind of loathing for her.

"Oh, John, hello," she said. She was so glad to hear from me.

It was really very painful. I told Alice that I was very sorry but I couldn't see her that night as a friend of mine from Wheeling, West Virginia, had suddenly arrived in town with his family, and that they'd invited me out to dinner. It was the only chance I'd have to see him, as they were all in for just one night. Every so often during the telling of the lie, I'd stop and listen to the silence on the other end, and I'd say, "Alice?" and she'd say, "I'm still here." I knew she was, as I could hear her breathing. It was obvious that she didn't believe me, and I finally said, "Well, I've got to go," and hung up.

I felt rotten. I took a deep breath, then walked over to the bookshelf, and after removing a book and opening it, I slammed it shut and put it back. I fell into an easy chair and tried to read the morning paper. But I threw the paper on the floor. I lay down on the couch and looked at the ceiling, and then I closed my eyes. Should I call Alice back and tell her the truth? That I was never going to see her again. But what good would it do? I'd tell her later.

After five thirty in the afternoon, I went upstairs and took a bath, and began to get ready for the evening. As I lay in the tub, I was fairly confident that Sheilah would go out with me. She wouldn't let me call her at seven thirty for nothing. I took my time getting ready. I put on a white oxford button-down shirt, and then I went to my father's closet and borrowed one of his ties—a fairly conservative red and blue stripe. After that, I returned to my room and I sat down on an old leather chair and put on a pair of lightweight charcoal gray socks, and then I put on a pair of dark brown wing-tip Bostonians, my best shoes. I was all set except for my suit. And then I put it on. It was my favorite—a gray, summer herringbone. I looked at myself in the full-length mirror on the closet door. I looked rather man about town, a little like William Powell as Nick Charles in The Thin Man. I gave my shoes a good brushing, and I combed my hair again. After looking in the mirror once more, I went downstairs to see Bessie, our colored maid, before I left for the Willard Hotel.

Bessie's been with us since before I was born, and she always looked me over when I went out.

She was in the kitchen, wearing her light blue uniform, her brown arms up to her elbows in soapy dishwater. She was medium brown, and a fairly hefty, large-boned woman. When I walked in, she smiled, then frowned.

"Honey, where are you going?"

I didn't say anything, but just did a little soft shoe routine on the linoleum.

She wiped her hands with a towel. "John, where are you eating? No fooling."

"Not here," I said. I suddenly felt great. "If anybody wants to know, just say I was invited out," I said, doing a little hop and slide.

"You taking out Alice?" Bessie said.

"No. Do I look all right?"

"You looking sharp. You ain't taking out Alice?"

"Not anymore," I said. I felt this little guilty pain, like a twinge, but it was very brief; then I was all right again.

Bessie took a lid off a pot and looked in, then she took a deep breath and smiled. I was waiting for her to say something.

"Oh, what are you smiling at?" I said.

"I just so glad you invited out," she said, putting a hand lightly on her cheek. I couldn't help smiling.

"I have a new girl, Bessie."

"I bet she's some girl, the way you acting," Bessie said. She pulled a loose cigarette out of the pocket of her uniform and lit it.

"She's from New York," I said. "She's very sophisticated—you know what that means, don't you?"

"Uh huh," Bessie said, smiling.

"She's been around, Bessie, and she knows what it's all about. She's not like any around here."

"Well, that's good," Bessie said.

"I'm really in love with her," I said.

"How long you known her?"

"Not long, but that doesn't matter," I said.

She smiled.

"Honey, I guess it don't," she said. "You just got all hot and bothered."

I gave her a hug, and then I left.

It was a little too early to meet Sheilah. It was six thirty, and the sun was still fairly high. There would be light for another two hours. When I picked her up at the Willard Hotel, the time of day would be perfect—a dusky twilight with just a little orange on the horizon. I got on the bus, which was going in the general direction of the hotel. On the way, it began to worry me that maybe I wouldn't have enough money. I had about fourteen dollars, but that wouldn't go far if she had champagne tastes. If both of us had dinner, and if we knocked around in taxicabs, it could be quite a problem. And there was always the chance I'd take her dancing later. So I decided I'd better have something to eat first, like a little soup. It would give me a little strength and partly kill my appetite at the same time, and later I could say to Sheilah, as we sat in the restaurant ordering dinner, "I think I'll just have the shrimp cocktail. But you go ahead. The steak is very good here." When I got within walking distance of the Willard, I got off the bus and went into a People's Drug Store and sat down at the counter and ordered a bowl of split pea soup. While I sat there, I tried to recall Sheilah's perfume, but I couldn't bring back the fragrance. It was just as well, as it made me weak in the knees. I wondered if we'd make love in the Willard Hotel. I finished half the pea soup and drank a glass of water, and then I paid the check. I felt very strange. As I left the drugstore, I looked in the mirror behind the cigar counter. I seemed to be breaking out in a nervous rash.

I arrived at the hotel at a quarter past seven, fifteen minutes early. I walked right to a house phone and asked the operator to ring Sheilah's room, then suddenly changed my mind and walked out of the hotel. It was too early. It doesn't look good to appear so anxious. So I left the hotel and I walked around the block. It was rather warm and sticky out, and I kept wiping my face with a handkerchief. My eyes were burning from the sweat. At seven thirty sharp, I walked back into the Willard lobby, but I didn't go right to the phone. I waited about seven minutes, and then about seven thirty-seven, I had the operator ring her room. I felt being five to ten minutes late was perfect—sort of casual and urbane, but not tragic or anything to get excited about.

"Hello," she said.

"Hello," I said. "This is John Lionel."

There was a pause.

"Oh, yes," she said. "Please excuse me for a second."

Then she covered the mouthpiece of the receiver, and I heard some muffled voices—Sheilah's and another girl's—but their voices weren't too distinct, and I couldn't hear what they said. Then I heard a kind of squealing laughter.

"Oh, yes. Well, how are you?" she said, finally.

"Fine," I said. "I'm all right."

And then suddenly she must have clamped the mouthpiece again. There was more muffled laughter, then a slightly hysterical scream, and the sound of something falling to the floor, then Sheilah's voice coming through again, sort of breaking and unusually high pitched. "Excuse me!" she said, then she covered the mouthpiece briefly again, and then came back on, sounding more in control. "Could you possibly call me back? Uh—Oh, God, Gloria, please! For God's sake!—look, excuse me, what did you have in mind?"

"Well, that we'd go out."

"Oh, I think that might be a little difficult. Tomorrow I have to catch an early train for New York, and really I don't think it would be a good idea—" I heard this scream in the background, and the sound of a thump, like a body hitting the floor. Sheilah laughed, then said, "It was awfully nice of you to call."

"Look, I thought maybe we'd have dinner, or just meet for a little while."

"I'm very sorry," she said.

"Or we don't have to have dinner," I said. "We could just meet and have a cup of coffee. I'm in the lobby."

"The lobby of this hotel?"

"I gathered we'd decided to go out at seven thirty, or that's what it seemed to me."

"I never said we were going out," she said.

"Well, not definitely," I said.

"Oh, what's the difference," she said. "Look, if you're in the lobby, why don't you come up. Room 543. My roommate from college is here."

The door to Sheilah's room was part way open. I knocked just to let them know I was coming, and then pushed the door all the way open. Inside, Sheilah was sitting on one of the twin beds next to a small night table on which there was a bottle of champagne. She wore a blue bathrobe, and held a half-filled glass. Her eyes were bright and sparkling. As I entered, she said, "Oh, look at him, Gloria. He's changed. He's nothing like he was this afternoon," and then with a little wave of her hand, she said, "John, meet Gloria Danz."

She was kneeling on the floor in her bare feet, a slightly overweight girl with short black hair; she wore a green dress with a bow on the back. Her face was fairly pretty, though she had a small pug nose, and she had a squinty, nearsighted look. A pair of high-heeled shoes and a champagne glass were on the floor beside her. She looked at me and said, "Oh, for heaven's sake, hello. I've been trying to stand on my head for twenty minutes, but I'm just too dizzy—" and then she began to giggle and collapsed on her side, knocking over the glass of champagne.

"Oh, n-o-o-o-o," she said, touching the wet spot on the rug.

"No harm," Sheilah said, getting up from her chair and picking up the bottle from the night table. She walked over to Gloria, who was holding up her glass, and poured her some more champagne. Then she said, "Won't you have some, John? Look, we'll have dinner together. OK? It's a very good idea. Well, please have some champagne, John. I'll get you a glass from the bathroom." She walked off with one hand on her head and holding the bottle with the other. I was really surprised and happy that we were having dinner after all.

I just stood there and looked at Gloria who lay back on her side and sipped champagne from her glass. She kept looking at me in this very serious way, and I felt a little uncomfortable. I put my hands in my pockets and tried to look unconcerned. Then Sheilah came back with the champagne.

"John doesn't like me!" Gloria said, suddenly, making this exaggerated downcast face. "He hates me!"

I took a sip of champagne, then sat down in a chair. I just ignored the remark, but Sheilah said, "No, John loves you. John, tell Gloria that you love her."

"He does not!" Gloria said.

"Please tell Gloria that you love her, John," Sheilah said. "She brought the champagne all the way from Philadelphia. Say that you love her, John."

I took another sip of champagne, and I looked over at Gloria. I was terribly embarrassed. I certainly wasn't going to tell her that I loved her. Instead, I tried to think of something fairly witty to say, a clever remark about champagne or even Philadelphia, but I couldn't think of anything, and I felt myself blushing.

Sheilah laughed.

"Now isn't John wonderful?" she said. "Isn't he simply grand?"

"Well, he isn't too bad at all," I said, suddenly, trying to sound superior and casual, but it was all wrong. I hated the sound of my voice. I sipped some more champagne and tried to appear interested in a picture on the wall. I suddenly stood up, and then I sat down again.

"John's bored," Gloria said. "He's very restless." Sheilah smiled at me. It was a wide and winning smile, and her eyes were sparkling. She wasn't at all like she was in the afternoon— all the cool reserve was gone. I didn't know which side of her I liked better. She seemed a little 'under the influence,' but it was all right with me. She suddenly looked at me very seriously, then held up her glass and said, "To friend John." Then she put the glass on the floor, stood up, and very calmly and naturally took off her bathrobe—all she had on underneath was a brassiere and a slip—and she went into a kind of a sexy pose, with one hand on the side of her face and the other on her hip. Gloria began to scream with laughter. I was never so surprised in my life, but I didn't move a muscle, and tried to be very nonchalant, but my heart was beating very fast. Sheilah was beautiful, her skin all copper brown from the sun, with fine shoulders and a really fine looking bosom, not too large or small, but just right; and her legs were fine, too. As far as I was concerned, she was a perfectly well-proportioned girl. I felt a little strange.

The last rays of the late afternoon sunlight were coming in through the window. I picked up my glass of champagne, and I said, simply, "To beauty," but then I felt so foolish—it was just wrong in every way—that I had to sit down.

"Oh, John is shocked," Gloria said. "He's really shocked."

"Oh, not at all," I said, trying to be matter of fact, but my voice was shaking slightly, and I hated myself.

Sheilah put on her robe and tied the belt. After going to a closet and removing a dress, she said, "Don't go away," and then went into the bathroom. I could hardly believe I was in Washington.

Gloria seemed suddenly a little let down and tired. Putting a hand to her forehead, she stood up and complained of a headache; then, without saying anything further, threw herself across one of the beds and went to sleep.

I sat down and sipped some champagne. I'd hardly drunk half the glass, and I wasn't at all 'high.'

A few minutes later, Sheilah came out in a blue dress that was simple and elegant at the same time. She really knew what it was all about, I thought. I suddenly thought of Alice in her cute little Washington 'girl scout' dresses. It was a sad comparison.

"Get up, Gloria," Sheilah said, going over to the bed and nudging her on the shoulder. "It's time to get the train."

Gloria rolled over on her side, opened one eye, then yawned and stretched. "Oh, God," she said, sitting up. "I'm a virgin again!" They both laughed, then Gloria looked at me with surprise, as though she'd seen me for the first time. "Oh, I remember you," she said. "You're John. Well, goodbye, John."

She sounded a little English all of a sudden, like Sheilah; she was fairly interesting and witty in a way, I thought, and sarcastic and amusing. I was almost a little sorry to see her leave.

"Au revoir, Sheilah," Gloria said, giving her a peck on the cheek. "See you soon."

"Thanks for coming," Sheilah said. "I was so sad, and you cheered me up—" She nodded and smiled. "Bless you, dear girl."

They said goodbye a few more times, and then Gloria left, waving and blowing kisses.

Sheilah looked at me without expression. She began to walk around and pick up glasses and stray clothing from the floor. I went over to the window and looked out. There was a dusky light with some orange near the horizon. I could see the old War Department. A pleasant breeze was coming in through the window.

I turned around and looked at her. It was a little strange being alone with her in a hotel room. For a second, I thought of trying to kiss her. After all, we'd been drinking champagne, and perhaps she was expecting me to try. I certainly didn't want to disappoint her. But then I thought, it wasn't the sort of thing a gentleman would do. It wasn't suave. I sat down in a chair and waited for her to finish cleaning the room. When she was through, she stood with her hands clasped in front of her. There was a look on her face that seemed to say, "I said I'd go out with you when I'd had too much to drink, and now I'm sorry." She seemed a little tired and let down. I was glad I hadn't made a pass.

"Well, shall we go?" she said.

"Fine," I said, trying to smile.

On the way down in the elevator, I tried to think of where I could take her for dinner. I needed the right sort of place for a sophisticated evening. I thought of the restaurants in the Hay Adams and Carlton. They are fine old distinguished places, but then, I thought, they may not be lively enough for Sheilah. For a girl like her, there had to be something rather special. I couldn't think of a place like that in Washington. As we walked through the lobby and out of the main entrance, I began to feel a kind of lightheadedness and panic. She was a girl who was not easily satisfied. God, I thought, if I only had a car. We could drive around and have a pleasant conversation at least. It would be fairly urbane.

The last of the twilight was turning to dusk. There were a few cabs lined up at the curb. While I was thinking about where to go for dinner, the street lamps came on.

"What's wrong?" Sheilah said. "Why are we just standing here?"

"Oh, we're about to go," I said.

"Where are we going?" she said.

"Well, it's rather early. I thought we'd take a walk first, and then go out to dinner," I said, stalling for time.

"Why don't we just go to a restaurant?"

"Sure, if that's what you want to do," I said. I still couldn't think of a restaurant that would be all right. I'd narrowed it down to Fan and Bill's, Harvey's, The Occidental, O'Donnel's, and the restaurants in the Carlton and Hay Adams Hotels. I really didn't want to go to any of them.

"Look, what are we going to do?" she said, slightly irritated. "We can't stand here all night."

I had to do something and do it fast, and I found myself hailing a cab. I opened the door for her and helped her in the back, and then I got in and closed the door and said, "Take us to Harvey's Restaurant, please." I don't know why I picked Harvey's except that it's over a hundred years old, and I always liked the atmosphere there. It's one of the best seafood restaurants in Washington, maybe the whole world.

It was about an eight-minute ride in the cab, and all the way over, Sheilah sat smoking on the left-hand side of the cab, as far away from me as she could get. I tried not to appear terribly concerned, and I made light conversation with the driver. By the time we reached Harvey's, I was feeling fairly confident again, and I gave the driver a half dollar tip.

Actually, it was the first time I'd ever taken a girl out to dinner. I'd always picked up my dates after they'd eaten, unless they'd invited me over to their house for a meal, like Alice did a number of times. Her parents treated me like a member of the family. The truth is, in Washington you'd never take a girl out to dinner, as it just wasn't the thing at my age. And I never could afford it anyway.

As the Negro headwaiter took us to a table, I said, "This may be the oldest restaurant in Washington."

"Oh, that's interesting," she said, in a faintly sarcastic way.

After we sat down, I looked around the restaurant. It's really a fine old place. All the waiters are rather old Negroes who are rather humorous in a dry way. I was looking for Branlee Hobbs, a dark brown wiry little man who always waits on my family. He saw me and smiled and nodded. He was picking up some menus in the back of the restaurant. It was really good to see him. I've known him since I was nine years old.

The lighting in the place was sort of yellowish-dim. There was the smell of old wood and turpentine and seafood and steamy clam chowder. It didn't go over too well with Sheilah. She looked slightly irritated. She opened her purse and took out a pack of cigarettes, and then she struck a match and lit one, and then dropped her head back and blew a fine stream of smoke toward the ceiling. She wouldn't look at me. Then she began to light matches and drop them in the ashtray and watch them burn down. She made no effort at all to enter into light conversation. I tried to ignore it all and pretended that everything couldn't have been better. After a few minutes had passed, she reached into her purse and pulled out a pair of dark glasses and put them on—it was very Hollywood—and she put her hands on her temples, as though she were just waiting for her head to explode.

She sighed, then took off her glasses and wiped her eyes.

Branlee came by the table and said, "How are you, Mr. Lionel?" and handed us some menus, and I said, "It's good to see you, Bran. This is Miss Lorraine."

"It's nice knowing you, ma'am," he said, and then he went to the back again. It was interesting that he called me, 'Mr. Lionel.' I guess he was trying to help me make an impression. He normally called me 'Old John.'

I looked at the menu, then closed it and looked around the room. Although it was fairly crowded, it was rather quiet. Sheilah was being very aloof. I was a little surprised at the way she was acting, but I wasn't disappointed. I even liked the way her moods kept changing. She was far from boring. I opened the menu again, and I said, "Look, the clam chowder is fairly good here." Sheilah covered her face with her napkin—she began to laugh—then she drank some water.

I looked down at the table, took a deep breath, and opened the menu again. The print ran together for a moment, and then became clear again. I concentrated on the words 'flounder' and 'Maryland Crab.' She put her hand lightly on my arm.

"Look, don't worry," she said, smiling.

"What do you mean?" I said.

"You're a wonderful boy, that's all," she said.

I drank some water. She was treating me like her little brother. I would rather have had her call me a 'dirty old bastard' than a 'wonderful boy' any day. It was obvious she didn't think I was a person to take seriously, and it was certainly no compliment when she called me a 'wonderful boy.' Naturally I didn't let on that I was upset, and I opened my menu again like nothing at all had happened—I was fairly close to tears—and I acted as though I was even faintly amused by what was going on. I certainly wasn't going to let her know that I was upset. I studied the menu like the only thing I really cared about was having a good dinner at Harvey's.

When I looked over at Sheilah, she suddenly laughed again for no reason at all, and then she shook her head and sighed. A very slight film of perspiration was on her upper lip. It made her look dewy and fresh. I drank some water and put the glass down.

She smiled again.

"You're awfully nice," she said, nodding.

I was really surprised.

"Thanks a lot," I said. "You're fine yourself."

I just blurted it out, and when I realized what I had said, I had a brief coughing fit. I was really embarrassed. I should have just said, "Thanks a lot" with a tone of slight sarcasm, and I don't know why I had to add, "You're fine yourself." There's nothing worse than overdoing it. It was the sort of thing that Alice would do. I really hated myself.

Branlee came over, and we gave him our order. We started off with a shrimp cocktail, and Sheilah ordered a lobster for the main course. I picked the halibut. I was fairly hungry, in spite of the pea soup I'd had earlier.

After the shrimp cocktail, Sheilah lit up a cigarette. She seemed rather happy and nervous at the same time. She was what you'd call a 'high strung' girl. I'm fairly high strung myself. I suddenly felt wonderful. I sat there in my gray summer herringbone suit feeling I was more than just fairly good. I felt I was 'a little bit of all right,' as Ewing would say. It's strange how great the right girl can make you feel. I looked at her, and for the first time noticed that her eyes were blue with little flecks of green, and she had a very smooth and nicely shaped forehead with a few freckles just below the hairline. She was so interesting looking sitting there in her blue dress, with her auburn hair falling over her shoulders. The more I looked at her, the more in love with her I became. It was a great feeling, but there was a kind of agony as well.

As she ate her lobster, she seemed to change in her attitude toward me. It wasn't just this sweet 'little brother' business, and I could tell that she was showing me a little more respect. She didn't smile so easily, and I could tell she was having a little trouble figuring me out. When people really think they know you inside out, they take you for granted, but Sheilah was having a hard time knowing me, because while she was eating her lobster, I was fairly aloof, like I was deep in thought about something, and I never gave her a chance to settle her mind on me. I was changing every few seconds. For example, I'd smile, then suddenly look very thoughtful and absentminded and place a hand on my chin. I'd pick up a spoon and tap the glass ever so lightly, and then I'd look at Sheilah in a very strange way, like she'd just become incredibly interesting to me again, almost too interesting for words. And just when it looked like I was going to say something, I'd gaze off at the people sitting in Harvey's Restaurant. Also, I'd look over at her and smile from time to time, to let her know I hadn't completely forgotten her. I used several varieties of smiles and tried to remember which one worked best. I was so busy thinking, I was under a terrible strain, and I got a slight headache.

"John, are you all right?" she said, putting out her cigarette.

I nodded. Branlee came over and filled our glasses with water. He smiled at me and nodded.

"How are you, Bran?" I said, for about the third time.

"Barely making it," he said. "How you doing, Mr. Lionel?"

"Fine," I said.

He picked up a tray and went back to the kitchen. Sheilah was looking at me strangely, but I managed to strike what I thought was a fairly careless indifferent pose—I leaned back in my chair, tilted my head slightly to one side and smiled. I was feeling somewhat lightheaded.

I ate some more halibut and some asparagus and a little mashed potatoes and green salad. For a moment I thought of poor Alice. I wondered how she was doing and if I'd really made her unhappy. Maybe I'm no damned good, I thought. That's what my father thinks at times, and he lets me know it, too. He'll say, "John, you're not worth a good God damn." Well, that's his opinion, I thought. He thinks I'm selfish and inconsiderate. My mother and sister agree. They're not altogether wrong, but they're not altogether right either. I could say a lot about what's wrong with them, but why bother?

The thought of Alice really upset me, and I tried to put her out of my mind. She wasn't going to ruin my life, I thought, looking at my plate. I concentrated on my food like a very cosmopolitan man who's been around and knows what good eating's all about. And I sort of savored it with this far off expression on my face.

When I finally looked at Sheilah, she was staring at me. It made me a little nervous.

"Well, how was the lobster?" I said, trying to be pleasant.

She shook her head and looked annoyed.

"What's wrong?" I said.

"Nothing—oh, everything. I don't like your whole attitude," she said. Her eyes were bright and shining.

"What do you mean?" I said.

"You're behaving foolishly, that's all," she said. "It's not very relaxing."

I didn't say anything.

She sighed.

"Oh, look, please don't mind me," she said, suddenly smiling. "Let's change the subject."

"Fine," I said.

We didn't say anything for a few minutes. I felt sick.

"Tell me, what have you read lately?" she said, finally.

I took a deep breath.

I told her that I was reading *Ivanhoe* by Sir Walter Scott and the stories and poems of Edgar Allan Poe and *Leaves of Grass* by Walt Whitman, which I recently checked out of the library.

"How nice," she said, with this smirk on her face.

I asked her what she was reading.

"*The Playboy of the Western World* currently—and of course, Proust."

I didn't say anything.

"Have you read him?" she said.

"Who?"

"Proust."

"Not really," I said.

"You mean, not at all," she said. "You're really so vague and indefinite, John." She laughed and lit another cigarette. I didn't say anything. The truth is, I'd never even heard of that writer. I hoped we'd get off literature. It obviously wasn't my strong subject with her, even though I'm fairly well read for my age. I've read Robert Louis Stevenson, Mark Twain, Bret Harte, James Fenimore Cooper, Nathaniel Hawthorne, Thomas Hardy, and Charles Dickens and some of Shakespeare as well as Jack London and a number of English poets. But how could I talk about literature with a girl who'd probably read nearly everything.

She drank some water and smiled.

"John, you're really amusing. I mean you're genuinely amusing."

"What do you mean?" I said.

"Well, you're rather naïve and innocent, that's all."

"Oh, I don't know."

I felt myself turning red.

She laughed.

"Don't be so sensitive. It's no disgrace to be a high-school boy."

I didn't say anything.

She lit another cigarette and smiled. I was really upset. I didn't like her calling me a 'high-school boy.' It was the truth, but there was something sarcastic in the way she said it. Jesus, it was really a joke on me, I thought, to pick up this lovely girl in the Willard Hotel and end up in a restaurant getting criticized. This pain went all through me, and it was like a black curtain was coming down over my eyes. I didn't like the part about being 'naïve and innocent' either. God knows what she meant by that. I briefly thought of Alice. Now Alice was naïve and innocent. She didn't know anything, but I've certainly been around some and have had a lot of experience for someone my age. I drank some water and took a deep breath, and I felt a little better.

Branlee came over to the table and filled our water glasses. He was looking a little tired. He was wearing a white coat, and there was a napkin across his arm. While he was pouring some water in my glass, Sheilah got up and excused herself in this very cold, formal way. She was going to the ladies room. I stood up out of politeness, and then I sat down again.

"Branlee, you're looking good," I said. "You the one who looking good," he said. "You got a pretty girl." He smiled. "How's your daddy?"

"Fine," I said.

"Your mother and sister, they all right?"

I nodded.

"Well, tell them Branlee said hello," he said, and then he walked back to the kitchen.

When Sheilah came back, she was smiling. She had powdered her nose, and her lipstick was darker than it was before. Her lips were so beautiful and inviting that I felt like kissing her right in the restaurant. It would have shocked plenty of people, but I'd have done it anyway, if I'd felt she'd have let me.

We had some coffee, and then I paid the bill—it came to about six dollars. I said goodbye to Branlee, and then we walked out of Harvey's.

It was about ten o'clock. We started walking south in the general direction of the Willard Hotel. I was thinking about taking her dancing, but I wasn't sure of the right place. I'd never taken a girl out dancing before, except to a school affair, but I'd been to a few Washington spots, like the Blue Room in the Shoreham Hotel, with my parents and sister, Carol. It didn't seem like the right place for Sheilah though. I'm not a bad dancer. I'm fairly good at the foxtrot, but I find those Latin dances fairly embarrassing. I don't know how to do them either. I was going over this in my mind, as we just strolled along.

She was in a much better mood now, and I was glad to see it. I took a deep breath and stopped and looked at her—she was so beautiful—and she turned around.

"What's wrong, John?"

"Nothing."

She laughed.

"You're being so dramatic," she said.

I felt myself turning red.

"Look, would you care to go dancing?" I said.

"Oh, I don't think so. I'm a little tired, and I have to get up early in the morning."

It was a relief. It had suddenly occurred to me that maybe they wouldn't let us in the Blue Room, as they served liquor there, and I think you had to be in the company of an adult. It was the same way all over Washington. I felt I had to ask though, as dancing was a fairly suave way to end the evening.

"Well, what would you like to do?" I said. I'd run out of ideas.

"Oh, we could take a little walk," she said.

"Fine," I said, and we started walking.

"I wish we could walk near the water," she said, as we strolled along. "Is the river far?"

"Well, we could take a cab," I said.

"Oh, let's do. That would be wonderful, John," she said, smiling. "I love the water."

So I hailed a cab and told the driver to take us to the Potomac River. He was really surprised. "Which part?" he said. I told him to go toward Haines Point. "I'll let you know when to stop," I said. I had to smile. He seemed rather confused, and I could hardly blame him. Sheilah's idea of walking along the river was certainly a novel way to spend the evening. Alice would never suggest anything like that in a thousand years. Her idea of a good time was going to a movie. Sheilah was full of surprises though. Being married to her, I thought, would no doubt make for an interesting life, with each day more exciting than the last.

I told the driver to stop near a grassy bank along the Potomac River. After I paid him, he looked at us in a rather strange way and then he drove off. It was very quiet. Some cars passed occasionally, and each time the light from the headlamps gave a glow to Sheilah's face. She was half smiling, with her teeth pressed against her lower lip. Her eyes were wide open. She kept staring at the water, her arms folded against her stomach. I wanted to say something to change the mood, but I couldn't think of anything to say.

We started walking toward the river, and when we got near the edge, Sheilah said, "I'd like to sit down here." I took off my coat and spread it out and asked her to sit on it. I sat down beside her on the ground, which was fairly wet from the dew. It was a beautiful night. There was a little breeze. The stars were out. You could see some of the constellations very clearly—the Big and Little Dippers, Orion, and the Pleiades. The Milky Way covered the sky with a kind of powdery light. It was all so calm and pleasant. Sheilah sat cross-legged on the ground. She lit a cigarette and handed me the pack. I lit a cigarette myself.

"Are you feeling all right?" I said.

"I guess so," she said, not looking at me.

I didn't say anything. After a while, she seemed to forget about her cigarette. It slowly burned down between the fingers of her right hand which rested on the ground. I got up and took the cigarette from her before she burned herself. Then I sat down again. She seemed in a daze. Her mouth was slightly open, and there was a faraway look in her eyes.

After a while, she looked over at me. She seemed a little more alert, but there was still a strange look in her eyes. I moved a little closer to her, still sitting on the ground, and then I placed a hand lightly on her shoulder—in a very casual way, as if to say, "Don't worry. You've got a friend here"—and then I slid my hand across her back, feeling a little nervous, not wanting to make a false move. I had my arm around her. She reached up and took my hand that was resting on her shoulder and held it for a few moments. Across the river, there were lights from Virginia. She placed her face against my shoulder, and I looked down at the top of her head, and then she slowly looked up at me. It was all so quiet and beautiful, sitting there on the grass by the river, under all those stars, and I never felt so scared and tender in my life. There was a smell of honeysuckle along with Sheilah's perfume. I placed my cheek against her cheek, and I could hear the water rippling against the bank, and I kissed her on the eyes and then on the mouth. It was a light kiss, and I was a little afraid I'd gone too far, but then she put her hand behind my head and pulled me down on her and kissed me hard on the mouth, and we just lay there in each other's arms for about two minutes on that kiss alone.

We got our breath, and then we kissed again. The second kiss lasted longer than the first, and it was all so warm and pleasant.

I looked up at the sky—there were a few fast-moving clouds sailing through the moonlight—and then I looked down at Sheilah again. She was looking at me with a faint little smile on her face, and I thought, God, I've never been so happy in my life, and I kissed her again. When I stopped for a few seconds, she began to murmur, "I care for you, John. Do you care for me?" and "Kiss me again. Don't stop kissing me," and while I was kissing her, I put a hand on her breast just for a second but I took it right away as I was afraid I'd gone too far, and then she took my hand and put it back where I'd had it, and said, as she pressed her forehead against mine, "I'm growing rather fond of you"—God, she felt so wonderful and smelled so good—and then she slowly sat up, and she was breathing deeply and sighing with her mouth slightly open in a little smile, and she was so pleasant and natural, not at all nervous like she'd been. I was rather wild with passion, but I managed to control myself, and we both just sat there, looking in each other's eyes, and not touching one another, and then we gradually began to breathe more quietly again.

We looked at the river and the sky, at the powdery starlight and a yellow-orange three-quarter moon that was reflected on the water. It was very quiet and still except for the sound of little waves lapping against the riverbank and an occasional car passing on the road behind us.

"John, do you like me?" Sheilah said, suddenly.

"Well, yes," I said, a little surprised.

"Would you just do anything I asked?" she said.

"Sure"

"I bet you wouldn't."

"Sure, I would."

"Do you really like me a lot?"

"Oh God, yes," I said.

She smiled, then laughed, taking my hand and squeezing it and then letting go. She bit her lower lip and stared at me for almost half a minute. I was never so happy in my life.

"Suppose I gave you some ridiculous command," she said. "Would you obey it?"

I nodded.

"Then take a solemn oath," she said. "Say, 'I solemnly swear to do any outrageous thing Sheilah Lorraine asks me to do.'"

I said it, smiling the whole time.

"Now you made an oath, John, and it's your sacred duty to perform it," she said, her eyes sparkling.

"That's right," I said, smiling.

"Then take a swim," she said, smoothing back her hair.

I wasn't expecting that. I thought it would be something fairly humorous, like "Kiss me, my fool," or "Sing a song, hopping on your left foot," and the like.

I didn't say anything.

"Are you speechless?" she said.

"No."

"You look so shocked."

"I'm not shocked."

"You are, too. Do you really like me?"

"Sure, I do."

"Then take a swim."

"But what for?"

"You promised, and I want you to."

She smiled and put her cigarette out in the grass, blowing out the smoke. She began to bite her lower lip and stare at me without blinking. I was crazy about her all right, but I didn't want to take a swim in the Potomac. What good would it do? I'd probably get typhoid or a bad case of cramps and drown. I just smiled and was very nonchalant.

"Well, are you going to do it?" she said.

"It doesn't make sense," I said.

"Stop being a little high-school boy."

I went into a momentary daze and felt these pins and needles all over my face and body.

"John, do you want to be a perfectly ordinary person all your life?"

"No."

"Then don't try to make sense all the time."

I didn't say anything.

She licked her lips and smiled slightly.

"Look, can't you do something that doesn't make any sense at all? Aren't you capable of a grand gesture? I asked you to go into the river, and if you like me, you'll do it, just because I asked you."

I liked the part about it being a 'grand gesture,' like Beau Geste, and I tried to kiss her, but she pushed me away.

"What do you say, John? It's great that you don't want to do it, but would do it anyway." She suddenly gave me a quick little kiss on the mouth. I tried to kiss her back, but she pushed me away. She lit a cigarette, dropping her head back and blowing the smoke toward the sky.

The sky was a great swirl of light. I saw a shooting star.

She smiled at me.

"Come on, what do you say, John? Do you like me enough?"

I felt very strange. I stood up and started walking toward the river. I prayed to God I wouldn't drown, then took off my Bostonians, then my socks. While I was taking off my shirt, Sheilah walked over and sat down at my feet. I was hoping she'd change her mind, but she just smiled up at me. The water was partly dark and partly shimmering in the moonlight. I wondered about the current. I was a good swimmer, but even the best have been pulled down by an undertow, and what about a stomach cramp? There was no defense against that. And the Potomac was one of the foulest, most polluted rivers in the world.

I tightened my belt a notch, then I stepped off the muddy bank and into the water. "Take a swim for Sheilah," I heard her say. I looked back at her. She suddenly laughed, then coughed into her hands. The water swirled around my legs. It was muddy and slippery underfoot, with small, smooth rocks on the bottom. As I moved slowly toward deeper water, I stepped on a can and a piece of glass, but fortunately I missed the sharp edges and didn't cut myself. I moved out into water up to my waist, keeping my arms straight out from my shoulders. It was a 'grand gesture' all right. I wanted to get it over with as fast as I could and get back on dry land. I waded out in the Potomac until the water was on a level with my chest. I looked back at Sheilah again. "Go on. Go on," she said. As I moved out, the current got a little swifter. The main thing I was concentrating on was to keep my mouth closed, and to keep my head above water. I didn't want to swallow any of the Potomac River. Suddenly, I couldn't touch bottom, and the current was much faster. I began to tread water, and then went into the sidestroke. The water was very cold, and my pants were getting in the way. I don't know why I didn't take them off on the bank. I guess I was a little shy. It was the end of my gray herringbone, I thought. I was about forty yards off shore, and I kept doing the sidestroke against the current in order to stay in one place. I looked over at Sheilah. She was waving my shirt, and she yelled, "Oh, marvelous!" I swam around a few more minutes, and then I made for shore. I would have sprinted in with the American Crawl, but I was afraid to get my face in the water.

Dripping wet, I walked the final few yards, and the way Sheilah greeted me, you'd have thought I'd swum the English Channel. She threw her arms around me, and then she began wiping my back with my shirt. It was cool with the breeze, and my teeth were chattering. "Your lips are blue," Sheilah said. I put my damp shirt on, and my coat over that, and then I put on my socks and slipped into my shoes. I felt all right, except for my legs, which were wet and very cold. I wasn't sure I smelled particularly good from the river, but Sheilah didn't seem to mind. What I could have really used was a bath and a hot cup of coffee. We sat down on the ground, and I continued to shake. Sheilah kept saying, "You did it for me." It was true. I'd done it for her all right. I sure wouldn't have done it for Alice, or any other girl I knew. Sheilah lit a cigarette, and we kept passing it back and forth.

"Would you do it again, if I asked you?" she said.

I didn't say anything.

"Well, would you?" she said, looking a little upset.

I was still shaking.

"Sure, I would," I said. "But I don't feel well right now."

She smiled. She was all aglow, just knowing that I loved her enough to do anything she wanted. In a way, I felt a little disgusted with myself, but as soon as I looked at her smiling at me, I felt all right again.

I put my arm around her and kissed her. We continued kissing for a while. I was really mad for her.

After a while, she began to cough and we stopped, and just

lay on our backs and looked up at the sky. While I was lying there, I thought of poor Alice. She'd never understand why I went into the river. Why, it's really the same kind of thing I once read about in a book called *Tales of Chivalry*—every knight does a task for his lady—not that I considered myself a knight or anything like that.

As I lay there on the grass, still shaking slightly, I almost wished that Sheilah would ask me to go jump in the river again.

We lay there and held hands and smoked. We talked about how fond we were growing of one another. I put my arms around her and kissed her, and she kissed me back. We lay in each other's arms for quite some time, and got rather passionate. I wanted to go further than merely kissing, but Sheilah said, "John, I think I better get back."

It was about one o'clock in the morning. There were a few thin, wispy clouds in the sky. Some birds flew low over the trees, circling and diving, then swinging high again. A breeze blew across the water, sending little rippling waves to shore, and causing the leaves to rustle and the trees to sigh and bend. It was wonderful how the grass was quivering in the breeze. Across the river, most of the lights in Virginia had gone out. I could have stayed there all night, watching the river and the sky, and kissing Sheilah, and occasionally smoking cigarettes and having these tender little conversations. But nothing lasts forever.

We started walking back to the Willard Hotel. I was feeling very light and happy. The streets were very quiet. We walked arm in arm. Every so often Sheilah would stop and look up at me, and I would kiss her standing under a tree or by a parked car. A block from the Willard Hotel, we sat on a bench in Lafayette Park, and I told her, feeling a little afraid, that I really wished we could spend the night together—it was a fairly suave thing to say, and it was the truth, too—and she said, "I wish we could, too, but perhaps not tonight—" and then she laughed, and said, "I'm going to kiss you whether you like it or not." And we kissed some more. I never really counted on spending the night in the Willard Hotel with her. In the first place, the way I looked, they'd have called the cops as soon as I walked in the lobby and had me arrested for vagrancy. Besides, my dad wouldn't quite understand my spending the night with the girl I loved. I have to come home every night.

We sat in Lafayette Park until a policeman came by and said that we'd better be moving on. So we got up and walked the remaining block to the Willard. It was about two o'clock in the morning.

Outside the Willard Hotel, Sheilah had the most interesting expression on her face. It was a little sad and strange—and affectionate, too. I told her I'd see her in the morning.

"I'm getting an eight o'clock train to New York," she said.

"I'll take you to the station."

"Well, goodnight, John. Please kiss me goodnight."

I kissed her again, and then I said, "Sheilah, I really care for you."

"I know," she said.

It was really hard to say goodbye.

"I'll come and see you in New York," I said. "Well, goodnight."

She went up the steps and turned around and waved. "It was a lovely evening," she said, smiling. "Au revoir." And then she went inside the hotel, turned once and waved again, then disappeared. As I started walking, I felt so light and happy and pleased with the way things had gone. It didn't matter that she was eighteen. I was going on seventeen, and the important thing was how we got along.

I walked all the way home, about five miles, occasionally breaking into a run, and when I arrived at our house, I felt so wide awake that I couldn't imagine going to bed.

I sat down under a tree and thought of Sheilah. My heart was practically exploding. I must have thought of her for hours. Later on I walked around the neighborhood, and tried to calm down. I was so happy, it was slightly painful. I walked for an hour or so. It was more like floating than walking. And then I sat down again under the tree in the yard. The sky slowly turned pale, until the whole neighborhood was in gray light. About six thirty, the sun came up, and the sky turned to light blue. There was dew on the grass, and everything was fresh in the morning.

I went in the house and very quietly went up the stairs and into my room. I took off my pants—they were still damp from the river—and then, turning down the sheets of my bed, I lay down for a minute to make it seem like I'd slept there all night. Then I got undressed and took a hot shower, ending up with a cold spray. I toweled dry and put on my bathrobe. After hiding my gray summer herringbone suit behind a box in the closet, I went down to the kitchen and made some coffee. I had a cup with plenty of milk and sugar, and I smoked a Camel cigarette. It was about quarter to seven. I had to start getting ready to take Sheilah to the station. So I went upstairs to my room and changed into my other summer suit, a gray glen plaid, and put on a blue shirt along with another of my father's ties, a light green with white dots. And then I put on a pair of plain brown cordovan shoes. I went downstairs and brought in the Sunday papers from outside. I looked at them for a while. Then I had another cup of coffee. I wanted to be alert for our farewell.

Sitting in the kitchen, I wondered if she'd been able to go right to sleep, or if she'd been thinking about me. Had she been tossing and restless and getting up and turning on the lamp? I stirred the sugar in the cup. I felt strange. I was a little delirious. Had she fallen in love with me on first sight? I wondered. It wouldn't be the first time, though usually a girl has to get to know me first. Of course, some have hated me on first sight, and even more when they got to know me, thinking I was conceited and selfish. I yawned. I was getting sleepy. I slapped myself on the face a few times to improve the circulation; then I went into the bathroom and placed a cold washcloth over my eyes.

It was about ten after seven. Wanting to make more noise than usual in leaving the house, I thumped up the stairs again, then ran down, hoping they'd hear me and know for sure I'd been home. But no one was up or stirring. I left a note on the dining room table. I said I was out taking a walk.

As I went out on the street, in the silence of the morning, and looked at all the old houses and trees, I thought of Alice. It was sad in a way. She'd been a very good friend. Standing there with the sun on my face, I lit a cigarette. I'd probably never see her again. I suddenly felt so strange and sad that I had to lean against a parked car.

I pushed off and began to walk toward Connecticut Avenue. I just wanted to be happy, I thought. I began to think about Sheilah. At the thought of seeing her again, I felt this tremendous excitement, but then, oddly, I began to lose some of my coordination and started weaving down the street. I slowed down and leaned against a tree. In the branches were some robins and Baltimore orioles and a few blue jays. They were singing away. Listening to them, I almost felt like my old self again. I started walking, and a few minutes later, I came out on Connecticut Avenue and hailed a cab for the Willard Hotel.

All the way down in the cab, I kept yawning and growing more keyed up at the same time.

As the cab pulled into the curb in front of the entrance, I told the driver to wait, and I jumped out and went into the lobby. It was seven thirty sharp. I picked up the house phone and asked the operator to ring her room. It rang for about two minutes, and there was no answer. I flashed the operator and asked her if she was sure that she was ringing Sheilah Lorraine's room. She said that she was certain, then gave me 'information,' and the clerk said, "Miss Lorraine has checked out." I hung up. I didn't even have her address or telephone number. I slumped forward on this little ledge and covered my face with my hands. She was gone, and I'd never see her again. As I took my hands away, I saw Sheilah over at the Cashier's window, paying her bill. What a feeling! I watched her with a kind of mad happiness. She looked so neat—so fresh and cool and sophisticated, while she talked to the cashier. She was wearing a very simple and elegant green dress, and her auburn hair was hanging loosely on her back. I noticed again that she had wonderful legs—maybe the best I've ever seen. I managed to walk over to her, and then, with this great smile spreading over my face, I said, "Good morning." She seemed startled, as though she almost didn't recognize me. It was like a knife in the heart. I thought I was beyond getting all upset if she didn't look at me just right, but I was as easily hurt as ever. Sheilah smiled quickly and said, "Good morning. I'll be with you in a minute." I took a deep breath and let the air out slowly. She finished paying the cashier, then went through some things in her purse, completely ignoring me. It was very painful. She kept going through her purse. I didn't know what she was looking for. We should have kissed when we met. I believe in that, particularly when you're in love, like I thought we were.

She pulled her room key out of her purse and left it with the cashier. Then she looked over at me. I tried to look rather indifferent, but it was a terrible strain, and I suddenly thought the hell with it. All this jockeying around for an advantage, it makes you tired.

"Hello, John," she said. She smiled, but it wasn't from the heart. It was impersonal and a little cold.

"You didn't have to come," she said, hardly looking at me. "It really wasn't necessary."

I wanted to say, I know it wasn't necessary, but I just wanted to see you again. But I couldn't get it out. She was so formal. God, I thought, didn't she remember last night? She'd been so warm and passionate then. Was her caring for me all a big lie? Was it just one of those 'brief interludes' I'd read about? I picked up her suitcase, and we walked through the lobby to the cab waiting outside. I opened the door, and she got in. I put her suitcase in the front seat, and then sat down beside her in the back, and we started out for Union Station.

I wanted to talk to her, but it seemed like the wrong time and place. There was no privacy. We hardly said a word to one another. I was a little tense, but she was perfectly at ease, and acted like she never felt better. It was obvious that she wasn't sad to be leaving.

When we pulled up to the unloading platform of Union Station, I opened the door and jumped right out of the cab. I helped

Sheilah out, then got her suitcase from the front seat and paid the driver.

As I started walking with Sheilah's suitcase, she said, "John, I can take that. You don't have to go in with me."

I kept walking with her suitcase, and we went into Union Station. It was about quarter to eight. There were a lot of travelers in the station, even at that hour, on a Sunday morning, sitting on the long dark wooden benches in the main waiting room. Though it was bright outside, it was dim in the station. It was like being in a great dusky cavern. There was a sound like the roar of the ocean, with sharp and muffled noises reverberating off the walls. As we walked through the waiting room toward the train gates, I suddenly stopped near the Traveler's Aid desk and put the suitcase down.

"John, what are you doing? Why are we stopping here?" Sheilah said.

"When will I see you again?" I said, feeling sick. I held on to the Traveler's Aid desk for support.

"John, I have to go."

"Will I ever see you again?" I said, looking down at the suitcase.

"I'm going to miss my train," she said.

I pulled out an old envelope from my pocket and picked up a pencil that was on the desk. "What's your address and telephone number?" I said. "I'll write. I'll come to New York. Look, I can come and visit you at Bryn Mawr in the fall."

She shook her head.

"Oh, what's the matter with you? Please. Let's go."

She looked very uncomfortable and somewhat annoyed.

I picked up her suitcase, and we went through the swinging door to the train shed, and walked toward the gate of the Morning Congressional to New York.

When we reached the gate, I wouldn't give her the suitcase.

"John, I've got to go!" she said. We stepped aside to let some people pass.

"When am I going to see you again?" I said.

"Oh, must you go on about that?" she said. "Will you give me the suitcase?"

"Not until I get an answer."

"John, I'm too old for you. Now give me the suitcase."

"Didn't you mean what you said last night?" I said, feeling sick.

She threw her head back and gave out this exasperated sigh. "We had a nice time, didn't we? Let it go at that—" She coughed. "I mean, it was amusing. Look, don't take everything so seriously, John—" She smiled in this very pained way. "Look, you're too young for me, and I'm not in love with you. Please give me my suitcase. I'll miss my train. People are looking at us."

I put the suitcase down and let her pick it up.

"Well, goodbye, John," she said.

I didn't say anything.

She went through the gate. Little eddies of steam came from under the cars and swirled around the platform. She walked down to a coach a good distance from the gate and climbed aboard. I was hoping she'd turn around, but she never looked back.

I went back inside the station, and sat down on one of the long benches. For a second, I closed my eyes. I felt myself falling to one side, and quickly sat up and opened my eyes again. I wished I'd never met her. I got up and walked a few feet to a water fountain and had a drink. Then I returned to the bench and sat down again. I was too young for her, and she wasn't in love with me. That was the truth. I was sorry I hadn't drowned in the Potomac.

I started to force myself to my feet—I was really drowsy—but then, I thought, the hell with it. I'm not going anywhere. I sat back down and folded my arms across my chest and slumped down a little lower on the bench. I dozed for a while. When I looked up, the station clock said twenty after eight. She was somewhere south of Baltimore. I began to stare at my hands. There were rows of calluses on the palms, just below the fingers.

It was from swinging the bat. I suddenly thought of the Johnstown Tournament up in Pennsylvania. It was double elimination. You lose twice and you're out. We had a fairly good chance to go all the way. My eyes got very heavy. I tried to imagine Sheilah sitting on the train, but before I could see her, I fell asleep.

I had a dream. I was in a green field in Washington. It was a summer afternoon, with a nice breeze and fleecy clouds moving across a blue sky. I was walking with Alice, and she was smiling and looking at me with great affection. On the edge of the field, there was a grove of trees. Skylarks were sitting in the branches. Their singing made me very happy, and I said, "Alice, you're really a blithe spirit," and she said, "Oh, John, I'm so happy. You're the most wonderful person in the whole world." When I woke up, about an hour later, I went right to a telephone booth in Union Station and called her up. We made a date for that night.

Later that evening, having slept in the afternoon, I took her to a fairly sophisticated movie at the Loew's Palace. Sitting in the darkened theater, I thought of all that had happened. It hardly seemed real and was more strange than the movie on the screen. I looked over at Alice. She looked so glad and innocent, and a little shy; and I thought, she's really a fine and tender girl.

Afterwards, we went out for a cup of coffee, and it was a very friendly, pleasant time. We were so relaxed, and the conversation flowed. Naturally, I did most of the talking, but Alice didn't seem to mind. I thought of Sheilah every now and then, and there was a little stabbing in the heart, but all things considered, I felt pretty good. There was no point being sad over what was gone. I stirred the sugar in my cup and drank some water, and I tried not to think of her at all.

Friend of Mankind

Early spring in Washington, 1941.

John Lionel, twelve, was being kept after school until four o'clock, and then he had to fight Frank Dugan.

He was alone in the room with his teacher, Lorna Babcock. Last month she'd called him a liar after sending him down to the book room to return a book. The book room was closed, and when he came back and told her, she claimed he'd never gone. "You always lie," she said. He could not remember that he'd ever lied. He was not a liar and never would be, and she was the liar for saying he was.

When she sent him down to the book room for the second time, he only pretended to go and came back in five minutes. "It's closed like I told you," he said. She'd told him to sit down and be quiet, but he was so angry he threw the book on her desk, knocking over an ink bottle. The ink spilled over a grade book she'd been writing in.

"Look what you did, you awful boy!"

He wasn't sorry. She'd called him a liar. He was glad he did it, and he'd do it again. Then he told her that he hated her because she was mean, and it made her eyes tear up.

She'd sent him to the principal's office. It was the fourth time he'd been sent to Mr. Liflett in a month's duration. Mr. Liflett called his father at work. "I'm losing patience with your son. Today he threw a book at his teacher. Tomorrow, who knows what?"

When he got home he got a whipping with a strap.

"You're a rotten kid. You're no damn good," his father said.

"I am good. I'm very good."

"You're going to military school. They'll knock some sense into you."

"I won't go! I'll run away."

His father cracked him again.

"That's enough. You're no damn good and never will be."

"I'm real good. But you're not. You think you're such a big shot!" John shouted, and he ran from the room.

That night he lay on his bed and cried. His mother tried to console him.

"Daddy has a temper. But he's a good man."

She didn't have to tell him.

"Daddy loves you," his mother said, but he knew it, he wasn't stupid.

His father was moody. When his father felt good, he'd say, "You're my boy, John," and he'd recite "Gunga Din."

"'Though I've belted you and flayed you, by the living God that made you, you're a better man than I am, Gunga Din.'"

He looked out the window. There was blue sky overhead, with dark clouds to the west.

It was so unfair, he thought. He got twice the punishment for being late that other kids got. It was a fact, he thought. That he was the worst offender did not occur to him. Every morning he was late for school.

"And no more gazing out the window. I don't want a day-dreamy effort," Miss Babcock said.

"Yes, ma'am, but how many times do I have to write it?"

"You just keep writing until time is up."

"But I have a sore hand."

"I think you'll live."

"If I could write left-handed, it'd be different."

"That's enough."

He began writing, 'Tardiness is a thief of time.'

And he thought of Dugan waiting outside.

He didn't like waiting to fight with time to think but would rather fight when he was hot to get even like when he'd fought Buck Taylor on the playground. Buck had whacked him on the back of the head and thought it was funny, and he'd hit Buck in the mouth, then took a fist in the eye before a teacher, Miss Rathko, broke it up. She said he'd started it and sent him to Mr. Liflett's office.

"I'm very disappointed in you. I thought we understood each other," Mr. Liflett said. John looked down at the floor. "Don't be shifty. Look me in the eye. Now, why did you hit Buck Taylor?"

John looked down.

He wouldn't say Buck had hit him first as he'd rather take the blame himself than rat on Buck. Mr. Liflett leaned forward.

"I'm waiting for an answer."

"I don't know," John said.

Mr. Liflett removed his glasses. "Your sister was so nice when she was a student here. It's hard to imagine you're from the same family."

John turned red. What did he know, he thought? He was stupid. He hated him.

"Look at me. Give me one reason why I shouldn't expel you."

He could think of more than one, but he wouldn't say it. He was modest. He wouldn't say, 'Oh, I'm good. I'm good.'

Mr. Liflett said, "You're a problem to your teachers and yourself. You've set a record for tardiness. And I've never known a boy with so bad a temper. You get into fights at the drop of a hat."

John shook his head. That was a lie. He'd had only three fights all year. The worst fight he'd had was in print shop with Norman Hunter, he couldn't remember why. They'd both had bloody noses and were sent to the infirmary and while there began to fight again because Norman had hit him for no reason. The truth was, he didn't care for fighting. If people were nice to him, he was nice to them. But if someone called him a liar or hit him for no reason he wouldn't say 'Thank you very much.' And if he was late for school it was because he slowed down when he thought of Miss Babcock, and he couldn't make it by the bell.

"I want to ask you something," Mr. Liflett said. "What sort of person would you rather be? Some barbarian at the gates or a friend of mankind?"

John looked down at his hands.

"You're not saying? You'd rather be some foul-tempered barbarian, is that it?"

Mr. Liflett opened the Bible on his desk. "I'm going to read you something from Proverbs." And he found the verse. "'He that is slow to anger is better than the mighty; and he that ruleth his spirit than he that taketh a city.'"

John looked down. He didn't need Proverbs. It was Buck who needed them and a whole lot more. It was so unfair it made him sick. He was minding his own business and Buck had hit him first and he'd hit back like anyone would. And they'd sent him down to the principal's office. And why was that? Because certain teachers had it in for him, and they were a bunch of liars.

Mr. Liflett leaned forward and looked at him for some time.

"I should expel you, but I believe in mercy and in the possibility of human redemption. I'll give you one more chance and place you on probation. But you must first promise to change your ways. Now I ask you, do you wish to stay here and be a civilized person? Or would you prefer that I call your mother and say, 'Mrs. Lionel, come for your barbarian child'? What? I don't hear you. Look at me. Your life at this school hangs in the balance. So what's it going to be?"

His hand was tired. He'd written more than a hundred sentences. He put his pencil down, made a fist, then hit the palm of his left hand and winced. He'd hurt his hand playing baseball, sliding into home.

The window was open. He looked out at the rooftops of old wooden houses. The sky was filled with gray clouds.

A moist breeze entered the room.

It was lonely sitting there waiting to fight Frank Dugan. He wanted to talk to someone, even if only to Miss Babcock. He raised his hand.

"What is it?"

"Why is tardiness a thief of time? How can it steal time? Time passes whether you're late or early. It doesn't matter what you do but time's going to move on. So tardiness doesn't steal a thing that I can see."

"It steals time from school, John. You know that very well. Next time you'll write, 'Tardiness is a disease.' At least, it is for you."

He kept writing. Then he thought he heard some thunder. He raised his hand again.

"What is it now?"

"It looks like rain. Maybe I should leave early to beat the storm."

"You're staying until four o'clock, and besides, a little rain never hurt anybody," she said.

"No, but what about lightning?"

"That's enough."

It wasn't the storm he wished to avoid. It was Dugan. Five months before, Dugan had come to public school after being thrown out of a Catholic school for cursing a nun. Joe Conroy told him. Dugan had cursed the nun and thrown a book at her. It was a religious book. Afterwards, he would not go to confession and show contrition. If he'd shown it, he could have stayed. That's what Conroy said, and he was Catholic himself.

"And he told a priest to go to hell," Conroy said. And this

priest had tried to help him. He'd said, go to hell, not even, go to hell, Father. It was a double disrespect, Conroy said. And they'd kicked him out and said he'd burn in hell. John was glad he wasn't Catholic. It was too hard. The priests hit you and so did the nuns, that's what Conroy said, and you'd go to confession and say, 'Bless me, Father, for I have sinned,' and you had to tell the priest what you'd done. You could never say, 'I've got nothing this week.' They'd worm it out of you. That's what Conroy said, and he was an altar boy.

Conroy said Dugan could outfight boys three years older, and he'd go into the ring some day and be champion. He'd fought Billy Morris outside the Boys Club in Georgetown. Morris was bigger and older, and Dugan about killed him. Conroy said so.

John had heard a lot about Dugan. He was scary, he was strange. Some nights he slept in parked cars to avoid going home.

He hated Dugan, and Dugan hated him. They had only one thing in common, throwing books at teachers. Other than that, you could find no two boys so different. John liked to talk for one thing, and Dugan hated talkers.

On that day John had been talking to Joe Conroy and Fatty Wolf in the lunchroom, while Dugan had sat at a table nearby.

"Can you remember the poem about the World War?" Conroy said. It was a poem John had recited by heart on Armistice Day at the school assembly. When he'd walked off the stage, he'd got an ovation; Winfrey Powell, his English teacher, had hugged him. "You're wonderful," she'd said. She was the only teacher he loved.

"Can you do the first part?" Conroy said.

John put down his sandwich.

"'I have a rendezvous with Death/At some disputed barricade,/When Spring comes round with rustling shade/And apple blossoms fill the air—'"

Then he said, "The poet's name was Alan Seeger. He was an American fighting for the French. It was 1916. We weren't in the war yet, but he got in early. Well, he knew he was going to die. He had a premonition—that's when you know something before it happens—and after he wrote the poem he died on the Western Front. But he didn't die in the spring but on the fourth of July."

Seeing Dugan out of the corner of his eye, he kept talking.

He told a story about his father. Conroy and Fatty had heard it before.

"In 1923 my dad was third in the Penn Relays in the four-hundred-and-forty-yard dash. He would have got second but he got a cramp in his leg. I have the clippings to prove it."

"Sure. But no one has ever seen them," Conroy said.

"They're in a trunk in a storage room. I'm going there soon with my dad, and then I'll get them."

Conroy shook his head.

"You're making it up."

"No, it's true. My father told me."

Dugan got up and walked over to him.

"Hey, shut up."

"No, I'd rather not," John said.

"You make me sick. You make me want to puke."

"I don't care what a moron thinks."

Dugan grabbed his arm.

"I'm going to bust you, boy!"

John shook free.

"Get off."

"I know you got to stay after. But I'll be outside. You better show up. I'm going to kill you."

Dugan walked away, then looked back and shook a fist.

John smiled at Conroy and Fatty Wolf. He hoped he'd shown no fear.

"You're in for it now," Conroy said.

"No, I'm not," John said.

"Are you scared?" Fatty said.

"No. Well, I got to go."

And he got up and returned to class.

He kept writing, 'Tardiness is a thief of time.' He thought he heard thunder. Maybe it would storm; they couldn't fight then, but sunlight came through a break in the clouds and lit up the wooden houses.

"It's four o'clock. You're free to go, John," Miss Babcock said.

After putting his paper on her desk, he picked up his school bag and left.

He came out the main entrance. The sky was gray again. The houses looked dreary and sad. After looking up and down the street, he reached in the pocket of his knickers, pulled out a handkerchief and wiped his face. Then he put down his school bag and loosened his tie. He thought of taking off his sweater and tying it round his waist; his mother would be upset if he tore it, but he left it on.

He pushed his right fist into his left palm. His hand hurt, the writing had made it worse. It was going to be sad, it was going to be awful.

He looked up at the sky and said, "I'm John Lionel. I'll never quit or beg for mercy. I'll give mercy but not ask for it myself."

He closed his eyes and tried to think of something pleasant. He thought of Cecil Travis, the shortstop for Washington. He saw himself going to Griffith Stadium to see him play. His father would take him.

Some birds flew out of an elm tree, and settled on a chimney. There was no sign of Dugan.

Conroy and Fatty showed up on their bikes. They liked to see the fights that took place after school. John did not say much to them, and they said things like, "You better keep your guard up" and "You better watch his right hand and his left, too" and "If he knocks you out, don't get up."

John waited ten minutes, then five more; and then he

thought, "I showed up on time and waited. I don't have to wait forever."

He said he was leaving.

"I showed up but he didn't. I'll see you," he said.

And Conroy and Fatty got on their bikes and rode away.

He started walking. He hadn't turned yellow but had shown up ready to fight, ready to die. Now he'd go home and turn on the radio.

He began to sing "Roll Out the Barrel."

When he came to the woods near the school, he thought he'd go home by way of the trail. He liked being in the woods; it was quiet there, and pleasant being near the creek.

After he walked in a way, he looked back through the trees, and he saw Dugan coming out of an alley, saw him look up and down the street, then slap the roof of a parked car. He was angry, he'd missed his chance.

John laughed.

"Well, so long, Dugan. I showed up on time, but you're just a tardy boy."

And he slipped deeper into the woods.

But then he thought, Dugan had showed up, and he was running like a coward in the war. He was sorry he'd looked back. If he hadn't, he could have gone home, but he'd seen him.

He thought about dying. There were death spots on the body. The Chinese knew where. If you got hit on one, your life was over.

Then he thought, 'Do I really need to get all smashed up and bloody?' He could put out his hand and say, 'I'm willing to forget it if you are.' But the thought died the moment it was born. It was asking for mercy. He might as well paint a yellow streak down his back as do a thing like that. He might as well put it in the newspaper that he'd lost his nerve, got sick with fear, and begged for his life. The English sent you a white feather in the mail if you turned coward, he'd read it in a book. And how could he ever look in the mirror after that?

Moving back toward the street, he felt both feverish and cold, his legs and arms felt weak. He was going to get killed.

Dugan had his back to him, looking toward the school.

"Hey, Dugan," John said.

Dugan turned.

"Where'd you go!"

"I was here. I waited," John said.

"You're a liar."

"No, you're the liar. I was here."

"You're a lying son of a bitch."

John's face felt hot.

"You better not call my mother a dog," he said. "You better take it back."

Dugan laughed.

"I better? Son of a bitch. Son of an ugly old bitch."

John swung and missed, and Dugan hit him in the ear and knocked him down. He got up shouting, "I'll get you!" and Dugan hit him in the eye, and he fell in the leaves by the woods' edge.

Dugan grabbed his school bag and backed on to the trail.

"Give it here," John said, getting to his feet.

"You want it? Come get it."

John followed him into the woods.

Dugan walked, looking back over his shoulder, then he turned and skipped backwards, and when John went for the bag, he started to run. And John ran after him.

They ran deeper into the woods. After ten minutes, they were in the midst of a forest. There was no sign of the city. They could have been in there with the Iroquois.

The crows were cawing.

Dugan stopped above a ravine. Some fifty yards below was a creek. John was breathing hard.

"Give it here," he said.

Dugan held it out. John lunged for it, and Dugan pulled it back.

"Don't you want it?"

"Leave it on the ground."

"No, I'm going to leave it some place else."

Dugan spun several times, then sent the school bag soaring toward the ravine. It landed on the lower slope, opening when it hit. Books and papers scattered; the school bag lay in the creek water.

Dugan laughed.

"Did you see that bomb explode?"

John thought of his report on 'Andrew Carnegie, Industrial Titan' in the creek along with his ruined books. He thought of Miss Babcock. She'd send him to see Mr. Liflett. His father would send him to military school.

He looked at Dugan, and he hated him more than he'd ever hated anyone.

"You're so low, Dugan. You're the lowest of the low."

Dugan laughed.

John shook his head.

"You're just so dumb. Is there anyone dumber than you? No, you win."

Dugan hit him in the mouth, knocking him into the ravine; John rolled down the slope spitting blood, and grabbed on to a tree to stop his fall.

Oh, God, he'd get him, he didn't care how, he'd get him good. He found a rock under the leaves, and came back up the slope.

Seeing this wild boy, his face streaked with dirt, blood, and snot, Dugan laughed; and John threw the rock with all his might and hit him above his right eye.

Dugan stood with his mouth open, raised a fist, and dropped to one knee. He strained to focus, then fell forward and rolled, ending up on his back.

John wiped his nose and the blood from his mouth.

"Don't you ever call my mother a dog," he said.

He was excited, felt giddy. He hugged his stomach, trying to calm down. Then he looked at the sky and said, "He started it, but I finished it."

He felt like crying, but he didn't.

The sky was growing darker.

Birds flew from the branches overhead, as the wind came up. Light rain began to fall.

John walked back to Dugan, nudged him with his foot, but he didn't move.

"Hey," he said. He looked at Dugan's face. The color was drained away. He looked peaceful, unlike himself.

"Hey, come on," John said.

He looked up at the sky.

"He asked for it. I didn't want to fight, I swear," he said. He looked at Dugan. "See what you did?" he said.

Two crows landed on the ground, walked bobbing their heads, then flew to a perch in the trees and began cawing.

He lay down in the leaves.

It was hard to breathe, he had a headache. His face and neck felt warm, his feet like ice. He had thoughts that scared him, then his mind shut down. For some time, he had not one thought. It was as though his brain had died. He could not move his arms or legs. Then after a while he thought of his school work in the creek, and he could move again.

He looked vaguely at Dugan, then went down into the ravine. He moved sideways down the steep slope to the creek.

Climbing up on a fallen tree that lay across the creek bed, he walked along it, then stepped out onto the rocks and picked some books out of the water. His notebook was still inside his book bag. The ink ran on the pages.

Farther up the slope, he found more books and papers. Then he walked back to the creek and sat down on a log, and wiped out the inside of his book bag with his shirttail.

He put his things away, then put a hand in the water and wiped the blood from his face. Some crows began to caw; he leaned forward and brought more water to his face. He thought of Dugan up on the trail, and tried not to think of him. Then he went back up the slope.

Dugan lay as before. John knelt down and shoved his school bag into his ribs.

"Come on," he said.

He could see by the slight rising and falling of his chest that he was breathing. He wondered if he was in a coma. He'd heard of people going into comas. His Aunt Alice had gone in and died three days after.

He waited for Dugan to open his eyes. Then it seemed that he had stopped breathing. He placed a hand on Dugan's chest to feel a heartbeat but felt nothing. He felt his own chest, and felt no heartbeat there as well; then he found his pulse. He tried to find Dugan's pulse, but he couldn't find it.

He crawled to the edge of the slope and threw up. He wiped his mouth with the back of his hand, then wiped his hand on his sweater.

Dugan lay with his mouth open. There was a huge bloody lump on his forehead.

"Open your eyes!" John said.

He knew he was dead. He'd never seen anyone dead before. Dugan was pale, he was death itself.

John tried to turn back the clock to when they were both alive but he couldn't. He tried to will Dugan to open his eyes. But they remained shut. Then he prayed to God to open them but Dugan's eyes stayed closed. There was nothing to do. If you're dead, you're dead. He wished he was dead himself. If he wasn't scared to die, he'd jump off the Taft Bridge.

Then he asked God to strike him dead so he'd die in a pain-less flash, and later on they'd find two dead boys in the woods and nobody would know he'd killed him. But he changed his mind as he said it. "No, I didn't mean it. It wasn't my fault, it was an accident. Please forget what I said."

He wondered if he'd burn in hell for what he'd done even

though he didn't mean to kill him. He began to cry, then stopped, shuddering, and rose to his feet.

He looked up at the sky.

"I'll never ever kill another thing. I swear. Not even a crow."

He'd go to the Eighth Precinct.

"We had a fight. He's dead. But it wasn't murder."

It began to rain. He raised his face to the rain, rubbed his fists into his eyes, and started off for the police.

Then he heard "Unnh Uhh" and he looked back and saw Dugan struggling up on his side.

"Hey," John said.

He wiped his eyes.

"Say, how are you?" he said.

Dugan would not acknowledge him. He took a careful breath, touched his wound, then rose slowly to his feet. Pushing hair out of his eyes, he stood with a dazed look, then began to walk in a slight weave and stagger before finding his balance.

They left the woods as they'd gone in, Dugan ahead and John trailing behind. They came out near the school.

John followed him home. It took nearly an hour to arrive at a neighborhood of old row houses. By then it had stopped raining.

Dugan walked up the steps to the porch landing.

A girl in the uniform of a Catholic girls school stood by a porch swing. It was Dugan's sister. John knew her name was Florence and that she was fifteen. When she saw her brother, she said, "What happened to your head, Frank?" He didn't answer, and she went inside the house.

"Well, I'll see you," John said from the street.

Dugan's sister came out to the porch and said, "He wants you to come in. He wants to talk to you. You better come."

"I'll come when I feel like it and not before."

"You better come now, Frank."

Dugan's father in his undershirt came to the door.

"What happened to you?" he said.

"Nothing."

"What happened to your head?"

"Nothing."

"I'll show you nothing. Get in here!"

"No!"

His father grabbed his ear and jerked him into the house, the door remained open.

"Take it easy, Dugan," John yelled. And then he heard Dugan cry out, "Lay off me." There was the sound of scraping furniture, and the father screamed, "I'll break your goddamn neck! I'll show you!"

Then a woman cried out, "For God's sake, Martin! You're going to kill the boy some day, and then you'll be sorry!"

"Like hell!"

John looked toward the open door.

"I'll see you, Dugan," he shouted.

It grew quiet in the house. And there was not a sound on the street but for a dog barking. Then the barking stopped.

John stood below the steps, looking at the door. He wondered if someone would come out. He thought of going up to the door and standing there. But then he thought, the father might come out and yell at him. Or the sister might appear and say, 'What do you want? Why are you hanging around?'

He was tired. He'd had enough. He turned for home.

And on the way, it occurred to him. Compared to Dugan he had an easy life.

His own father was different than Dugan's father; his own father might yell, might whip him for his own good. But his life was not like Dugan's life. If he'd slept in parked cars and not come home for days, his own father would call the Missing Persons Bureau; and when he became outrageous and lost his temper and insulted him, he'd regret it later and try to make it up to him.

He stopped walking and closed his eyes. And he saw his father and himself. They were in a restaurant, and his father said, 'Would you like a steak? Whatever you want. But don't fill up on bread.' And he had steak and bread, too, and ice cream for dessert, and they talked about life, and after coffee his father lit a cigar, and he looked at him, and he said, 'My boy, John.'

And then he saw Dugan, his head wrapped in bandage standing on the school steps, and he saw himself, and he went up to him, and he said, 'Hello, Frank, how are you feeling? It's good to see you again.'

On Experience

It was 1940, in the city of Washington, and John Lionel's English teacher, Winfrey Powell, the one teacher he loved, had the class read the essay "On Experience" by Ralph Waldo Emerson, and afterwards they talked about it in class. Hardly anyone understood a word of it, but John thought he understood some of it, or he understood it and then lost it as if it went up in smoke, and then he'd understand some or thought he did, and then it all turned into smoke again. After the discussion, she said that she knew the students were too young to understand it, they were only eleven after all, and even some very intelligent adults couldn't quite get it straight so it was no disgrace to find the essay hard going. But the reason she had them read it is that she wanted each of them to write his or her own essay "On Experience," just as Ralph Waldo Emerson had done, and not to worry if they were getting it right but just to write from the heart and not be concerned about what anyone might think.

After her talk, a boy named Alex Hunt said, "You mean you want us to write about an experience we had?"

"Well, that can be part of it, Alex, but what I really want is that you write about the nature of experience itself, what it is.

Do you think you can do that? That's what Ralph Waldo Emerson did."

"I didn't understand one word. I can't do nothing like that," he said.

"Don't worry, be brave. Do it your own way. Do your best."

John loved Winfrey Powell, the way she looked, the way she talked, the way she was smart and kind; and after class he started thinking about what she'd said, and he'd write about it and wouldn't be scared. And if he made a fool of himself, he'd done it before, and he got over it. Miss Powell liked to say, "Be yourself and take a chance," and she was right.

He had been going through a difficult time, and now he could put it down on paper.

Two months later, the essays were turned in. Only John Lionel volunteered to read his essay to the class.

Last year I nearly died of pneumonia. I had it in both lungs, and it was fifty-fifty if I'd pull through, and then I broke a night sweat, and I didn't die after all. And I'm happy I didn't. For it's great to be alive and have experience. That's what living's all about. And when I have experience, I like to think about it afterwards.

What is experience? It's what happens to you when you're alive. There may be experience after you're dead but who can say for sure?

After I recovered from pneumonia, we went down to Florida for a vacation.

Now I'm going to talk some about drinking whiskey. I'd never seen anyone drunk before except one time I saw two guys weaving down the street in Washington. They were laughing and shouting and then they stopped and pounded each other, and then started weaving down the street again. My father said they were 'falling down drunk' as the alcohol had gone to their brains. My dad always has a drink before dinner to relax after a hard day. But he doesn't weave around or fall down in the gutter.

My mother drinks cocktails now and then. I had never seen her even tipsy, what women get, until this vacation in Florida when she had a drink with rum in it at the hotel bar. It was called a zombie. Not long after she drank it, we stood waiting for the elevator to our floor, and my father said, "For God's sake, Mary, you look cross-eyed." My mother, she looked like her face was frozen. They called it a zombie because it nearly turned you to stone after you drank it. That was last year when I was ten, and I'm eleven now.

You can never know what experience will be like. It can be fun, it can be scary, it can be so confusing that you can hardly stand it, it can make you crazy, if you let it.

We were staying at the Dempsey-Vanderbilt Hotel over the Christmas holidays. My sister hadn't come, as she was visiting a friend in Vermont.

The day after my mother drank the zombie, my father got too much sun lying on the beach. I had told him to watch out, as he had very fair skin, but he didn't listen. He'd turned red like he was on fire, and so he had to lie in the room covered with salve the hotel doctor put on him. He was in a lot of pain. We offered to hang around and keep him company, but he didn't want it.

"There's nothing you can do for me," he said. And then he said, "John, take care of your mother."

Mother and I went in the ocean. I was a good swimmer but she couldn't swim at all. She waded out to where the water was up to her waist, but then suddenly she drifted out farther, it was an undertow that took her out, and I swam out to her just as she sank and the water covered her. I dived under and pushed her up and started yelling, "Please help me, my mother can't swim." There were two men nearby treading water, but they looked at me like I wasn't there. It was like they were blind and deaf too because I kept yelling, and they couldn't see or hear me either. I went down under and kept pushing my mother up, and every time we came up I'd yell, and finally some lifeguards rowed out and saved her.

I'll never forget the two guys treading water. I didn't understand it and never will.

You know what my mother said? She said, "I thought I was going to drown and ruin the vacation." If it wasn't so sad, I'd have laughed.

In the spring, this man who worked for my father took a shine to me. His name was Joe Woodman. His nickname was Woody, and he was from North Carolina. It was funny he had a name like Woodman because he was a carpenter and cabinetmaker, an expert with wood and glue. He could make anything out of wood. He made me a periscope out of wood like they had on submarines with two glass mirrors, one at each end, and you could duck down in a trench, say, and put the top opening above the trench and look through the bottom part and see everything on the ground above the trench, so that you couldn't get shot in the war because you were under cover. I'd come to the shop in my father's place and hang around with him. He'd been a marine and fought in China; he had stories about the Yangtse River and fighting the Chinese or maybe the Japs. I never got it straight.

On some nights when my parents couldn't be home, my father had Woody pick me up at school and take me out to dinner. We got hamburgers at the Little Tavern, where they're small and tasty and you can eat five of them easy. One day we crossed over the river to Virginia, and Woody bought a shirt and a pair of pants for himself, and he bought me a shirt like his. He said I was a nice boy, and if he ever he got married he hoped to have a son like me.

But Woody drank. My father said he couldn't stop with one drink but had to keep going. It was like he was in love with whiskey, my father said. He'd stop drinking for a while and then he'd start up again, and he'd get drunk on the job. My father told him that he couldn't overlook it anymore as he'd given him lots of chances, but the next time it was strike three. And then Woody got drunk on the job again, and my father called him into his office, and he fired him.

I was standing by the door.

Woody started screaming, "You're firing me? Like hell you are! Why, I'll knock your teeth down your throat."

I was never so surprised.

"I want you to leave right now," my father said. "Come back tomorrow to pick up your pay."

"Go to hell. You think you're better than me? I'd like to kill you as soon as look at you. I just might kill you."

My father stood up, and he told him he'd better go and sober up. I was surprised how calm my father was. He might have been scared like me, but he didn't show it.

Woody left his office. As he walked by me, he said, "Your father's a no-good son of a bitch."

I'd really liked him once, but I hated him then.

I got a hammer and destroyed the periscope he'd made and tore up the shirt and threw it in the trash, but then a month later I'd think of how nice he'd been and half forget what he'd done. But then I'd remember, and I'd feel angry and scared all over again. And it went back and forth like that.

Just when you thought you knew what you felt, you'd feel something else. But that's experience. It won't give you any rest.

It wasn't but three months later that my father was in Chicago, and he got in a taxicab, and who was the driver? None other than Woody. What are the odds on that, getting in a cab with someone who'd wanted to kill you? About a million to one, I'd say. Woody was sober and friendly. "Well, how are you, Mr. Lionel? And how is your family? Hey, be sure to give my best to John," he said. That was quite a surprise. Or more like a shock, if you ask me.

But not long after I had some real shocks, the experience that takes your breath away. There was this friend of my mother, a woman named Constance Mandrell. She was beautiful, one of the nicest people I'd ever known, and she jumped from the seventh floor of her apartment building and fell to her death. She left a note that she was dying from a disease, and she didn't want to suffer.

And then about a month after that, my father's cousin Arlene's husband, Harold, was shot and killed by a holdup man in Baltimore. I hardly knew him, but it was real upsetting. My parents went to the funeral.

Someone said that Death came in threes. I started waiting for the next one.

I went away to summer camp up in Maine. There was a counselor there, Bobby Walkenecht, one of the tennis instructors. He took a shine to me. He was real nice and very smart, always encouraging you, the kind of guy you'd want for your big brother. He taught me tennis every morning, but one day he came late to the courts and I took instruction from Charley Fox, and when I passed Bobby's tent later, he called to me and asked me to step inside, and so I went in the tent and he dropped the flaps down so nobody could see, and then he grabbed me and shook me, and called me a little bastard for taking a lesson from Charley Fox instead of him, and he slapped me in the face, and slugged me so hard on the arm I saw stars, and then he threw me out the other side of the tent, and I landed in the pine needles. I was in tears, and I got up and started running until some counselor stopped me. "Hey, what's wrong with you?" he said, and I said that I didn't know but later I said what happened, and the next thing Bobby was packing up, and he left in a taxi that took him to Portland. I heard that later he got put in a mental hospital in Boston. It looked like Bobby had everything to make him happy, but he didn't.

Experience can be happy, and it can be sad. You never know what until it happens.

When I got back from camp, I went to New York with my parents and sister to see the World's Fair. I'd never been to New

York before, and I was looking forward to it. We went up on the train. My grandmother gave me two dollars for the trip. She said before we left that I was her favorite. She was always saying that, and I loved her for it.

When my parents and sister went to the dining car, I said I wasn't hungry but would join them later, if that was all right. "Well, don't be long," my father said. I waited fifteen minutes, then started on the way to the dining car. In one of the cars I saw a man with this flat board on his lap. He seemed to be playing a game. Another man was watching. As I was about to pass them, the man who was watching said, "I can't always follow it. Do you think you can?"

I looked at the board. On it were three shells and a pea, and the man put one shell over the pea and then he kept switching the pea from one shell to the other, and then he said, "Do you know which shell the pea's under?" I pointed to the middle shell, and the pea was under it, and then I tried again and got it right the second time. Then the man who was watching said, "Say, you're good. You got good eyes. I tried twice and couldn't get it. I lost two dollars. I don't have quick eyes like you. It's too bad you don't have no money to bet." And I said, "Well, I have two dollars."

"If you bet a dollar, I'd bet a dollar on your pick," he said.

"All right, I'll sure try," I said.

I knew I had good eyes and could follow that pea, and the man shifted the pea from shell to shell, and when he stopped I was sure the pea was under the shell on the left, but it was under the middle one, and I lost my dollar and the other man's too. I apologized. "I'm sorry I lost you your dollar," I said.

"Aw, don't worry about it. You can win it back for me. You got real good eyes," he said. And we put our dollars down, and the man started shifting the shells like before, and I followed the pea, and when he stopped I was sure I knew which shell it was under but I was wrong again, and I'd lost both our dollars. I felt sick about it. I told the man if I had two more dollars, I'd hand them over to make up for what I'd lost for him.

"Don't worry about it, that's just how it goes," he said. "There's no hard feelings on my part."

We shook hands, and I said goodbye, explaining I had to meet my parents and sister in the dining car.

I got to the dining car, just as the train pulled into Philadelphia, and they were all eating lunch.

"You don't look well. What's wrong, dear," my mother said.

"Nothing. I don't know."

"You don't know what?" my father said.

"I don't know."

"What don't you know? Answer me."

"Well, I lost this man his money. If you could loan me two dollars, I'd pay him back."

"What are you talking about?" he said.

"I bet on this game where you guessed which shell the pea was under, and I guessed wrong and this man had bet a dollar on my pick, and I lost his money twice."

"Did you bet on it, too?" my father said.

"I had good eyes, but he was too fast for me."

"How much did you lose?"

"What Grandmother gave me. Two dollars."

My sister laughed.

"I can't believe what you did. I'll never believe it."

I told her to be quiet, as she was getting on my nerves.

"Come on. We're going to find those men!" my father said.

And I took him back to the car where the men had been, but they weren't there. My father talked to other passengers in the car, and one man said, "Those guys got off the train in Philadelphia. They're bunko artists."

My father explained what happened.

"You got taken by two confidence men. Con men. Do you understand? You didn't lose that man's money. He was partners with the guy doing the shell game. They lured you into the game and took your money. You fell for it because you have no experience."

We arrived in Penn Station in New York and went right to the Waldorf-Astoria. It was a swell hotel, one of the best in the city. The lobby was like the main floor of a palace.

At the World's Fair, we saw what the future would be like, and we went to few pavilions and saw exhibits from other countries, but my sister got tired and had a headache so we left early.

It was about five o'clock when we got back to the hotel. Mom and Dad were going out for a while, but they'd be back in time for dinner. They told me and Carol not to go wandering off and to stay in the room until they returned. Before they left, my mother talked to me in private. "I don't like you not having money in your pocket. Here's five dollars, John. You can give it back to me later. Well, not all of it, keep two dollars for yourself, but I wouldn't mention it to your father," she said. The two dollars was to make up for what I lost to the con men.

When they left, I told my sister that I was going out.

"What do you mean? They said to stay here, John. They don't want you wandering the streets."

"I'll see you later," I said.

"You better stay. Or I'll tell them what you did."

"I don't care. I want to see New York."

"But you'll see it tonight when we all go out to dinner."

"I want to see it now," I said.

"Then I'll come with you."

"No, I want to see it by myself," I said, and I left the room.

I went down to the lobby and walked out into the street and began walking around New York. I was in the greatest city in the world, and I didn't want to sit in a hotel room. I looked up at the buildings. I'd never seen them so tall, you could hardly see the sky unless you looked straight up, and the people walked much faster than they did in Washington. There was so much noise and traffic that it got me all worked up, and I wished I could live in New York and have a lot of experience, and I kept walking and the sun had dropped down and dipped behind the tall buildings so it got darker faster in New York than if you were living out on the Indian plains, where you could see the sun all the way to the horizon, and I walked toward the sun and then I was in a different part of the city. I walked one way for a while, then another, and then I saw a street sign that said I was on Tenth Avenue. It was getting late, so I hailed a cab so I'd get back to the hotel in time for dinner.

"Where to?" the driver said.

I told him to take me to the Astoria.

When we got to the hotel it didn't look anything like the hotel we were staying at. It looked like an old dump.

"Say, this isn't the Waldorf-Astoria," I said.

"You said the Astoria."

"That's right."

"What's wrong with you. You don't call the Waldorf-Astoria the Astoria. You call it the Waldorf. This is the Astoria. So you want to go to the Waldorf. Am I right?"

"That's what I said."

"Nobody calls it the Astoria. Get that straight."

It was a lousy ride. The driver kept shaking his head and mumbling under his breath. I knew he didn't like having me as a passenger. When we got to the Waldorf, he said, "How many times you been in a cab?"

"A few," I said.

"You pay what's on the meter, and then you give the driver a tip. You understand that?"

"We don't have meters in Washington."

I'd been watching the meter the whole time, and I didn't know about a tip. I thought maybe it was another con game, and he was pulling a fast one.

So I just gave him what was on the meter, and I got out of the cab, and he got so mad he turned his head and screamed that I should go back to the hick town I came from, and he pulled off screeching his tires.

"Was I supposed to give him a tip?" I said to the doorman who'd opened the cab door for me.

"Well, that's usually the case," he said. "But you didn't know so don't worry about it."

But I felt bad. Because right after he pulled out, I remembered my dad tipping cab drivers; I'd known it the whole time but it had slipped my mind. I was so upset I couldn't think. If I could do it over, I'd give him a dollar tip which was more than was on the meter for the whole ride. One thing about me, I'm not cheap.

They were waiting for me at the hotel.

"I told you to stay in the room. Where have you been?" my father said.

"I wanted to see New York, and I walked around and got lost. And then this cab driver took me to the wrong hotel. How would I know you can't call this hotel the Astoria? The driver said I had to call it the Waldorf."

Carol laughed.

"The Waldorf's the most famous hotel in the world, and you called it the Astoria?" she said.

"I didn't know exactly what they called it. But now I know, and I won't make that mistake again. I love it in New York. You can make mistakes all you want, and you're learning things all the time."

We went out to dinner. It was nice. My dad was in a good mood. "Well, you're 'Wrong Way' Corrigan," he said. He was smiling.

You remember 'Wrong Way' Corrigan, don't you? He thought he was flying west but he was really flying east. He meant to fly to California but his compass was broke so he flew across the Atlantic instead and landed in Ireland. That was two years ago.

He got a ticker tape parade down Broadway. I saw it in the movie newsreels. My father said sometimes they give you a parade and sometimes the bum's rush, and you never know. It's all fate.

It was some restaurant. I had a shrimp cocktail and roast beef. New York was great. I never had so much fun in my life

But then it all changed. A day after we got back, my grandmother died in her sleep. It was like a wall fell on me or like I got the breath knocked out it was such a blow. We were friends, we'd talked about life. I remember her saying, "John, I still feel like a girl of sixteen. But then I look in the mirror and see an old lady."

And then out of the blue she just died. I wasn't ready for it. Can you ever be for news like that?

Sometimes you have a good time and others a bad time. Life surprises you. It cheers you up, then knocks you down. It's always changing. Sometimes it can seem like bad news will last forever, but a day later or the next hour it's just a bad dream and you're feeling on top of the world.

Experience is the unexpected, like you think it's going one way and it goes another. It's like a shell game, full of confusion, and takes you by surprise. You can learn from experience, but you can't learn it all. You can never think you completely understand it. You can get in water that's up to your knees, and before you know it, it's over your head, and the world is spinning around and time passes, and then one day you look in the mirror and you're old, if you haven't died of disease or got killed in the war.

People disappear and you never see them again, and it's sad. Or they disappoint you, and then they disappear. Or somebody shows up and makes you happy, and then disappears, and you're sad all over again. Or you disappear yourself. You can die young or drown or fall down an elevator shaft. Or get killed in a car wreck. Or get shot by the bank robber 'Pretty Boy' Floyd because you handed the money over too slow. It doesn't matter, because you're going to die anyway. It could be today or in twenty years or maybe you can live to be a hundred. You can never understand it as long as you live.

But one thing's certain. If you get born, you're going to die.

It's sad when you think about it, so try not to think about it too much, just be happy in the day. It's good to tell jokes and laugh. Is there anything better than a good laugh? I have joke books for when I'm feeling sad, and they really help. Experience is what you're feeling, and right now, if you want to know, I'm feeling great, and I hope you feel the same.

There was silence. On some faces there was perplexity. On others anger or fear or something of both.

Winfrey Powell asked them to consider what John had said.

When the class ended, Oscar Ritz came up to him and said, "That was stupid. How can you show your face?" And Loreli King said, "What you said was so disgusting it makes me want to vomit." And Alex Hunt said, "You made everybody feel sick. I hope you're satisfied." And Maxwell Flaverman, never a friend, said, "You should throw your essay in the fire and jump in after it."

And not one person liked it or could say one good thing about it.

John wondered if they were jealous because he'd read his and they were scared to read theirs. We all get jealous and scared sometimes, it's part of experience, he thought. But it hurt him. He liked being popular, and he felt alone in the world.

He was the last to leave.

Winfrey Powell was waiting at the door. She regarded him closely, and she began to nod, and then she put out her hand and smiled at him.

"John," she said, still nodding.

Neither of them said a word more, and it was enough for him.

Storm

Leaving the sunny, open field, John went into the shadowy woods. He walked for miles along a dirt trail partly covered with brown, dead leaves. The trees were tall and thick with foliage, and the sunlight was spotted and flickering on the trail. It ran along the side of a slope which rose several hundred feet to a rounded crest with high, wild grass growing along its rim. The trees on the slope were thinner than the trees near the trail, but on the crest amidst the grass, the trees were larger still, with thick trunks and heavy branches. Another hundred feet down the slope from the trail, there was a quiet, meandering creek with large rocks in its bed. The water was very clear. John threw a rock at the creek, and then he looked up at the sky and threw another rock as high as he could. Above the trees, the sky was blue with small, puffy white clouds moving eastward. Farther west the clouds were black and billowing.

He stopped and leaned against a tree and carefully examined the terrain—the creek, the rocks and underbrush, the fallen trunks. He wore a yellow polo shirt and short blue pants and a pair of torn sneakers. He was a thin, gangling boy, with his brown hair short from a recent summer haircut. His arms were slightly suntanned, with the whiter skin showing just below the short sleeves of his shirt. A folded newspaper was tucked in his pants. There was a sense of sadness about him, though on his wide, full mouth, there was a hint of a smile. He was nine years old.

He walked down the slope through piles of dry leaves to the creek and then stood on the muddy bank watching the water gurgling and splashing over the rocks. He sat down on a log by the creek. Now and then he could hear the caw caw of a black crow or a squirrel running through the leaves. It was pleasant to hear the sounds coming out of the silence. He wished he could live in the woods and be happy always. It would be a lot better than living at home, he thought, digging a toe of his sneaker into the soft mud. As he sat on the log, he withdrew from his pants the *Washington Times Herald* and opened the paper to the front page. There was a picture of Mussolini and a story about the Maginot Line. It was something he had studied earlier at school, in current events. The Germans would never get through the Maginot Line, John thought, and the British Navy was the best in the world. According to his father, there wouldn't be a war at all. He tried to read a news story about the Danzig Corridor, but he couldn't concentrate, and he folded the paper up and shoved it back in his pants. He didn't feel well enough to read the newspaper, so he must feel pretty bad, he thought, as much as he enjoyed reading them. He covered his face with his hands. He just couldn't get along with anyone, and now he was in a lot of trouble. That morning his father said they were sending him away to military school in Virginia. His father had already spoken to the commandant of a school about fifty miles from Washington. It was rotten, John thought, to be sent away like that. He had tried to get along with everyone, and now they were punishing him. He wished he could put up a tent in a little clearing above the slope and never go home. It would be wonderful to make friends with all the birds and small animals, and sleep inside a little tent in a blanket roll, and read by the light of a coal oil lantern. Perhaps, quite late at night, when he was normally

asleep, he'd come out of the tent and just sit around the campfire. It was pleasant to think about all the canned food he'd have.
He enjoyed using a can opener, and liked eating out of cans. He
particularly liked canned peaches and pears, and pinto beans
and jellied madrilene and chicken gumbo soup. As far as he was
concerned, things were better cold than hot. He could eat off of
tin plates or right out of the can. It would be perfect. He'd call it
John's Camp. He could see the lean-to close to the tent, and
under the lean-to would be the logs and kindling wrapped in a
tarpaulin. Inside the tent would be his seaman's chest packed
with his tools and a flashlight and his socks and raincoat, and a
sweater and an extra pair of pants. He already had a Boy Scout
knife with a can opener, bottle opener, long blade, short blade,
and corkscrew, and he'd keep his matches dry in a Prince Albert
Tobacco can. It would be swell to get up in the morning with the
birds singing, he thought, and go down to the creek and wash
in the cold water. It was a dirty trick if they sent him away, but it
was all right with him. He would miss his best friends, Ewing
and Hal, and his colored maid, Bessie; but he would be glad to
leave his mother and father and his older sister, Carol. They
didn't care about him anyway. His father said there was no man-
aging him anymore, and that the time had come to cure his
rudeness and bad temper. Military school wouldn't tolerate his
being rude, unmannerly, and disrespectful. They would knock
some sense into him. It wasn't true, John thought, he was none
of those things. They said he was rude to their friends, but he
didn't know what they were talking about. He wasn't rude, but
he wasn't friendly either. He was just polite. If you were polite,
you couldn't be rude, John thought. He wished he could live in
the woods for the rest of his life where no one would criticize
him. His mother didn't like the expression on his face. Usually,
he didn't know what his expression was until she told him. She
was often displeased by his tone of voice, and the way he ate his
soup. Eating soup was an art that he hadn't mastered, she said.
She didn't want to pick on him, but if she didn't tell him, then

who would? It was hard to breathe. She was always grabbing him and saying, "John, I want your shoulders parallel to the ground." He hated that. She felt that he had an irritating habit of dipping his right shoulder lower than his left. It was because he threw right-handed, he told her a hundred times. When she was through yanking him into a level position, he would let his right shoulder sink again. It didn't feel natural level, he told her, and she felt truly that he was being spiteful and contrary, in order to hurt her. He didn't care. It didn't feel natural. He liked her a lot, but he wished she'd leave him alone. His father was fine, John thought, but he got angry a lot and beat him with a strap, for his own good. They were always doing him a lot of good, and now they were sending him away. Military school, his father said, would teach him to be neat and orderly in his person and in the care of his room. The parading and drilling would help improve his posture. If he didn't measure up, he would get demerits, and that meant punishment. 'Oh, I don't want to go away,' John thought. He loved Washington. If they had to send somebody away, let them send his sister. She was so perfect, he thought, that it would be real luck for the school that got her. He smiled at the thought of her leaving and kicked some leaves. If she ever showed up in the woods with her girlfriends and made fun of him, he thought, he'd kick her right in the back side, and then he'd shove her in the creek. She got all the credit, he thought, and he never got any. That was the worst thing, how they never gave him credit. His mother always wanted to change him. He wished his father would give him credit sometimes. He did a lot of good things, and he deserved it. Ewing's mother once told him that he had a 'very good personality,' and his athletic coach, Ken Moore, called him 'Flash' Lionel after he had done something particularly well. He enjoyed getting compliments, as he never got any at home. It was fun to get a compliment and be modest afterwards, he thought. Sometimes he'd tell his father about a thing he had done well, so he'd get some credit, but his father would say, "Let other people praise you. Don't praise yourself," or "You're showing off again, John," or, with a look of slight irritation, would ignore him altogether. His father could hurt his feelings more than anyone, as he admired him so much. Why couldn't he say "nice going" for a change? John thought, or just say something pleasant out of the blue? Bessie always gave him credit, even when he didn't deserve any. She would say, "Honey, you a sweethearted boy. You always all right with me." He thought of her and smiled. It was swell how she always liked him just the way he was. Just because she was colored didn't mean that she was dumb.

The sunlight came down through the trees, rays of light that lay softly interspersed with shade on the ground sloping down to the creek. Suddenly, he heard a hoot owl. It startled him. Bessie said that if you heard an owl hoot seven times in a row, then somebody you knew would die before the day was gone. He tried to smile. Maybe the owl was telling him that he was going to die, John thought, as he was somebody he knew. Bessie said that her mother and father had each died, years apart, on a day she'd heard the owl. He should have counted the hoots, he thought, not that he believed in it. He turned and looked up the slope through the trees to the crest of the hill. It was so beautiful, he thought, that it was hard to imagine dying. He got up from the log and lay down in a bed of leaves and looked up at the sky. Some dark clouds were beginning to appear, and he could barely hear some distant thunder.

John got to his feet and brushed off the leaves, and then climbed the slope all the way to the top, to the small clearing of high grass that overlooked the creek. It was the place where he'd set up his camp some day, on the slope's edge under a large tree in the wild grass. He stood looking down the hill he had just climbed to the creek below. On the other side of the creek, the slope rose more sharply, and the trees were thinner and closer together. The tops of the thin trees swayed gently in a fresh breeze. There was the sound of a crow which died away into the silence. It was very still. The sky was getting darker. Listening carefully, he could gradually hear the sound of flowing water in the creek and the wind in the trees. He sat down and placed his elbows on his knees and his chin in his hands. A squirrel moved quickly through the grass a few feet away, stopped suddenly, and looked at him with startled eyes, then bounded twice and scurried down the hill. John could hear her moving excitedly through the leaves. He closed his eyes and smiled. They were really funny, he thought, the way they looked at you. He put his feet under some dead leaves, then lay back on the grass. The shadows of tree branches and leaves covered his face and body. He looked up at the sky. Parts of it were still blue. He could see three large birds very high, moving with a slow, steady flapping of the wings. John thought they were geese on the way south from Canada. He thought all big birds were geese from there. A quick, fluttery breeze moved through the tall grass and swirled some leaves down the slope. There was a wild, rustling sound in the trees. You don't have to love your parents, John thought, feeling a little scared. Nobody can make you. That's what Ewing said, and it was the truth. He listened for a hoot owl, but there was no sound. With the quickening wind, it had gotten cooler. The breeze got under his yellow polo shirt and caused it to billow slightly. He felt cool all over, and goose bumps appeared on his arms.

He watched the sky grow darker. There were a lot of birds flying very fast. They knew a storm was coming, he thought. A flash of lightning streaked across the sky, and there was a distant rumble of thunder. He wished he had his tent all set up and tied down. He imagined crawling in while it rained and reading by the light of his coal oil lamp. A bird suddenly alighted on the branch above his head, then flew away. He thought of his mother and father, and he felt immediately warm with irritation. Maybe they were right about him, he thought. There were pain and dizziness behind his eyes. He was sick and tired of everything.

He stood up and watched the sky. There were no more blue

places. It was all black and dark gray. A bolt of lightning darted across the sky and was followed a few seconds later by thunder that came in four separate registers, becoming a low, dying rumble at the end. Feeling suddenly angry and vaguely disappointed, he picked up a rock and threw it at a tree. "Damn you, Daddy!" he said. Oh, damn them, he thought. He picked up another rock and threw it down the hill. That was for his mother and sister. Suddenly, there was a bolt of lightning and a loud crash of thunder. The wind was very strong, bending the grass flat against the ground. He was frightened. It began to rain, and John moved closer to the trunk of the tree, pressing himself against the side nearest the slope as protection against the wind-blown rain. It was raining fairly hard, but the trunk and great leafy branches gave him partial cover.

Ten minutes later it began to pour a torrent of wild rain. Rivulets of water moved down the slope, emptying into a small ravine which formed a channel to the creek. The rushing water in the creek moved higher up on its banks. It was no longer clear but muddy, and sticks and branches moved rapidly against the rocks and boulders in the creek bed. The thin trees on the slope were wildly swaying. A loud crash of thunder caused John to hug the tree and close his eyes. It was raining so hard that it sounded like a waterfall. There was another bolt of lightning, very close, followed immediately by a very loud report of thunder. He heard something crash down in the woods, and was afraid to look, opening his eyes only enough to see the water going through the ridges in the bark his face was pressed against. There was a prolonged crack of lightning and thunder. It was as though the ground was exploding beneath him. The thunder was right on top of him now. The vibrations were tremendous. He knew he was going to die. The lightning was very close, and God was going to kill him. He knew that God was sending the lightning for him. He suddenly opened his eyes and let go of the tree and yelled, "I don't care!" There was a very loud crash of thunder, and he hugged the tree again, sinking to his knees, and pressed his face against the trunk. He knew he was going to die. God was going to kill him right there in Rock Creek Park in Washington.

The thunder and lightning continued for another half an hour. John lay curled at the foot of the tree with his hands cupped over his ears, and his eyes closed. The rain beat down on him. He waited to die, but gradually the thunder diminished and the lightning moved farther away.

He sat up, feeling dazed. The smell of the earth and grass and the trees all washed with rain made him nearly faint with happiness. The thunder became continuously fainter, and the rain, coming nearly straight down as the wind had lessened, hit the trees with a loud, pattering sound. The woods were soaking. John looked up at the leaves and branches, glistening and shining, and at the water moving down the gleaming wet bark of the trunk forming a puddle in the hollow at the foot of the tree. He prodded his sneaker into the muddy ground at the edge of the water. He was completely soaked. His shirt was smeared with mud, and there were, on his arms and legs and face, bits of leaves and bark and streaks of dirt. His newspaper, soggy and unrecognizable, was still stuffed down in his pants. John looked up through the trees. Faint flashes lighted up the sky. The rain was letting up and turning fine and misty.

Gradually, the rain stopped altogether. A light mist hovered over the creek. The wind had died down, and it felt hot and steamy in the woods. John watched the creek through little patches of mist. The water was swift but not as rushing as before, and the rocks that had been covered began to appear again as the water slowly receded. There was a lovely, fresh smell in the woods, and water was dripping off the leaves. John opened his mouth, catching a few drops. He looked at the thin trees on the far side, so quiet and still now, and thought how much he loved the woods. It was always changing and never the same, and always lovely in different ways.

It was twilight. The dark clouds were breaking up and moving eastward, and white puffy clouds tinged with orange slowly drifted from the west. He supposed he'd better be getting home. He gave a final look at the creek, then turned and began to walk through the high grass toward a trail that did not wind high above the creek as the one he had come in on, but went more directly home. For a while, he thought he could hear the flowing creek still swollen with rain. As he walked, an occasional gust of wind sprinkled him with water from the leaves. He passed through a small glade and then, half sliding over wet leaves, went down into a shadowy ravine, moved along the floor of a hollow, and climbing a hill, came into the light again. He could see part of the city looking blue and orange in the twilight. It wouldn't be long before he'd be coming out, he thought. He was looking forward to seeing everyone, and he hoped they'd all be glad to see him. Maybe they wouldn't send him away if he promised to improve. Looking at some dim, red buildings in the distance, he wished he could always feel as he felt then in the woods. He and his dad were pals, he thought, and his mother was swell, and his sister wasn't half bad when you got to know her. He picked up a stick and removed some caked mud from his shoes. Then he pulled out the soggy newspaper from his pants and buried it under some leaves.

John came out into a small clearing in the dusk. Looking back for a final glance at the darkened woods, he then entered a street of old houses and broke into a trot for home.

Hal in Colorado

Durango

I'm a writer of tales, a poet, and a scholar on the life of Edgar Allan Poe, a genius of his age. You might have seen my work under the authorship of C.W. Halliday. C.W. stands for Carlisle Worth. I'm called Hal by my friends.

Mary sometimes called me Prince Hal. She was a romantic person.

In a restaurant in Baltimore, I asked her to marry me. It was not the first time.

"I love you," I said.

"Oh, you poor boy. I feel sorry for you," she said.

Charming and detached, Mary had deflected me again. She did not want marriage, she'd been married before, she did not wish to repeat the experience; she liked her freedom, she did not want a life that would make impossible demands; she did not want to have to ask for permission or feel restraints or have to compromise or accommodate in any way; and most important of all she did not want to be bored.

I understood her so well. I had an advanced degree in the sort of life she required. And I knew it to be a recipe for disaster.

I wanted to live a normal life.

"We could be happy," I said.

"Hal, you're like all men. You want some woman to take care of you."

"I want us to take care of each other."

"That's what men say. They say all the right things before marriage. But afterwards, watch out. I could tell you plenty of stories, my own and those of my friends. Look, I'm happy now. I'm free as a bird. Let's enjoy what we have. We have a nice friendship. What could be better than that?"

But I saw it differently. I saw marriage as the road to wisdom, an antidote to selfishness, a moral education. One learned to take life as it came, living with quiet ease in each other's company. I saw married life as an unsung expression of courage and endurance. As a reality of the most difficult kind.

I no longer wished to live in the spheres; I wanted a simple life, without pretension. And to live in the light of the everyday.

Is there really any choice but to accept life as it really is? I'd been for a short time a convert to the mundane.

Mary loathed ordinary life, while I was a recent pilgrim to its charms.

She had no monopoly on disillusionment. I'd been married three times, I'd gone through hell, but I was hopeful, while she lacked all confidence.

I had first met Mary four years before in Baltimore, at the Edgar Allan Poe museum on Amity Street. The museum was in the house where Poe had lived with his aunt, Maria Klemm, whom he called Muddie, and her daughter, Virginia, who became his wife when she was but thirteen. The time he lived there was, I feel, the happiest period of Poe's life, which lasted until Virginia died eleven years later.

While standing in one of the rooms, I heard a woman say, "Are you here out of mild curiosity, or is it more than that?"

I turned and saw an attractive woman in her early forties.

"Well, I'm writing a book on an aspect of his life," I said.

"Are you from Baltimore?"

"I'm from Richmond but I've lived in Baltimore, too."

"Poe lived in Richmond as well as Baltimore."

"And other places," I said.

Poe died in Baltimore, but he was born in Richmond and lived much of his life in Virginia and the South. In Richmond, he had been for a time the editor of the *Southern Literary Messenger*. He lived in many places, among them Charlottesville where he attended Mr. Jefferson's university but was forced to leave over gambling debts. Shortly thereafter, he enlisted in the army in Boston and later served in an artillery regiment at Fort Moultrie in South Carolina, as a non-commissioned officer; he left the army with the rank of sergeant major. Not too long after, he went to West Point for a time but left under strained circumstances. He ranked high in the study of classics at the time of his dismissal.

I introduced myself.

"I'm Mary Everwell," she said.

"Did you know that Mary was Poe's favorite name?"

"No, but thank you for telling me," she said.

I did not tell her that Poe was once in love with a girl named Mary Devereux. The relationship did not work out and nearly gave him a nervous breakdown.

Mary said that she adored Poe, everything he wrote and stood for. He was for her a hero of the first rank. She wanted to know about the book I was writing, and invited me to have a drink.

I told her a few things about the book, the sort of things that she might want to hear, but I did not tell her my real reasons for writing it.

Why did Poe's life appeal to me? Apart from his literary genius, I was fascinated by his relationships with women and how his romantic views and fevered imagination made it hard for him to live in the real world. He often fell in love and, on occasion, with two women at the same time.

I, too, had the taint of the romantic imagination, and like him could not live easily in the real world.

My very life was so similar to Poe's that it was uncanny.

Like him, my real parents were both actors who died when I was young, and I, too, was brought up by a stepfather who was harsh and critical and by a stepmother who adored me.

But as much as I admired Poe and felt a kinship with him, I began to view his life as a cautionary tale which provided insights into my own life. Admiring his genius, I feared his example.

My real parents, Nora and Alistair Halliday, were very romantic people. They were always playing parts, even when they weren't on the stage; I got into the habit myself. I had a natural flair for the dramatic.

Imagining ourselves in certain situations, we'd take on roles and play out the scene. It was a lovely time, even when we were on relief in Chicago or Memphis or God knows where. For we lived in our imagination; when it was raining, we imagined the sun. I loved the life, but the problems came later, when as a grown man I was still acting, with no idea of who I was except for the part I was playing at the time.

I had no desire to go on the stage. I liked to do my acting in real life, and I drifted into poetry and teaching and the writing of tales; that's all I was good for. For I had no sense of reality or how to live in a mature and balanced way.

When my parents died in a car accident on the way to a job in a summer playhouse on the Finger Lakes, my happy life of make believe ended, and I became an orphan at the age of twelve.

A cousin arranged for my adoption by the Worth family down in Richmond. I did not get along with my stepfather, Calvin Worth, though I loved my stepmother, Aristide, beyond all measure, for she enjoyed my imaginative nature as much as my stepfather despised it. He thought I was good for nothing, and he was mainly right, from his point of view.

One of the greatest sorrows I have ever known was the death of Aristide Worth. My stepfather survived her and continued to persecute me, deny me money, and make my life a living hell.

When I was seventeen, I ran away and joined the army. I ended up in the artillery, and I served for four years. After that I went to Charlottesville and studied at the University of Virginia, and I was thrown out in my sophomore year for gambling and riotous behavior. But in my dissolute life, I'd found my true calling in the world of literature.

In my study of Poe's life, I discovered to my amazement that he too had been in the artillery, and like me he had been thrown out of the University of Virginia, and had lost his beloved stepmother. We were so alike in much of our lives and our very temperaments that I felt that in his map of sorrow lay the secret key to my own happiness. I simply had to avoid the ideas and way of life that had led to his ruination.

Poe had been in love a number of times after the death of his young wife, Virginia, but all of his efforts to marry again and find the domestic contentment he had once known came to nothing. Near the end of his life, engaged to be married to one woman while being in love with another, he was in a state of complete nervous disorder, the natural fate of a romantic who had lost his grip on reality.

He could not find a comfortable place in the real world. He imagined his way into other worlds but could not live in the real one. That was my problem as well.

When I met Mary, I had been divorced briefly from my third wife, and I was feeling sad over the breakup. Another failure, and I wondered if I'd ever get it right.

"Hal, nobody ever gets it right. Not you, not me. Nobody on the planet. Anybody who says he likes being married is a fool or a liar. What starts out as love or sexual feeling ends up in boredom and weariness and a sickness worse than death. I look around at all my married friends and I don't know one that doesn't wish they were free and independent like me. I'm the envy of my old crowd. And for good reason."

I had a totally different view. It wasn't that marriage had failed but that I had failed at marriage. I had picked the wrong woman each time because I did not understand myself well enough to know the sort of woman I required. When I told her that, she laughed. "Oh, you poor man," she said.

After I went back to Richmond, I thought about her at odd times. I began to come more frequently to Baltimore, in part for my study of Poe but mainly to see Mary.

She attracted men as honey attracts flies. Romantic sorts like myself, with a touch of another world. I won her affections, I imagine, because I gave off more than any other that quality of Poe that she so admired.

She lived in the Federal Hill section of Baltimore, in a large apartment that overlooked the harbor. It was her haven and refuge from the real world. I was allowed to enter there because I was a Poe scholar, and therefore I had for her a touch of romance.

It was ironic. All I wanted was to be an ordinary man.

Then an odd thing happened, though odd is perhaps not quite the word, but it was strange and rare. I bought a lottery ticket and won a million dollars.

It made up for my disappointment in being disinherited by my stepfather, who had left his fortune to the Daughters of the Confederacy.

I gave up my teaching position at a college outside of Richmond and moved to Baltimore to be near Mary. She was all I really cared about apart from my literary career.

I purchased a house in the historic district of the city. Although we became lovers, it was only later that I moved in with her; but I kept my house, as our life together was uncertain.

"Marry me. We could be happy," I said.

"We're happy now, Hal. How many times must I tell you? Things change when people get married. We have a nice situation. We won't grow weary of one another."

I knew something about marriage. Married three times, I'd hoped for heaven but found only hell.

I wanted peace, as Poe did, but all I got was grief and disappointment.

My first two marriages were disasters. Dazzled by beauty, I married women who were completely wrong for me. But when I married for the third time, I thought I was more aware of what I required in a wife.

Faith said she would love to be married to an author, and she seemed to care for me and wished to provide a home. Not a feminist, she found fulfillment in domestic life. I couldn't have been happier.

After we married I discovered that she had no deep respect for literature. She found my work a fraudulent, pretentious affair, and she found me the greatest fraud of all. "What are you doing, Hal. What do you think you're doing? Writing, is it? You think anybody gives a damn about what you write or think? Why don't you get a real job. Then you'd know what life is all about."

Once when I was resting on my couch after a morning at my desk, she started in on me. "Oh, the author at work. I've been cleaning the basement, and you just lie there like the parasite you are."

I knew I wasn't perfect. But who is? I made an effort to change. I began to clear the table after dinner. I went to the store for cereal or milk. I even bought a book on practical repairs. I liked being helpful and unselfish. I tried to explain that to her, that I got a moral benefit from what I did and pleasure as well. But she said that all my talk was nothing more than a cheap writer's trick.

I nearly became a handyman in my efforts to please her, but it was all for nothing.

What was my greatest fault? Like Poe, I tended to exalt and idealize women. And like him, I had certain writerly tendencies that made me unfit for the real world.

Alexander Renfoldmain, a late nineteenth century scholar of some repute, summed it up nicely:

Writers of a romantic cast lack the emotional balance to be good husbands. They expect too much, and become too quickly disillusioned. Creatures of moonlight, the light of day destroys their dreams and hopes. Irresponsible and selfish, concerned only with their work, as though their talent made them special and privileged, they feel exempt from ordinary human concerns. Unable to endure the everyday, they are masters of desertion. Endless passion, freedom from every human responsibility, are what they yearn for. They create havoc in every human relationship, always wanting what they can't have; and then feeling sorry for themselves because life is disappointing.

Marriage is hard enough, so how could it last with people like that?

Renfoldmain's portrait of the vain romantic applied to me. We sleepwalk through the real world. The one place we are completely alive is in the private kingdom of our imagination. But the avoidance of real life leaves us bereft, cut off from humanity.

It was during my failed marriages that I began to have the insights that would change my life, and my study of Poe's sad history merely confirmed the lessons I'd learned.

I came to value the ordinary, the mundane. That was where salvation lay. "Ordinary" became the most beautiful word in the English language for me. I wanted to be married and live an ordinary life.

I felt I'd changed so much. Looking back at my old selves, I felt I was looking at strangers. Why did I change? Life broke me and I accepted my lot, then embraced it as a friend.

"Why do you want to get married?" she said. "What do you expect of me? Do you expect me to make dinner every night, to be the little woman, that old time slave wife who took care of her man? Well, don't look at me. I have my own special needs. I mean, suppose I'd like to go to Italy for three weeks? Would you take me? Or would your concerns always come first?"

"Marriage is give and take."

"You mean take from me and give to you."

If I could take her to Europe, of course I'd take her. But I'd have to consider everything, the whole context. I don't like hypothetical questions.

"We ought to get married. It could be wonderful, Mary."

"How do you know? It could be awful."

"I'm crazy about you. And I have no illusions about marriage. I know it's hard work."

"I don't want hard work. I've had enough hard work. I'm tired of all that."

"That's what makes a marriage. The effort. It gives life purpose. And do you want to be alone for the rest of your life?"

"We're not alone. We have a good thing, Hal. Let's keep it that way."

When you're not married, you live in a kind of dreamland of fantasy and illusion; but in marriage, you live with the real.

"Marriage can stretch you," I told her.

"No," she said. "It twists you. If it stretches you at all, it stretches you out of shape, and it brings you to unhappiness, not enlightenment."

That's how it went, back and forth, day after day. I was like a salesman making his pitch, and she wouldn't buy any of it. I didn't want to live a superficial life. I did not want just to skim the surface of things. I wanted reality. That's what I told her.

"You're like a character in a Russian novel," she said. "Those people were their own worst enemies, always making themselves unhappy. We don't have to be like that. We're Americans, not Russians. And what did they finally come up with, anyway? That life is suffering. What a waste of time. Of course, life can be difficult, but most of their suffering they brought on themselves because they cultivated it. Impossible people!"

She misunderstood me. I wanted to live simply as an ordinary man.

I loved her; and I hoped that we could work things out, so that we could marry and live in the light of reality.

"You get married and you're asking for trouble," she said.

"But I love you. I want to be with you."

"Of course, you do. Because we aren't with each other all the time. Do you know what a burden that is? Time and routine grow heavy. My first husband was just as ardent as you about wanting to get married. I had a dog, and before we married he used to walk the dog. I'd say, 'Honey, you don't have to walk my dog,' and he said, 'I feel he's our dog, and I like to walk him because he's part of you. I get a family feeling when I walk him.' But after we married, not a week had passed when he said, 'Why should I walk him? He's your dog.' Democracy and sharing are all well and good before the wedding, but once the knot is tied, watch out. Hal, I love what we have. I don't want it ruined by boredom and routine. Then we'd be like all the other unhappy couples in the world."

She had a horrible fear of the boredom of ordinary life.

"It's an enemy of imagination. It kills everything creative. Boredom is crushing. And being with the same person day in and day out, I don't even want to think about it."

I did not fear boredom. And why? Because I worked at it. If you embraced the mundane, boredom simply vanished, for your mind was closely engaged and regarded ordinary life with new respect, so that it became interesting and significant. That's what I tried to tell Mary.

"Marry me and I'll transform your boredom. I'll teach you how to do it," I said.

"Oh, give me a break."

Mary liked to send me away. She'd get nervous and restless, she'd want to be by herself.

"I need room, Hal. I need my space."

Why did she do this? Apart from needing to be alone, she liked to miss me. To her, missing someone was like oxygen for her soul. The phrase "far away" had a strange appeal for her.

On those occasions, I'd go away and do my research on Poe. I'd go to Richmond or Fort Moultrie in Charleston or to Philadelphia or Boston and look into different phases of his life, and wherever I was I'd call her at night before bedtime or early in the morning. "I miss you, Hal, I really do," she'd say. "I wish you were here. Why did you leave me?"

There was for her a kind of poignance when I left her, in the possibility of never seeing me again. That heightened for her the experience of my essence. She loved essence more than reality. She once explained it to me.

"I'd rather see Monet's paintings of Giverny than Giverny itself. I'd rather see his vision than the source of its inspiration."

She loved me more in thought than in real time. But I wanted us to marry and have a real life together in the here and now.

Was it a sickness that she couldn't endure the humdrum of everyday life? Is there a term for that condition in the lexicon of psychiatry? When she was confronted with things exactly as they were, she went into a kind of panic; she felt that she was disappearing. Ordinary life diminished her.

When she became restless and remote, I knew it wouldn't be long before she'd say, "Well, Hal, this old girl is tired. I need my solitude. I need to rest and contemplate. I wish I had your energy. Maybe you need a younger woman. I'm sorry. But I think you should leave for a while."

Once during a separation, I began walking to Washington forty miles away. I thought I'd spend an hour there and then walk back to Baltimore. Poe had done this in 1829. He had walked to Washington to see John Eaton, the Secretary of War, about his appointment to West Point. Poe walked because he had no money for transportation, having used what his stepfather had sent him to pay off debts. At the War Department, Secretary Eaton informed him that a personal interview was not required in his case. And then Poe walked back to Baltimore.

I started out for Washington but after I'd walked only a mile, I pulled a muscle in my leg, and I hailed a cab to take me to a hotel where I remained several days before returning to Mary.

In the late spring, feeling beset by ordinary life, when her mind went dull in the everyday, she sent me away again, and for the first time I did not visit a place that I associated with Poe. I went out West.

But perhaps, unconsciously it was related to Poe after all, for he had died in 1849, the year of the Gold Rush.

In New Mexico, on the outskirts of an Indian reservation, away from their dreary shacks and poverty, I saw mesas and buttes. I phoned her that night and told her what I'd seen.

"You're out West, Hal? How wonderful. I've never been to the real West, only the coast. Were you on the plains? Were you wearing something Western? No, don't tell me. Let me imagine. I can just see it. Take me out there, Hal. Will you promise? I feel such passion for you now."

It turned out that she was serious about wanting to see the West, and when I came back, we began to make plans for the trip.

"Hal, do you realize that this is our first trip together?"

I loved that she was happy at the thought of being with me instead of wanting to send me away.

In the summer, we flew to Albuquerque and rented a car and drove north. We stopped in Santa Fe for a day and went to the Spanish Market and then continued north toward Colorado, stopping at the Ghost Ranch and Echo Cavern on the way. At Echo Cavern we took a long walk over uneven terrain in incredible heat and yelled into the hollowed out side of a hill. We got a quick reply, and then we struggled back over the same ground to our car.

By the time we arrived at Mesa Verde to see the Anasazi site, we felt a bit weary from the altitude. It was a hard time for Mary; she had periods of lightheadedness where she felt she was about to faint; and she found the mountain driving so unnerving that she could not look out the car window. She crouched down in the front seat and covered her eyes, as I drove the curving mountain roads with the sheer drops beyond the guardrail.

"I can't look," she said.

"It's a beautiful view. I hear it helps if you try to see two dimensionally. You lose the sense of depth that way."

"Don't say anything. Please!" she said, hands over her eyes.

Farther up the mountain, I pulled over into the parking lot of the tourist center for the long-deserted Anasazi pueblos. We got out of the car. She appeared unsteady, pale and slightly ill.

"I'll stay in the bookshop. You can explore by yourself," she said.

I followed the path down into the ravine. It was a long, steep climb down to the site. There were a lot of tourists, mainly family groups with young children. I looked around, climbed down a ladder to look at a large room, and then climbed up again; and then, feeling tired from stress and altitude, began the ascent up to the tourist center. By the time I reached the top, I was exhausted and wet with perspiration. Feeling overcome by the ordinary, I managed to transform my fatigue and discomfort into an interesting world of its own. When one fully accepts reality, however unpleasant, it becomes interesting in itself. Of course, it takes practice. And one can't be impatient.

She was sitting outside the bookstore on a bench writing post cards.

"How are you?" I said.

"I don't know. How were the ruins?"

"Wonderful. It's all wonderful, if you see it in the right way."

When we drove down the mountain, the experience for her was worse than coming up, as we drove on the edge of the precipice, and there was no room for error or to avoid an oncoming car without moving toward what she considered certain death. I drove slowly down the mountain road and encouraged Mary to look at the view, but she wouldn't open her eyes.

After Mesa Verde, Mary seemed to grow bored and restless. We'd never been together for so long, at close quarters for three days, and much of the time in the car; she began to complain of headaches, and I sensed that she was suffering her old feelings of entrapment.

When we came to Durango, she perked up.

"Oh, Hal, it looks like a real Western town, right out of the movies."

We were on Main Street right outside the Strater Hotel, a sort of Victorian-type building of an earlier time. It was a typical Western hotel of the better sort. Mary was right. We could have been on a movie set. Down the street was a similar hotel, the General Palmer. I'd never seen Mary so happy in the here and now. We had lunch in Durango and walked around. It was an interesting place, part Western and part hippie; but it was the Western aspect that excited her.

"We must come back here, promise me," she said, and I agreed that we'd return later in the trip, after we'd seen more of Colorado.

We pushed on to Pagosa Springs. All the way there, Mary talked about Durango, and I tried to get her to calm down and live in the moment, to find pleasure in the present.

"Look about you," I said. "We're not in Durango anymore. Forget Durango and move on."

"Hal, I simply enjoyed it there, and I was talking about it. What's wrong with that?"

"Nothing, if you don't try to hold on to it. You should try to live in the present without all that romantic meandering. You'd feel better."

"That's enough, I don't want to hear that stuff."

"If we got married and lived a normal life, you'd be happy."

"No. You'd tell me what to think. You'd start bossing me around, just like you're doing now."

I stopped talking. I concentrated on the road.

In Pagosa Springs, we drank the waters. The waters are thought by some to be an elixir of life. They didn't do anything for me. It was just water and nothing more, but Mary hoped it would have magical properties, like the Indians said, but she was disappointed. Like all romantics, she'd had inflated expectations.

I thought of Poe. What a wonderful man and writer but how deluded and misguided about how to live in the real world.

After Pagosa Springs, I told Mary that we ought to go to Leadville. It was to the northeast, a long way from there. We could reach Salida by nightfall and then go on to Leadville the following day. I'd read about Leadville in some Western travel literature. Among other things, it had the highest altitude of any incorporated city in the country, 10,000 feet above sea level.

"And it has a romantic history," I said.

I caught myself using the word 'romantic,' finding it interesting that I'd used a word that I'd long wished to abolish from my vocabulary; perhaps, I wanted to make the trip more appealing to Mary. I told her how there once had been a gold rush in the area around Leadville and when the gold gave out and the prospectors went away, a man named Tabor discovered that in the black sand that had clogged the sluice boxes of the prospectors there was carbonate of lead which was full of silver, and Tabor later became the rich owner of silver mines, and the money went to his head. He divorced his wife of many years and married a young beauty named Baby Doe and moved to Denver. The story excited me, in spite of myself, for the sheer drama of it. And I told Mary that we could get a kind of Rocky Mountain high up in that altitude. I found myself growing animated, but I kept a tight hold on my mind, watching it like a hawk.

Mary said that she'd go to Leadville but that her heart was in Durango.

It was a long way to Salida. We stopped at some restaurant on the road and we ordered roast chicken sandwiches to eat in the car.

"Hal, this isn't roast chicken," she said, after were underway. "It's pressed chicken. I'm really upset."

"Don't get so worked up. Make the best of it. Just eat the sandwich and move on to the next thing in your life."

I was getting on her nerves. It was being together, day after day. She couldn't take it. After we'd driven a while, Mary complained of stomach pains and a touch of nausea.

"It's the sandwich, Hal. I knew it."

"Don't get upset. It'll just make it worse."

"Stop the car. I want to throw up."

I pulled over, and she got sick outside the car. I hoped that would be the last of it. But not long after, Mary asked me to stop again, and it was the same.

It rained for about an hour, and then it stopped, and we saw two rainbows in the eastern sky.

"Look at that," I said.

When the rainbows vanished, and the skies cleared, I didn't linger on the rainbows or write a poem in my mind. I moved on.

In late afternoon, I began to feel sick myself. OK, I was sick, I thought. I concentrated on my breathing, and I accepted it. I refused to feel aversion.

I pulled over. I told Mary I had to get out of the car.

"Don't worry. It's nothing," I said.

"I need to get out myself," she said, and she got out, and we were both sick on the side of the road.

"We'll find this amusing in retrospect," I said, as we drove along. "Sure, it's not funny now, but later on, we'll laugh at it."

She slumped forward, her head in her hands.

"God, I hate this," she said.

It rained again in the late afternoon and then cleared up with another rainbow arch that was even more brilliant than the others we saw.

Dusk came on as we passed between mountains, and then night fell. It was dark except for the light of stars and the moon, and we drove in silence, Mary asleep in the front seat. I found it all mysterious, the darkness and the silence, and then a twinkling of lights from a few houses set well back from the road, and then passing into darkness again.

It was cold and I had to turn on the heater. I enjoyed being cold but it was also pleasant being warm.

We came into Salida and found a place to stay for the night. In the morning, being careful, we had dry toast and tea for breakfast. Mary did not look well. She was sickly pale.

"I feel awful," she said.

I did not feel well myself, but I was living in the moment. I tried to comfort her.

"You'll be fine. I know you feel bad, but try not to feel aversion. It'll only make it worse."

I should have kept quiet, but I had the weakness of a natural teacher. By repeating the message, I hoped it would sink in somehow.

We left Salida after breakfast and began to climb north toward Leadville. We moved along the Arkansas River, with a mountain peak to our left of over 14,000 feet.

In the midst of great beauty, Mary was unhappy.

"I think we're near the Continental Divide," I said.

But she did not reply.

"The Continental Divide, that's beautiful, isn't it? The very sound of it," I said, and then I checked my impulse to be poetic, and forced myself to view the passing scene without holding on to it, letting it go where it would.

Our sickness grew worse. We had to stop several more times on the way to find relief in restrooms.

We continued to climb, the air got thinner. When we arrived in Leadville, ten thousand feet above the sea, we were lightheaded from vertigo and exhaustion.

I thought of Poe and his illnesses. He suffered bouts of nervous depression and terrible exhaustion and numerous physical complaints, which he tried to relieve with laudanum (or opium, as it is called today) and alcohol that played havoc with his nervous system. I only wish he could have employed certain mental exercises in their place.

It began to rain. Before going to sleep in our motel, we went out for dry toast and tea. We were dehydrated. We sipped water and let ice cubes melt in our mouths.

"Well, we're in Leadville, Mary. It could be interesting tomorrow. Remember the story I told you?"

"I don't care, Hal. I don't give a damn about that."

In the morning, we had only tea and a little water before leaving for the Mining Museum. I thought we should see it, having come all that way, but Mary resisted.

"Why? Who cares?"

"Remember Tabor and the silver mines and how after he got rich he let go of his wife and married Baby Doe?"

"So what. I don't give a damn. I'm sick. I need a hospital."

"No, you're fine. We're both fine, Mary. "

In the museum, we spent most of our time in the restrooms. I have no recollection of the exhibits; I was using what energy I had to steady my mind. I concentrated on my breathing.

I thought of Poe, always in the suburbs of my mind, and wondered how he would have fared in my place? Could he could have survived this trip with his faculties intact? And then I thought, why waste time thinking? Live in the present. Do what has to be done.

I helped Mary to the car. She was so weak, drained, and unhappy.

"We'll get some Coca-Cola. It's good for this sort of thing. Don't worry," I said.

In an old-fashioned drug store on the main street of Leadville, we sat at the counter and drank Coca-Cola.

Mary was in tears.

"Oh, God, what's happening to me?"

"You're under the weather, that's all. We're living real life. It's not always pleasant. Just drink your Coke, Mary. Look around you. Don't reject anything. Let it come, let it go."

"Be quiet, will you. I want to get out of here. I want to go home. We're not far from Denver. Let's catch a flight out."

I didn't want the trip to end this way.

"Mary, try to be calm. We'll go back to Durango. Remember how much you liked it? I'll take you there, just as I promised."

"Oh, I don't care. Just get me out of here."

And we left Leadville and went back the way we came, down through the mountains. As we dropped down in altitude, the sickness went away; we could eat again, and we recovered our strength.

Two days later, we arrived in Durango and checked into the Strater Hotel. We felt good, and Mary was smiling.

In the morning, we walked around the town. We passed stores that sold Western regalia. At a store called Farrell's, Mary saw cowboy hats in the window.

"Oh, this is perfect. You're getting a hat, Hal."

"Why do I need that?" I said.

"Please, do it for me."

Inside the store, I bought a hat. I didn't want to, but it was her idea, and I wanted her to be happy. And it wasn't a bad hat. It looked pretty good on me. So I bought it. Why not? It pleased her, and they put it in a hatbox. A slogan on the box said, 'Whether you ride a fast horse or not.'

It was amusing, I have to admit, I enjoyed the time in the store, but I understood what was happening, and I wasn't worried about losing my sense of balance. I was rooted in time and place, not off in the spheres.

Mary insisted that I get a pair of cowboy boots as well, and I bought some Luchese boots. After I bought her a hat and boots, we went to another store, and Mary bought me a Western shirt and one of those bolitos to wear around my neck. I got a buck-skin vest as well, and I bought Mary some things for herself. She couldn't wait to get back to the hotel to try everything on.

We got dressed in our Western gear and walked through the streets of Durango. It was amusing, even absurd. I was laughing to myself the whole time.

I was concerned for Mary. She seemed a bit delirious, a bit too dazed with joy. But I was glad she was happy; the Leadville trip had been hard on her, and she could use a break from all that.

I felt that it would pay off, that reality would take hold in the end.

We walked down the street. Mary was a picture of delight. I was enjoying it all myself, though the boots hurt my feet; they were at a high angle to the ground. This caused me to walk differently, and my hips ached from the change in my stride, but all that mostly disappeared in less than a day.

And Mary commenced to see me in a new way.

"I loved you before, Hal, but I'm mad for you now."

She started calling me the Durango Kid. It was really funny, in a way. I was glad she was happy, but I hoped she'd come back to her senses, when she got the romance out of her system.

We went back to the store where I'd got my vest and bolito, and I bought a wide Western belt with a tooled design and a silver tip. It was Mary's idea.

"Get rid of your old belt. That's your old life," she said.

"You know, the boots are really getting comfortable," I said.

"I love you, Kid," she said,

She bought me a holster to go along with my belt.

"What will I do with this? I don't own a gun."

"You can get a gun later."

Actually, I liked the holster. It was a handsome piece of leatherwork.

OK, I was the Durango Kid. Let her have some fun. It was harmless. And who was I really, anyway? I had no idea. I wasn't the Kid, of course. I was just an ordinary guy. But it was as good a handle as any other.

On our third night in Durango, we went into the bar of the Strater Hotel, and I put a booted foot on the rail, and ordered whiskey with water. Mary watched me from a nearby table as though she were seeing a movie.

"It was thrilling to see that," she said, when I sat down with her. "Well, how are you, Kid?" I had to smile.

The boots brought out all the passion in her. She wished I could wear my boots in bed. She told me that, laughing, but she was serious.

When I took off my boots while sitting on the bed, she said, "Put them on again, and then take them off. I love watching you."

It wasn't life. It was theater. It was like the old days with my mother and father. I was an actor in a drama of which Mary was the author.

It was just amusing, that's all. The boots made her happy, my hat made her happy, though when I thought about it, I wasn't sure that 'happy' was the word. I didn't want to think about it too much. We were going in a direction I couldn't control, in a blissful state that I hadn't foreseen. It had, as they say, a life of its own.

The West was her weakness, she said. It was pure and honest. She loved John Wayne almost as much as Poe. She loved the poetry of the lone rider in the plains.

I hoped that what she was going through was simply a way station on the road to real life. That one day we'd be living in that underrated paradise, the world of ordinary life, without pretence or illusion.

The days went by, each day like the other. It was pleasant for a while, but it didn't last.

The time came when she wearied of our little drama. The Durango Kid had had too long a run.

It was in the late afternoon. We'd been there for a week. I was standing outside the Strater Hotel in my cowboy gear. When she came out in her eastern clothes, I felt that something was up. She asked me to come up to the room; she had something to say to me.

We sat around for what seemed like a long time. She kept looking at her hands, then looked up at me without speaking. Finally, she spoke.

"Hal, I'm tired of this masquerade. It was fun for a while, but it isn't fun anymore."

"It isn't?" I said.

"No. And it will never be fun for me again," she said.

I knew it was getting old for her. Everything gets old and stale if you try to hang on to it. I knew that so well. You could try to outrun reality; you could stay ahead of it for a time, but it caught up with you in the end.

I hardly knew what to say.

"Hal, something happened to me. While you were out this morning, I was sitting in this chair I'm sitting in now, and everything started to feel strange, the way the air feels right before a storm, something had been building up inside me for some time. And then it happened, it was as though I'd been struck by lightning. And I fell to the floor and lay quite senseless. I started to shake. Then I began to cry and moan. I was out of my mind. I thought I was dying. I lay there terrified, filled with horror. Then the terror faded and I felt the deepest sorrow I've ever known, and then that, too, slowly passed away, and a feeling of great peace came over me. I'm still in the grip of it now. I feel reborn, Hal. I'm a new person. I had a shattering insight that nearly killed me, but it brought me to a new and wonderful place. I know now what you mean about a normal life. It's what I want. I want to live that sort of life with you. Nothing special, just being ordinary together. Can you believe it? I want us to get married."

I was stunned. I struggled to find the words.

"Well, what's the big rush?" I said.

"Big rush? What do you mean, big rush?"

I couldn't speak.

"What's wrong, Hal?"

"I don't know."

"Of course, you know."

"Well, it's a big move."

"A big move? What are you saying? It's what you've always wanted."

"I know, but something's stopping me."

And then she broke down and cried. I'd never seen her like that before. She was a different person. I didn't know what to say. And then I said, "Mary, it's nothing personal."

"Nothing personal? That's all it is. You don't love me."

"It's not that," I said.

I said maybe we could just leave things as they were and go on in our old way.

"I don't want the old way. I'm sick of running from myself. I've had a conversion. I want reality. Just as you've always said. So are you going to marry me or not?"

"I thought you loved not being married," I said.

"Are you deaf, Hal? Didn't you hear what I said? So what's your answer?"

I tried to reply in a way that would make sense to her, that would comfort her, but I couldn't find the words.

"It doesn't feel right, Mary," I said, finally.

And she began to sob again, and then she got her suitcase out of the closet and started packing; there was nothing more to say, and I left the room and went outside to the streets of Durango.

I stood there wearing my boots and hat and buckskin vest and a bolito around my neck and a pair of chaps that I'd bought that morning. I was losing her for good. But it was all right.

When she came out of the hotel with her suitcase, I put my arms around her.

"I'll miss you, but it's the right thing," I said.

"Why is it the right thing?"

"I don't know, but I'm sure it is."

She began to cry again; it made me sad, and yet I was relieved. It was for the best.

"Hal, what happened to us?" she said.

I had no idea.

A taxi picked her up for a ride to the airport at Cortez, and I stood there as the cab pulled off. And it was as though I was in a dream and I watched the cab disappear into the dusk and oblivion leaving only the light of my imagination, and it unsettled me, and I tried to resist. 'Don't do this,' I said to myself, but it was no use.

Maybe it was the altitude and getting sick and all that business in Leadville, or the sheer exhaustion from trying to become a better person, but I heard this voice inside me, and it said, "Be yourself, Hal, don't fight it anymore." And I stopped thinking and I watched the night come on, and I put my hand in my holster, and I thought, where's my iron? And then I went to the bar in the Strater Hotel, and the piano was playing and I ordered straight whiskey and I drank it down, and then I ordered drinks for the house, and this pretty lady came up to me and said, "Say, aren't you the Durango Kid?" and I just smiled and touched the brim of my hat, and she kept talking and I kept saying, "Yes, ma'am," and then I couldn't hear her anymore, and I wondered where I'd put my horse.

Walter Desmond in Virginia

The Lost Cause

Walter Desmond had been a banker. Banking for him had held but one drawback, the problem of foreclosure when the debt could not be paid. He'd done all within his power to delay that awful time, given extensions, refinanced the loan, anything to save the man his property; and if all efforts failed, he'd state his own distress at how things had turned out and tell the man, whether colored or white, farmer or merchant, that he hoped he'd soon be on his feet again. He had hated to foreclose; and no one had ever left untouched by Walter's kindness and goodwill. "Don't you worry. You'll be all right, just have some faith now," he'd say to each one, meaning every word. But when the economy went bad and stores closed on the main street of town and people left to find work elsewhere, he sold his interest in the bank and retired to his house on the hill. Not long after that, his wife died.

"I just don't *believe* you, Walter," Rose Lee had said. "I can't believe what comes out of your mouth. You are outrageous in your views."

"Well, honey, I don't know what's so hard to believe. My views are nothing but moderate," he'd replied.

They were from Virginia, of the same background, but had long differed in their views of the South. Even when first married and very much in love, they were aware of their differences; but it hardly mattered then. Other things were more central to their happiness. But as time went by and the world changed, as she grew more politically aware and joined liberal groups and subscribed to left-wing publications that offended his sense of proportion, he felt their growing estrangement. The things about him that had once pleased her, his affability and charm, his way of deflecting unpleasantness with a smile and a kind word, had only come to irritate her, for she saw them as an unconscious deception to maintain the status quo and they represented for her a style and way of life she had long abandoned. Their main disagreement was about the Southern past. Rose Lee'd felt it was best forgotten or remembered only with regret. "See it as a morality play, Walter, or cautionary tale. But don't dwell on it. Don't *sentimentalize* like your poor old mother, that mad heartless woman you defend day and night just because she is your mother. You are a nice man, Walter, but the Southern past is an albatross around your neck."

"Honey, we must look back with sympathy," he'd said.

"You have too *much* sympathy. You've got to break with all that—and change. One must often be ruthless to be moral."

But it was not in him to be ruthless. He feared rapid change. The change that she desired would destroy the social order and create chaos in its place. It would destroy continuity, and life would lose its meaning. Change had to come slowly; a man had to understand where he'd come from. It did no good to hate the past or to condemn those who had gone before. He preferred to look back thoughtfully and give due respect and honor. He did not wish to stand in the way of progress but rather to move forward with care and deliberation.

The word she'd loved more than any other was 'new.' She spoke of entering a new day, being part of a new world, newness was everything; her greatest desire was to give up the "sad old backwater ways" of their parents and the "dead hand of past generations." She favored every kind of liberation, intellectual, emotional, political, and sexual. She hated tyranny of heart, mind, and soul. In that regard, she likened herself to Thomas Jefferson, though she disapproved of him for owning slaves. As for sexual matters, she desired that "the act of love be always fresh and new." Walter had tried to make allowances for her thinking, he knew she was nervous and high-strung, but he'd been upset by her insistent modernity.

"Why, you just don't have to make love in the bedroom, Walter. You can make love all over the house—there's no rule against it. You can make love on the floor, on the dining room table, for God's sake."

"Well, honey, why would we want to do that?"

It was her burden, she often thought, to have been born in the South and to have married a man like him.

At the beginning he was her project and at the end her hopeless task. "If I die first, I'm going to haunt you, Walter," she'd said with a kind of rueful affection. And after her death in the spring of 1962, she did haunt him through his memories of their life together.

It was his mother's birthday, on a cool fall afternoon.

He started out for the cemetery. It was not too far from his house, a white frame building with a gabled roof and a long porch. The house rested on a hill. Looking west from the porch, one could see farms and fields and farther off the Blue Ridge Mountains. The ground in front sloped down a good distance to a narrow winding road. Behind the house was an open field of wild grass, then an expanse of woods. A path through the woods led to the cemetery, which could also be reached by car, taking the road below a quarter mile to the north and then turning right and driving on past a church, a general store, and an old wood structure, one wing of which had collapsed. Just past that abandoned building in a clear meadow on the edge of the woods and surrounded by a white board fence lay the cemetery.

On this day he walked through the woods.

The sky was overcast. It had rained the previous night, and the ground was soft underfoot.

He climbed over the white board fence, then stood under a tree by the graves and looked at the headstone with the name "Desmond" and at the footstones of the dead. They were all there, his mother and father and younger brother and his wife, Rose Lee. His mother and father had been dead for three years, dying a month apart. His brother, Weber, had died in a car wreck in the Shenandoah Valley ten years before the death of his parents. Walter's own footstone with his name and the year of his birth was beside his wife's. She'd been dead a little more than a year.

Rose Lee had died of a stroke while at the home of her sister, Cora, in Newport News. Walter had been in Richmond at the time.

At the funeral, Cora had said, "Rose Lee was the most unselfish person I ever knew. She was good and caring and brave—and so misunderstood."

A year before she died, he had spoken of separation. He had wished to live a more serene life. He was not blaming her, but he was worn out by contention; he needed breathing space. He thought it would be better for both of them, for he could never please her.

She'd been hurt and surprised. She could not imagine him leaving. He was such a loyal person, but then she knew it was a matter of divided loyalties, and she felt bitter.

"I know we can thank your old mother for this. Well, she'd be happy now."

"Rose Lee, I'm sorry for any wrong I might have done you."

She pushed her fists into her eyes.

"Oh, be quiet. You are tormenting me. I can hardly breathe! Oh, yes, she's happy now lying in her grave. Well, go ahead and leave me, Walter, if that's what you want!"

But he did not leave her, he discovered he did not know how to walk away for good; he could not give up the habit of their married life with its familiar rhythms, strains, and opposition. He loved her in his sorrowful way, and he could not imagine life without her.

He could hear his father saying, "What does Rose Lee mean? Wasn't I good to the colored? They are people just like us and God made them and I helped them out when I could. George Mobley worked for me for thirty years. And he was more than my employee. We were friends. George had a very refined sensibility. You know I often felt he was spiritually superior to me. He'd been deepened by suffering and travail, and he had a wisdom, Walter, that I could never possess. We weren't on an equal footing to be sure. Each of us understood his place, but that helped us feel natural with each other. I knew he was a colored man, but I still got to know him as a person. Of course we've kept the colored down. We are not without blame. But at the same time I have loved some of those people like they were my own family. I took care of George. I took care of his medical bills, and I paid for his funeral and later helped out his wife, Rayola. Don't you know I cared about them? I would have liked to uplift the whole colored race if that was possible. Why, my own father taught this Negro Obadiah Parker how to read. Obadiah was old. His parents had been slaves in Westmoreland County. He'd come up to the house and sit in the parlor, and my father taught him the alphabet, and then how to read. Don't you know he'd have laid down his life for my daddy? Sure, we did wrong, there are things that need fixing. But we could straighten it out, if given half a chance. It's all got out of hand. The white extremists and Negro agitators are wrecking the country, and I don't know where it will end. It's hard to make friends with the colored now, not the old ones but the young ones coming up. They hardly look at you when they pass in the street, or they have a scowl on their faces. It's all so sad, this passing of good feeling. You know why Obadiah loved my father? He knew he was *appreciated*.

My father valued him. You don't find that in the North. I know Rose Lee means well, and if she wants to judge me, it's her right, but, Walter, here's the truth. I love my colored friends. They have humor, they have grace, and they know how to laugh and tell a joke and see the sunny side of life. We don't need outside agitators spreading discord and confusion."

Walter remembered Calpurnia, the colored woman who had helped raise him and Weber. He recalled his mother saying to Rose Lee, "When they were small children, they loved Callie as much as they loved me. Maybe more. I didn't resent it at all. They loved her for a good reason. I loved her, too, and in her later years I did all that I could to make her life comfortable and pleasant. When she died, we were all sick with grief."

Rose Lee had shaken her head with irritation.

"What's that have to do with anything? I was discussing civil rights. You are not saying you'd give rights to the colored because you loved Calpurnia. You are not saying anything. What is left unsaid is that you just miss the old ways, and want to turn back the clock."

"I implied no such thing. What's gone is gone, and I know that as well as you. I was just saying that we loved Calpurnia. My, how you twist things, Rose Lee."

Walter and Rose Lee had gone to New York in 1959 to visit her Wellesley College classmate Irma Braverson, and he remembered how she had pleaded with him to watch what he said.

"Don't embarrass me with your reactionary views, don't try to correct anyone or *explain* things," she'd said, but during a dinner party in their honor the discussion had gotten around to the South and the race issue, and Walter, shy at first and reluctant to speak, soon found himself talking at great length on the "complexity of this sad old problem."

"Oh, I can't believe what came out of your mouth," Rose Lee said, later. "What must they think of us now? Why must you justify all the prejudice intelligent people have against the South?

It's hard enough to live down our past, and you just play into their hands. Who cares that your grandfather was a good friend to a Negro named Obadiah and how Obadiah loved him, and how your grandfather taught him to read and write? And how he said, 'Obadiah has more wisdom than I.' It was embarrassing. No, humiliating is more like it. And then you had to go on about old Calpurnia. I wanted to die."

"Rose Lee, I just tried to say that there was much mutual affection between the races. And that some lovely Negroes came out of that society of discrimination."

"What are you saying? You want to create more lovely Negroes? My God, I can't believe you wouldn't have had the sense to sort of tailor your remarks."

"I only said we have to forgive each other and move on."

"Oh, your fake old piety! Whatever do we have to forgive the Negroes for?"

"For their anger and impatience, Rose Lee—for their hysteria. We have to forgive them, as they should forgive us."

"But we were unjust to the Negroes! They don't need our forgiveness."

"We are very much together, and we are very much apart—we require a new spirit of brotherhood."

"Oh, be quiet."

Walter held up a hand.

"We must seek understanding and goodwill between the races."

"What does that *mean*? Nothing! You are not saying anything. God, you are just like your father. You are both *so comfortable* with yourselves. And your old mother! The thought of her has nearly ruined New York for me, as she has ruined everything else. She is a living symbol of everything that's wrong, Walter, and you are getting just like her."

His mother, Grace Desmond, had loved history and had been a member of the Daughters of the Confederacy. When he and his brother, Weber, were children, she had taken them to Virginia plantations and to the battlefields. She had talked often about Robert E. Lee. Once they'd gone into Westmoreland County to visit Stratford Hall, Lee's birthplace, and she'd told them how Robert at the age of four had to leave his beloved home. "His father had lost the property due to poor investment and rash speculation. But before they left Stratford Hall, Robert went into one of the rooms and said goodbye to the little angels carved on the fireplace."

And she'd taken them into that room to see the angels that he had seen when he was four.

Walter could remember almost perfectly her lecture on Lee. He had heard it so often in his youth, and later on as well.

"Robert E. Lee was the son of Henry 'Lighthorse Harry' Lee, a hero of the Revolutionary War and a friend and confidant of Washington and Lafayette. When Lafayette came to Virginia some years after the war, he paid a call on his old comrade-in-arms at his home in Alexandria. But though a great hero and loved by all, Lighthorse Harry had suffered many financial reverses. He did not have a good head for making money, and he squandered his entire estate. His life was tragic, and he died when young Robert was only twelve. Robert was his son by his second wife, Ann Carter, who grew up on the Shirley Plantation. His first wife, Lucy, died young.

"General Lee's mother devoted herself to the raising of her children, and when she later became an invalid, Robert cared for her with great tenderness until her death. Later in his life he cared for his invalided wife, Mary. She was the daughter of George Washington Custis, the grandson of Martha Washington and the adopted son of General Washington. Mary was not an easy person to live with. She was difficult and temperamental, and did not show General Lee the proper respect even when he commanded the forces of the Confederacy, but Robert loved her and treated her with understanding and compassion. He was a man who gracefully bore his burdens.

"Next to Lee the greatest soldier of the War Between the

States was Stonewall Jackson, but he died at Chancellorsville, shot mistakenly in the dark by his own men. His left arm was amputated. He seemed to recover for a time but later died of pneumonia. His last words in delirium were, 'Let us cross over the river and rest under the shade of the trees.' When Lee heard the news he said, 'I have lost my right arm.' I do not care much for General James Longstreet. He was not a Virginian—I think he was from Georgia or South Carolina—and he did not have good manners—and he had blamed Lee for the defeat at Gettysburg. Lee had been good to Longstreet, had called him 'my old war horse,' but Longstreet betrayed him. It was Longstreet who lost Gettysburg, not Lee. As you can gather, boys, James Longstreet is not in my pantheon of heroes. If Longstreet's corps had attacked at sunrise on the second day, Lee would have been victorious, and the North would have sued for peace. But Lee's orders had been disobeyed, and Longstreet did not attack until late in the afternoon. By then the opportunity was lost. For the Yankees had gained time to strengthen their center at Cemetery Ridge. On the third day, Pickett's division moved out toward that ridge in some desperate attempt to break through the Yankee lines. Oh, you know what happened there, boys. They charged right into the Yankee guns. It was heroic and futile, like the Charge of the Light Brigade. Weaknesses that could have once been exploited by rapid movement had disappeared. If only Longstreet had attacked early on the second day, there would have been no need for Pickett's Charge, and victory would have been assured. If only Jackson had lived! He would have arrived on time!"

They were all together at his mother's home.

"Why, Southern boys and girls are becoming nearly as rude as Yankee children. They are losing sight of courtesy," Walter's mother said.

Rose Lee smiled.

"It's a good sign. They are not so cowed. They are thinking for themselves."

"They are not thinking at all. Children need not show disrespect to prove they are independent thinkers. But of course, Rose Lee, you mock courtesy. It had once been bred in you by your dear parents, but you went north to college and got ruined."

Rose Lee laughed.

"Mother Desmond, you are so *provincial*. You ought to travel some and get a broader view."

"I don't need a broader view, thank you. I know what I believe. I believe in *loyalty*. And I don't mean loyalty to the NAACP. Why, I can't believe that you are sending them money and acting so *moral* about it. You are just flaunting your liberal ways."

"Why, because I send them a little money? Well, I see no need to apologize. I hope it helps the colored advance."

"It is unseemly how you push your views on my friends. It is embarrassing to me."

"What are you saying? You are more concerned about embarrassment than morality?"

"I said nothing about morality, Rose Lee, but I know it gives you pleasure to twist the meaning of my words."

"Your meaning is quite clear, and I twisted nothing."

"I will not answer you. I leave myself open to your malice and contempt."

Rose Lee shook her head.

"Lord you are so *devious*."

"I am in no way devious. You take pride in being a renegade. You are disloyal to Virginia."

"Disloyal? Last I heard, Richmond had fallen. The war has been over near a hundred years."

"I dislike your tone."

"The war is over, that's all."

"Oh, yes, but think of our sorrow and loss!"

"What sorrow, what loss? This is 1959."

"The Confederacy died at Appomattox. And we have not recovered to this day."

Rose Lee shook her head.

"We are one nation, Mother Desmond. You ought to thank Mr. Lincoln."

"Please don't speak of Lincoln."

"Oh, I forgot. Here I must speak only of General Lee."

"No, I prefer that you not speak of him, for there is something sardonic in your tone and offensive in your manner."

"Oh, forgive me. I'll go to Richmond tomorrow and *genuflect* before his monument."

"Your sarcasm is unbecoming. And you are his distant kin."

"So what. Who cares?"

"I care, Rose Lee. He doesn't deserve your scorn and mockery."

"How you go on."

"Yes, I go on. You are so unfair. All through his life he was nothing but good, a devoted son, a model cadet at West Point, a loving husband and father. And you mock this man. Yes, all through his life, at every stage, he was exemplary. He was a hero of the Mexican War. General Winfield accorded him the highest praise in his reports."

"Oh, please calm down."

"In the ordeal of surrender at Appomattox, he thought only of his men."

Rose Lee shook her head.

"Just calm down, will you. I say he was *selfish*. His daughters never married because he wished them to nurse him when he got old."

"That is slander! They never married because they were loyal to their dear father, and they could find no man to match him."

"I can't believe you, Mother Desmond. You are so blind, so naïve."

Walter's mother sighed.

"Rose Lee, you are so predictable. Everything Southern is *bad* . . . I know you so well."

"I live in reality, and I won't buy your old myths. I am so sick of Robert E. Lee. I find your adoration sickening. He was no saint."

"Why must you tear him down? What pleasure can it give you?"

"I do not *romanticize*. I will not invent."

"I invent nothing. I romanticize nothing. After the war, he allowed no one in his presence to speak unkindly of General Grant, that's the sort of man he was, magnanimous and good! I do not declare him to be a saint, Rose Lee. He was flesh and blood. He was human. He loved the company of pretty young women, and he had a tender correspondence with a number of them, but there was never a hint of scandal. I find it hard to accept how you slander him, your own distant kinsman. I cannot understand how you slander him and betray the cause for which he suffered. I am still affected by his life. I am consoled by his memory and the beauty of his character. Yes, he was too good to be true, but there he was, true and good, and neither envy nor spite nor the calumny of small-minded detractors can change a thing."

Rose Lee laughed.

"Oh, how *dramatic* we are today! Lee is no model for the modern age. He was tied up with duty and self-denial. He was neurotic, a depressed personality."

"Oh, how up-to-date we are! He was not *neurotic*, Rose Lee, not a *depressed personality*. He had lived through great tragedy and suffered from the long strain of war, but he bore it with grace and he never burdened others. And what's wrong with duty? It's a virtue, not a crime. It entails sacrifice for others. I'm in distress at your remarks. God might forgive you for them but I never will!"

"Oh, I was wondering when God would appear. Come on, Walter, I can't deal with God *and* General Lee."

Walter, standing with his father in another part of the room, walked over.

"Mama, we're leaving. Don't be upset now," he said.

"Take her out of here."

Rose Lee put on her coat.

"I'm leaving, Mother Desmond, and I will not set foot in your house ever again."

"I know you will not, for you are not welcome here."

"I would not come, even if I were welcome."

"Well, don't worry. You're not and never will be."

"Good! I'm so glad to be relieved of your tiresome company."

And three days later they were all together again at his parents' home.

His mother was speaking.

"Stop talking of the Civil War. This was no rebellion, Rose Lee. It was the War Between the States. We seceded, we had a right to secede, and we became a separate nation, and for this we were brutally invaded. And we defended ourselves as was our right. And after four years of resistance, worn down by superior numbers and materiel, we could fight no more, and we lay down our arms, our land and people in ruin."

Rose Lee sighed.

"Spare me your orations. The truth is obvious. Southern society was based on the practice of slavery, and all our problems came from that."

"Our forefathers did not invent slavery. They were born into it. Slavery was part of the time in which they lived. I do not mourn its passing. Had I lived back then, I'd have opposed that peculiar institution, as did General Lee. As you know, he believed in gradual emancipation."

Rose Lee laughed.

"I'm sure you like the *gradual* part."

"Out of concern for the slaves. He wished them prepared for freedom when it came."

"Oh, why don't you admit it. You'd love to turn back the

clock. 'Oh, how nice to hear the darkies singing. Is there anything more lovely than to hear them in the dusky light? Oh, they really love us. We've been so *good* to them.' "

"Is that supposed to be funny? Well, it isn't, not one bit. I despise your sarcasm and your bitter mockery. Of course, slavery was wrong, but I want to tell you something, Rose Lee, and please don't throw a fit—many slaves *did* love their masters. Yes, there were some very nice plantations. And loyalty and affection between slave and master were not uncommon. It's possible to say that, and yet not condone slavery."

Rose Lee pushed her fists into her eyes.

"I don't believe the stuff that comes out of your mouth! You are outrageous!"

Walter walked in the room.

"I wish you ladies would stop."

He was greeted with silence. Rose Lee's face was flushed red. His mother sat grim-faced and angry.

A little later, they sit down at the dining room table.

His mother, still upset, finally breaks the silence.

"Rose Lee, you are too acerbic in your tone. You lack the gentle Virginia way."

"I do? Well, good for me!"

"You have forgotten your manners."

"Hurray! I don't aspire to be a Virginia hypocrite."

Mr. Desmond raises his hand.

"Courtesy is not hypocrisy. It is a serious moral matter."

She shakes her head.

"I beg to disagree. In Virginia it's just a smokescreen to conceal our inhumanity."

He smiles at her.

"Well, I must take exception to that, Rose Lee. In Virginia, courtesy is morally ingrained from birth. We are the heirs of the genteel tradition."

Rose Lee laughs.

"Oh, yes, we are of a purer strain. We are descendants of Cavaliers. Well, I'm sorry, but if you believe that, Father Desmond, you had best see a good doctor." She raises her arms. "I say, we are not Cavaliers. We are not even genteel. And nothing's ingrained from birth in this commonwealth but prejudice against the colored and a sense of our own superiority."

Walter's mother sighs.

"Yes, go on and mock *everything*. It's just so like you."

Mr. Desmond regards Rose Lee with a look of calm forbearance.

"We are a moderate and balanced society. After the war, we acted with restraint. We had a good relationship with our former slaves. In all the Old Confederacy we had the fewest lynchings. There were states in the North that had more lynchings than Virginia."

Rose Lee laughs.

"Oh, we are truly progressive. We lynched *moderately!*"

Walter's mother shakes a finger.

"You are always *judging* someone! You can't judge all the people of the South by the barbarous actions of the ignorant."

Rose Lee smiles.

"How can you speak of the ignorance of *others?*"

"I beg your pardon."

"What about your ignorance? Look how you treat Mattie."

"I treat Mattie fine. Why she loves me to death."

"Oh, really. I say she's little more than a slave in her subservience to you."

"How insane you are!" Mrs. Desmond calls to the kitchen. "Mattie, come here."

Mattie, a slim dark-brown woman in her early thirties, comes out.

"Yes, Ma'am."

"Tell Miss Rose how I treat you."

"You treat me fine."

"Am I fair in my dealings? Am I good to you?"

"Yes, Ma'am."

"Has anyone ever treated you better but for your own dear mother?"

"No, Ma'am."

"Thank you. You can go, Mattie."

Mattie leaves.

"Are you satisfied?"

Rose Lee sighs.

"Well, what's she going to say? She has such low expectations—and she needs a job."

"I care for her, and she cares for me. I would do anything for Mattie that I could."

"Why don't you have her for dinner one night? Let her sit at the table with you."

"What is the matter with you? She *serves* the dinner."

"Well, you serve it, and she could be your guest."

Walter's mother shakes her head, then calls to the kitchen again. "Mattie, come here, please."

Mattie returns to the dining room.

"Yes, Ma'am."

"Miss Rose has a wonderful idea. We are having the Waybrights over tomorrow night. Well, we are going to do things differently. I'm going to serve, and you'll sit at the table. Wear your best dress now."

Mattie smiles.

"Miss Grace, I ain't going to sit down with white folks, and you ain't going to serve."

"Well, if you don't want to, we'll do it the old way."

Mattie leaves.

Walter's mother nods at Rose Lee.

"I would not cause her such pain and embarrassment. I would not make her a figure of fun, and she understands better than you."

"Oh, she understands all right. She knows to stay in her

place. Well, I *enjoy* talking to Mattie. I *like* sitting with her. I have sat with her many a time."

"That is in the kitchen. But she does not sit down at the table. On a social level we have nothing in common."

Walter's father stands up from the table. "Walter, let's leave the ladies."

They go into an adjoining room.

"Why that is so heartless of you, Mother Desmond. And *so condescending.*"

"It is nothing of the sort. It is kindness. It is reality. We would all feel uncomfortable. She could not carry on a conversation."

"Then invite the genteel colored to sit at your table. They would not feel embarrassed, for they could speak as intelligently as you."

"I'm aware of the refined colored, but we all seek our own kind, Rose Lee."

"God, I feel sorry for you."

"I dare say. You are such a liberal now. You think you're smarter than everyone else."

Rose Lee sighs, then shakes her head.

"If you are party to an evil, then you had best separate yourself from it or you cannot call yourself a moral person."

"What evil are you talking about? If the races are unequal, is that my fault? We are not all equal, Rose Lee. Inequality is the nature of life. Some are good in art. Others in abstract thinking. Some at working with their hands."

"Lies and evasions! You just want to keep the colored down. No, we just have to do the right thing."

"Excuse me, lady. I don't need moral instruction from you."

"You are *devoid* of morality. It's disgusting how you delude yourself from morning to night. All your sick reverence for the Confederate dead! All that putting flowers on graves!"

"I pray that I am loyal. I won't desert them to please you."

"How you obfuscate, how you *glorify* your ignorance!"

"I wish you would not shout at me."

"I will shout at you! You are *evil*!"

"Rose Lee, I have borne your enmity for many a year."

"I am just so *sick* of you."

Walter's mother nods.

"I think you are sick of yourself. If only you'd had children. It might've made you more tender."

"Why, how cruel you are. You know I can't have children— and through no fault of my own."

"Poor Walter is the last of the Desmond line."

Rose Lee half laughs, half sobs.

"God, you are crazy."

Mrs. Desmond looks toward the adjoining room.

"Walter, come and get your wife. You have to live with her, I don't."

Rose Lee takes a deep breath.

"I find the atmosphere in this house *oppressive*."

"Well, then leave."

"I will, gladly."

"Good. Then do so at once."

"I am going, happily."

"Then why don't you."

Walter comes into the room.

"I wish you all would stop it."

Rose Lee begins to walk away.

"Come on Walter. Let's leave this old museum."

His mother leans forward in her chair.

"Yes, let's not keep her waiting. I feel so *sorry* for you, son."

"Mama, please. Goodnight now. Goodnight, Daddy."

He was in the cemetery with his mother. She held flowers wrapped in newspaper.

"Walter, I know she is your wife and your first loyalty is to her. But I won't endure her rudeness to Father and me."

"Mama, she means well. But she is high-strung and impatient. She can't help it."

"Don't make excuses. She is hateful." She took a deep breath and sighed. "I know you must defend her. You are too good. And she takes advantage of your kind nature."

She placed the flowers at the foot of Weber's grave.

"Poor Weber's gone, but he is not forgotten," she said, nodding. "When my life is done, I hope you'll come here and visit. Maybe each year on my birthday. You could read something, Walter." He nodded vaguely. "I'd prefer something by General Lee. I'll leave word in my will on just what. But say nothing to your wife. I can do without her mockery, thank you."

"We better go, Mama," he said. He adjusted the shawl around her shoulders. As they walked away, she moved unsteadily and held on to his arm.

"I don't like the way she treats you, Walter."

"It's all right."

"No, it's not all right. She does not treat you with respect. You deserve better. Much better."

He smiled and shook his head.

"Mama, if I outlive you, I'll read whatever you like, but you'll be here a long time yet."

"You're doing what? I can't believe you. But I know it will give you pleasure. Are you going to sing "Dixie," too? You are *pathetic*."

"Be kind, Rose Lee. Let's try to forgive and forget."

"*Forgive!* Is that all you can ever say? I do not wish to forgive. I will speak out. I'll not be cowed like you. You are so blind, Walter, and crippled in your devotion."

Rose Lee shook her head.

"I want to tell you something, Mother Desmond. It was Lee who lost Gettysburg. I spoke to professors in Charlottesville and they said that Longstreet had been unfairly blamed for the defeat. Longstreet had a superior plan that would have won the battle, but Lee wouldn't listen. Lee blundered, Mother Desmond. He lost the battle and the war. Of course, I'm glad he did. I would not want to live in the Confederate States of America. But I just want to say that I have it on good opinion that Longstreet was right and Lee was wrong."

"How dare you speak of matters you know nothing about. You know nothing of military history and care less. You are saying this only to provoke me. I know you so well, Rose Lee. Longstreet's views have long since been discredited."

"Only by Lee worshippers like General Jubal Early, that's what my professor friends said. Early was a malcontent, he made mistakes himself at Gettysburg, and he tried to recover his reputation by blaming Longstreet and defending Lee. No. I'm sorry to inform you that General Lee was at fault."

"What joy you take in spreading slander. I'm truly distressed by your attitude. General Lee was the greatest man of his time. Some say he was too good to be true. But his sort of greatness would always be attacked by those who feel threatened by a true man. He hated war and he did not wish it, but he was loyal to Virginia and the South. It was his duty to resist the invasion of its borders. There are those who say that he had one flaw as a military leader, that in his desire not to offend his subordinate commanders he was perhaps too lenient and patient with them, and not firm enough in his insistence that they follow his orders precisely, that he gave them room if not to overtly disobey him, then at least to frustrate his intentions. I say that this was not done out of weakness but out of the respect he accorded his brother officers. He allowed them some free play in their interpretation of his orders, for he knew that in the heat and confusion of battle things changed rapidly, and he relied on their judgment to respond to a changing situation. It is true that General Lee lacked ruthlessness. His good manners prevented him from wounding the feelings of others. He was the politest and most courteous of men. Of course, Rose Lee, you mock courtesy and call it a sham display. But true courtesy is not something one wears for an hour like a coat but is inherent in one's being. It arises from the deepest wellsprings of kindness and compassion, virtues that General Lee possessed in abundance but which sad to say are fast departing from our world."

Rose Lee laughed.

"Oh, how you do go on. I can't believe you're real."

"Goodnight to you, Rose Lee. I don't wish to see you anytime soon."

Walter stood by a tree in the cemetery. Putting on his glasses, he removed a paper from the side pocket of his coat.

The sun came through a break in the clouds. Shading his eyes for a moment, he leaned against the tree. A breeze passed through the branches, and his mind drifted. He could hear his father. "The important thing, Walter, is to take your time. Don't be rushed. And never lose your composure." And then he heard his mother say, "A gentleman does not reveal to others the burden of his sorrow." Some sparrows landed on the ground, then quickly flew away, and Rose Lee's voice went through him. "I hate your courtly restraint! I despise your moral confusion. Oh, I know, everything's so *complicated*. You make me tired, you really do. You dishearten me! You battle and frustrate me from morning to night! For God's sake, Walter, liberate yourself!" He bowed his head and sighed. 'Rose Lee, I know I'm not perfect. I truly regret any wrong I might have done you,' he thought. "Oh, be quiet, Mr. Saintly!" she replied.

The sun disappeared in the clouds. Walter looked at the woods, at the road, then out toward the Blue Ridge. A small truck passed by. He heard the cawing of crows. He did not feel well. He had not for some time. Looking out at the mountains, he thought, "I'm the last of the Desmond line."

Overhead some geese flew south.

Adjusting his glasses, he took a deep breath and looked at the paper in his hand.

"Well, happy birthday, Mama," he said, and feeling life's brevity, and wondering where it all had gone, he commenced reading Lee's final order to the Army of Northern Virginia.

"'After four years of arduous service marked by unsurpassed courage and fortitude, the Army of Northern Virginia has been compelled to yield to overwhelming numbers and resources.

"'I need not tell the brave survivors of so many hard-fought battles who have remained steadfast to the last that I have consented to this result from no distrust of them; but feeling that valor and devotion could accomplish nothing that could compensate for the loss that must have attended the continuance of the contest, I determined to avoid the useless sacrifice of those whose past services have endeared them to their countrymen.

"'By the terms of the agreement, officers and men can return to their homes and remain until exchanged. You will take with you the satisfaction that proceeds from a consciousness of duty faithfully performed; and I earnestly pray that a Merciful God will extend to you His blessing and protection.

"'With an unceasing admiration of your constancy and devotion to your Country, and a grateful remembrance of your kind and generous consideration for myself, I bid you all an affectionate farewell.

"'R. E. Lee.'"

The Modern Age

On a warm and cloudy morning in May of 1962, Walter Desmond, a retired Virginia banker wearing a seersucker suit and Panama hat, approached the entrance of an office building in Washington. He was walking slowly, with a dignity more appropriate to an earlier and more self-assured age. It was his view that any sign of haste was bad manners that might offend the sensibilities of others. A man should lift the spirits of those around him by his own demeanor, for that's what he'd been taught when he was a boy.

But on this morning his own spirits were as low as they'd ever been. As he entered the building, he thought of his late wife, Rose Lee, and what she'd said years before. "You know what you are, Walter? You are an elegy to a lost time. Why don't you let go of the past? It's about time you let go and became a progressive person. I'm not anything like my parents were. I'm not in thrall to the Confederate dead, or beholden to the Old South. I'm part of the New South that is now just arising." And then he thought of his mother as well, for she and Rose Lee had been bitter adversaries; his mother had been a defender of the old ways, and she had often told him, "Walter, no matter how trying life becomes, let this be your consolation and your guide.

You are a descendant of the planter aristocracy. Our people served with Lee and Jackson. Your great uncle Albert Desmond died in the battle of Cold Harbor on his eighteenth birthday." His mother and father had long since passed away, as had his brother, Weber; and Rose Lee had been dead for several years. There was little left of the world he had known.

He entered the building and took the elevator to the fourth floor, then walked down a corridor to the office of Frank Hartwell, a private detective.

"I understand how you feel, Mr. Desmond. But it's the uncertainty that's causing the problem. You don't have the facts. As the saying goes, the truth shall set you free."

"Yes, sir, it will set you free or depress you to death."

"Let's hope it's a happy truth."

"I'm sorry it's come to this. I never thought I'd employ a detective, and I feel it's unworthy of me. I'd like to talk to my wife directly, but I can't find a way to put it gracefully. If she thought I was jealous or suspicious, she'd lose all respect for me. I am jealous, and I do have cause for suspicion, but the idea of spying makes me ashamed." He shook his head and sighed. "If she found out, she'd never forgive me."

"Mr. Desmond, if your suspicions have no basis, then no one will be the wiser, but if your doubts are borne out, you won't be concerned about her forgiveness." The detective removed a ballpoint pen from the breast pocket of his jacket. "Now, may I ask how old you are?"

"Seventy-one."

"And your wife?"

"Twenty-seven. She's my second wife. My first wife died. Her name was Rose Lee."

"And what is the name of your present wife?"

"Lucy."

"Do you have any children by either marriage?"

"No, sir."

"All right. Now could you please go over again, Mr. Desmond, what you told me on the phone, and then tell me about your wife, the sort of person she is, her likes and dislikes, her hobbies and interests, and I'd like to hear something about your marriage. What was it like as an older man being married to a much younger woman? Were there sexual tensions? Or tensions of another kind? I know I'm prying into your personal life, but I must know things in order to find out other things. Now I hope your fears are groundless, but if not, you'll still have the truth, and what you do with it is your affair." He paused and nodded. "But before we go any further, we should discuss my fee, and the method of payment. That's customary. And you might have concerns on that score."

"No, sir, I'm not concerned about that. My sole concern is knowing the truth. For my life now is pure heartsick hell."

When he left the detective's office and walked out into the gray light of that morning, he again thought of Rose Lee. She had died in the midst of their contentious marriage, and he saw her in his mind as clearly as when she was alive, and he thought, 'Rose Lee, though much against my will and natural disposition, I have managed to do what you had always wanted for me. I have entered the modern age.'

After his interview, Walter left Washington, where he'd been living with his young wife, Lucy, in a house in Cleveland Park, and returned to his old home in Virginia. Lucy was then in New York.

He drove down to his house on a hill more than a hundred miles south of Washington, in the rural outskirts of a town east of the Blue Ridge.

He felt a need to go to the family cemetery, to spend time with the dead. For Walter it was a communion with the past and a comfort for the present.

Early the next morning, he passed through the fields and woods behind his home to a small graveyard bounded by a white board fence.

A car passed on the road, and as the sound slowly died away, there was a stir of a breeze. He looked around and seeing no one, he began to speak.

"Hello, Mama. Hi, Daddy. Hey there, Weber. Well, I hardly know where to begin. Yesterday I saw a private investigator. I fear that my wife is unfaithful, though I pray that I am wrong."

Five years before, he had spoken to his first wife, Rose Lee, about a separation and divorce. He'd been feeling his mortality, his heart was giving him trouble, and he seemed to feel less well with each passing day. In the time left to him he'd wished to live in a new way. "Rose Lee's a fine person," he'd said to friends. "But she's not been happy with me, and I have to say I've not been happy, either. It's nobody's fault, really, we are just incompatible, but if there is some fault, it's surely mine."

He felt bound to take the blame on himself; it's what a gentleman would do. But he was longing for something she wouldn't provide, warmth and human affection. Any man needs that, any woman, too, he thought. He needed to be appreciated, but she was dissatisfied with his politics, with his slow ways and courtly manner; there was nothing about him that escaped her critical eye. He was worn out from contention. 'I love Rose Lee, and I'll always love her, we've been married now for thirty years,' he thought. 'But is it wrong or selfish to want a new life? I'm not feeling too well of late. I could use a rest. I need some peace in the time I have left.'

And he'd heard his father's voice inside him. "For God's sake, be good to yourself, Walter. If you are not getting along with Rose Lee, if you are both unhappy, then leaving is right. How long do you have to suffer? And you got to consider your health; if she keeps nagging you she can put you in your grave. There is nothing worse for a man than a fault-finding wife."

Rose Lee had not desired the separation, she had accepted their differences as a natural part of married life. Perhaps she'd made him miserable at times, she told him, but often he had the same effect on her. "It's the nature of life, Walter. You can't avoid differences, you have to work through them somehow; and if you can't work through them perfectly, you make the best of things. That's what people of real character do. They are true to their marriage vows. There is no such thing as perfect bliss between a man and a woman. Don't you know that? You can't solve your problems by leaving me. You may think that someone else can make you happy. But she'll have flaws, too, worse flaws than mine, and then you'll be sorry. You'll beg me to take you back, but I won't, Walter. I'd not give a Confederate dollar to save you."

"Rose Lee, there is no one else. That is not an issue here," he said.

He moved out, went to Richmond and checked into the Jefferson Hotel.

She phoned and berated him for his inconstancy and moral blindness. He apologized for causing her distress, but he wished to live alone.

"You are tormenting me, Walter, just making me so sick I can hardly breathe."

"Oh, please, Rose Lee, you are making yourself sick. I'll help you in any way I can, but I can't live with you anymore. I need to lead a quiet life. I've got to rest."

"You got all eternity to rest."

At the week's end, she drove to Richmond. He was relieved that she'd come. They had a tearful reunion and reconciled.

"I'll not let you be a fool," she said.

He could not leave her. He was bonded to her by long habit and ties of affection. How could he have even considered it? He'd always been a loyal person.

So they remained married and lived together as they had before, in a state of tension, relieved at times by an odd exasperated affection. Their kind of marriage was all he'd ever known, and he resolved to remain with her until death parted them.

Rose Lee continued to have fits of hysteria, ranted against the

South, and spoke bitterly of his late mother. "It's all her fault, Walter, that you are so unreconstructed in your thinking. Yes, she is gone but not forgotten. She lives on in you."

"Honey, I ask you. Let Mama rest in peace. I do love you, Rose Lee."

He had come to feel compassion for her difficult nature. He was truly sorry he could not make her happy.

Almost a year after they'd reconciled, Rose Lee died in her sleep while visiting her sister in Newport News.

"Her heart gave out, Walter, that's all there was to it," the doctor said, but Walter blamed himself. Her heart gave out from living with him. A day after her burial, he went to her grave.

"Rose Lee, I was a living torment to you. Day and night. I don't know how you stood it." He'd not been modern or progressive as she'd hoped, and he'd thwarted her at every turn. That he'd spent much of his life trying to please her, did not in his grief occur to him.

As time passed, he tried to lay his sorrow aside and move on. But most days he felt too lonely and lost to think he'd ever feel well again. "I know what you're feeling," a friend told him. "The pain is something awful. And you can't sidestep it or push it down but you've got to go through it. And it's slow going, Walter, but nothing lasts forever, not grief or sadness or anything else."

On a late summer afternoon, more than a year after Rose Lee's death, as he stood on the porch of his house set back on a hill, he saw a light blue car pull over on the road below. A young woman got out and looked at the left rear wheel, shook her head, then opened the trunk of the car. She was about to remove something but changed her mind, then happened to look up toward his house. Seeing him, she waved and pointed to her car. Walter waved back and walked down to the road.

The rear tire was flat, and he offered to put on the spare.

"That's so kind of you. I'm not even sure I know where the jack is, and besides I don't know how to use it."

He found the jack and changed her tire, only to discover that the spare was as flat as the other. Walter jacked the car up again and removed the spare. Then he leaned the tires against the front bumper of her car.

"I'll take you into town and we'll have air put in the spare, and then I'll put it on for you. After that I can show you where you can get a new tire to replace the flat, if that's necessary."

"Oh, I hate to put you to all that trouble," she said.

"It's no trouble at all. It's nice to have a chance to be useful. I'll go up and get my car. Now don't you go away."

He put the spare tire in the back seat of his car.

As they drove into town, he introduced himself.

"I'm Lucy Dawes McCausland," she said. "But McCausland is my ex-husband's name, and I'm not sure I'll keep it."

It pleased him that she was not married.

After he put air in her spare tire, they drove back to her car, and he put the wheel back on; and then they drove again back to town in her car to a tire place, where she bought a new tire. By the time the new tire was placed on, the wheels balanced, and the spare returned to the trunk, they'd been together for more than two hours.

"I want you to know," she said, smiling, "it's so nice to meet a really kind person."

"Well, I don't know about that. I have simply enjoyed myself with charming company."

She laughed and touched his hand.

"I just love courtesy. It's so nice and Southern. Even if you don't mean what you say, it puts a nice glow on life."

"I believe in sincerity even more than courtesy," he said. "And I was thinking, Miss Dawes, if I could delay your departure for a while yet, we might dine together. I know a restaurant in Charlottesville you might like. And if you agree, I'd like to go back to my home and dress for the occasion. It would not take long."

And they went back to his place, and she waited in her car, while he cleaned up and put on a suit and tie.

He had not been to a restaurant since Rose Lee's death. And he felt slightly giddy at such a departure from his routine; he likened it to a body's sudden change in direction and the light-headedness that followed. He was surprised at how hungry he'd been for the smallest adventure.

"Well, please tell me more about yourself," he said at dinner, after a glass of wine.

"I'm from Roanoke, but I live in Richmond now," she said. Educated in fine arts in New York, she had become a commercial artist, her present occupation. Her late father had been a doctor and an alcoholic. She'd loved him, though she'd suffered much pain and humiliation as his daughter. Two years before, her mother had died of cancer, and she'd married the lawyer, McCausland, who had handled her mother's estate. "I felt lonely and bereft, like an orphan, Walter. And he was so thoughtful and consoling that I agreed to marry him, but it didn't last a year. You should never marry someone you don't love. Or maybe I thought I loved him. I was so confused."

Walter told her about his own griefs and sorrows, about his marriage, and the death of his wife, Rose Lee. "We did not have an easy time. It was not her fault, it was mine. I want you to know, I'm far from perfect," he said.

"Well, we are none of us perfect, but you have humility, Walter."

He was touched by her compliment. This lovely woman nearly young enough to be his granddaughter, and mature beyond her years, seemed to appreciate him. He felt she was someone in whom he could confide, and he wondered if they might become friends, even more. But exactly what, he could not ponder for more than a moment without becoming alarmed by physical longing, and feeling himself on dangerous ground.

'Oh, God, yes, she is lovely, but I'm not such a fool to think I can go forward with this. I hope and pray I have some judgment left.'

But when she asked for his address and gave him her own before driving off to Richmond, and said in parting, "Walter, I'd dearly love to hear from you," and then pressed his hand with a tenderness that surprised him, he felt something give way inside him, and what judgment he had left did not help him. He had fallen in love with her.

In the morning, as he sat on the edge of his bed, with the sunlight pouring into his room, he felt embarrassed at the recollection of the evening. What could he have been thinking to allow himself to have such feelings for a woman more than forty years younger? It wasn't love, it was physical attraction; it's what happened when you mixed wine and loneliness. Good sense went straight to hell.

He knew he'd not hear from her. As strangers often do, they'd shared stories of themselves they'd not share with friends, but back in her ordinary life she'd not think twice about him.

He felt disappointed. His days lacked novelty; he had little to do and no one to live for; he resigned himself to loneliness.

'She came into my life as a great and fateful surprise,' he wrote in his journal. 'Feelings long suppressed overwhelmed me.'

But he still had some judgment left. Life was confusing, temptation could play havoc with your mind. As his father said, "Walter, man is a weak reed. Only self-restraint can save him from disgrace and tragedy."

In the afternoon, he received flowers from Lucy, with a note of thanks.

"What a pleasant way to begin a friendship," she wrote.

Moved by the flowers, by her note, by the promise of friendship, all the feelings he'd tried to reason away came over him again. He'd done nothing wrong. He'd not sought their meeting, it had come unbidden. Without his lifting a finger, happiness had appeared on the road below his house. And why should he deny what the fates had so graciously bestowed? "I'm in love with her. I'm not ashamed," he said to the air. And sitting on his porch, the flowers beside him, he sobbed into his hands.

He phoned her that evening.

"Walter, what a wonderful surprise," she said.

"It should be no surprise, dear lady, for I've thought of you often since you left, and you must have sensed how I felt. Am I right? Oh, don't answer that. I just want to know one thing. Will I see you again?"

"Of course, I'd like that," she said.

He laughed.

"Well, that is just too wonderful for words."

On the weekend, he went to Richmond and stayed at the Jefferson Hotel, where he'd lived during his brief separation from Rose Lee. The irony was not lost on him. As he sat on the bed in his room, he wondered what Rose Lee would think of him now, and then, feeling he'd betrayed her in some way, he heard her voice.

"Walter, you are such a fool. Though you had a hold on my affections once, I just can't imagine why."

He took Lucy to dinner. As they entered the restaurant, it occurred to him that it was their first planned time together, not an accidental meeting but an occasion they'd both agreed upon.

"Well, here we are," Lucy said. "And I owe it all to a flat tire."

"I would call it a fate tire," he said, taking her hand.

"Walter, I thought you were wise, but I see you are witty as well."

He liked her bantering tone, there was much affection in it.

She smiled, he felt lightheaded. He felt so much at that

moment. Where it was all going, he couldn't say, but he knew that mere friendship could not be enough for him.

After dinner, they took a walk through Old Richmond.

They held hands and talked with a freedom that he found joyful. They were for each other a consolation for all the sorrows they had known. Old griefs dropped away. He felt a lightness that made him want to go dancing.

A month passed.

He continued to see her, always staying at the Jefferson. Arriving on Friday in the early evening, he'd pick her up at her apartment and then take her out to dinner.

He always took her to the same restaurant, until she suggested a change.

"I'm a man of habit," he said, and apologized for being so thoughtless.

"Walter, you are no such thing. I just thought you'd enjoy a new place."

"Being with you is the only place I require."

There was no physical intimacy, only the holding of hands and light hugs when he arrived and departed. He desired her but would not rush into things before their natural time, if such things were possible at all.

They took walks around the city. Once he took her to the Confederate Museum and gave her a lecture on the burning of Richmond. It moved him so in the telling that it was as though he and his own mother and father and brother had been dispossessed by the war.

They had their meals together and sat in historic parks.

"Walter, what I love about you is you're old-fashioned," she said, after she'd known him a month. "I find it somehow dear and charming. I hope I don't offend you by saying so."

"Oh, no, I'm thrilled to death that you like me at all."

He liked that she found him old-fashioned, for that's what he was—and stodgy, too, he could not claim otherwise. It mattered only that she cared for him, and he did not have to dissemble or play a part. He had never felt so appreciated by anyone as he did by this young woman who hung on his words and loved his talks on the old virtues that were dying out.

"In the older generations the quality of courtesy had an important value. It just wasn't good manners that it reflected, but it was an expression of moral qualities. It was kindness and restraint, embedded deep. Not something that you wore on your sleeve for an hour but part of your being. Of course, I may be idealizing here, there were obviously bad manners, too, but I'm expressing the ideal that people had, even when they didn't live up to it."

"That's so beautifully put, Walter."

"I don't say I'm that way. It would be immodest to say that. I'm just saying it was my tradition, and I value it."

She nodded.

"It's wonderful as long as it lets you be honest, so you're just not hiding behind some facade of good manners."

"Yes, it's important to be honest but with kindness. Life's a struggle, but you try to act decently."

"That's right, Walter. There's so much stridency and ugliness today. What people value is shouting for their rights. With no concern for duty."

"Well, you know in some ways the world is changing for the better. People who have been denied rights are getting them, like the colored, and that's only fair. My wife, Rose Lee, disapproved of my cautious approach to social change. I said we couldn't move too fast or we'd create disharmony between the races, we had to go slow or we'd ruin everything, I said. 'But you're not even going slow, Walter. You're standing still,' she'd say. And I'd say, 'Honey, we got to evolve into it or we'll have anarchy.' She said I was the worst kind of fool. She was probably right."

"Oh, don't talk that way. Rose Lee didn't appreciate you. You are just the dearest of men. I love you, Walter."

It startled him. What did 'love' mean? It might not mean the same to her as it meant to him. He wanted to tell her how he felt, but was afraid he might frighten her away.

After he left her and drove home, he felt he should have risked everything and confessed his true feelings.

In the morning, he went to the cemetery and sat down by the graves.

"I love a young woman. She's more than forty years younger, and I want to marry her. Have I lost my mind? All my life I've been guided by social convention, but I don't think there's just one right way to live, do you?" He waited, then heard in his mind his father's voice. "Walter, forget convention. It don't mean a thing. It's one thing one day and another the next. So she's a good deal younger than you, but maybe she needs an older man to steady her. You love the lady. That's all that matters. Rose Lee is gone. Time is passing. Be happy while you can."

He did not wait for the weekend to see her again, but arranged to meet her the following day.

"I have something urgent to say to you," he said on the phone.

She was alarmed by his tone.

"Are you sick, Walter? It's nothing bad about your health, is it?" she said.

"No, but I must speak to you, and the phone won't do."

He drove to Richmond, arriving in the afternoon. She took the day off from work. He did not check into the Jefferson Hotel. If she refused him, he could not bear to remain.

He met her at the entrance of the apartment building where she lived.

"Why, Walter, how novel to see you on a Tuesday," she said, smiling.

It was warm. He wore a seersucker suit. She wore a new dress and white gloves.

He took her hand, wanting to tell her at once what was on his mind, to just blurt it out and end the suspense. But all he could say was, "Shall we take a walk?"

They walked. She said nothing, waiting to hear what was troubling him. Finally, she said, "Walter, are you all right?"

"No, I'm not all right. I've got to talk to you."

"Well, I'm here," she said.

"I can't talk while standing. I have to sit down."

They ended up in a tearoom. They ordered tea and cake.

He waited for the waitress to leave, then stood placing his hands on the table, then flustered, sat down again.

"What's wrong, Walter?"

"Lucy, I can contain myself no longer. I love you. I have this hope to marry you. If you find this wildly presumptuous, tell me now, and I'll leave and never trouble you again." She looked at him without speaking. He looked down at his hands, waited for her to say something, and when she made no reply, he looked up red-faced and said, "I'm sorry. I know I'm way too old for you. I don't know what I was thinking. Forgive me. I ask you to forget what I said."

"Forgive? Forget? What are you saying?" she said.

"I have no right."

"You have no right? Well, you can marry me like you said."

"Marry? But I'm way too old for you."

"Walter, I thought you were proposing. And no sooner said than you start backing out."

"I'm not backing out. But you better sleep on it."

"I don't require sleep. I know what I'm saying."

She got up from the table, leaned down and kissed him. Covering his face with a napkin, he sobbed, then stood up and hugged her to him.

"I was unprepared for such good news," he said.

He thought of reserving a room and asking her to stay, but feeling tired and drained of emotion from all he'd been through, he felt he must go home. He needed to rest and reflect on how radically his life had changed. He was amazed at the man he'd become.

As he left, he kissed her.

"You are my dearest heart," he said. "We are now engaged to be married."

On the drive home, the elation wore off after twenty miles. The old doubts returned. He was too old for her, she'd tire of him, he'd not have the energy to satisfy her sexual needs; and there was the problem of his health. She could be a widow in a year.

By the time he arrived home, he knew he must end it. He did not trust happiness. Passionate love was uncharted waters in which a body could drown.

He wrote in his journal. 'I have mainly avoided extremes, prized moderation and self-restraint. I have enjoyed the society of friends, a drink on occasion, a good story, and harmless flirtation, but if the truth be known, my true pleasure in life is the faithful exercise of my moral duty. What I require most is a clear conscience.'

He was too old for her, and each year he'd be older still, while she'd have her youth for a long time yet.

He'd return to Richmond to break it off. He called her to arrange the meeting but gave no inkling of its purpose.

He waited for her in the same tearoom where he'd proposed.

Lucy arrived.

"I'm so happy," she said.

They sat across from each other.

"What's wrong, Walter?"

"Honey, I'm too old for you."

"No, you are just right for me."

"I'm far more than twice your age."

"Oh, don't be literal. True love is outside the realm of time."

"I'm not overly well. I have heart trouble. I could die on you."

"You won't, Walter. I'll never let that happen."

"But death comes when it pleases."

"You're being morbid, Walter. If you're trying to back out, just say so. Oh, look, if you don't love me, let's just forget the whole thing. You just go on back to where you came from."

In the fall, they were married in Charlottesville by a judge, a friend of Walter's family.

They went to North Carolina on their honeymoon, to the Outer Banks, staying at a beachside motel in Hatteras. It was cool and cloudy, and they had the beach nearly to themselves.

It was the most romantic time that Walter had ever known. They walked along the shore, saw shipwrecks from past storms. At night they slept in each other's arms. It felt strange to be married again. He'd been married to Rose Lee for thirty-two years. She'd been of his own generation, of the same background; but now he had a young wife with whom he did not always know his role; he was her lover and friend, her mentor and guide; and sometimes she appeared more like a daughter to him.

After their honeymoon, they returned to Virginia and lived in the house on the hill. They saw few people, were mainly their own society. She painted and planted a garden and shopped for groceries and supplies for the house. He read novels by Thomas Hardy and books on the Civil War, and on most afternoons took walks through the woods to the cemetery.

"I did marry the young woman," he said to his parents. "We are living in the old house. It is a new life for me. I'm a changed man. I think I'm happy, but we are still a little shy with each other." And he went to Rose Lee's grave, near the graves of his parents and brother. " Rose Lee, I hope you are glad for me. I have married again. I've been lonely without you." Then he heard Rose Lee's voice inside him. "Walter, if there is a right way and a wrong, you will find the wrong. I am sorry for you."

After a month in seclusion, Walter took Lucy on a trip to Washington. He was fond of the city. It still retained for him something from the days when it was not so important in the world, when it was a sleepy Southern town.

They stayed at the Hay Adams by Lafayette Park. From their room they could see the White House.

When they'd arrived on a Friday afternoon, she'd become upset when he carried his bag into the lobby.

"You musn't strain your heart, Walter. That's doctor's orders. You should let the bellboy carry your bag."

It moved him that she was so concerned for his health.

"You are precious to me, Walter, and you must not take chances," she said.

She took pains with his diet, made sure each morning that he took vitamins and his medication. She mothered him in a way his mother never had. For his own mother had loved him with respect and pride for his quality, but without much outward affection.

Lucy wished to tour Washington.

On Saturday morning, they went to the Phillips Collection. She held his hand as they walked from room to room. She was thrilled to see the paintings. Art had not improved much beyond the impressionists, she said.

They went to the Lincoln Memorial. As they stood looking at Lincoln in his throne-like marble chair, Walter thought of his mother. She had not cared for President Lincoln, considering how his troops had burned and looted Virginia, particularly Fredericksburg, her native home. But Walter admired Lincoln, who like Robert E. Lee was a man both noble and humane.

Afterwards, they walked along the mall to the National Gallery and looked at more paintings.

In the late afternoon, they sat on a bench along the Mall. Tired from all the touring, he was glad to get off his feet. He noted that she was as full of energy as she was first thing in the morning. It occurred to him that, after making love, it now took him nearly the whole day to recover.

"I love Washington, Walter," she said. "It's not too big or too small. It's just right. Wouldn't it be nice to have a place up here, and come up and visit, and even live here for a time?"

He was not sure it would be practical, but he did not wish to discourage her.

"Maybe we can someday."

She hugged him to her.

"I'm afraid to be so happy. It's not what I'm used to. Does that seem strange to you?"

"No, I understand the feeling. But I'll not let you be unhappy. I'll devote my life to your happiness."

She took his hand and kissed it.

"And I want you to eat right, you hear? I want you to watch your old diet and listen to your doctor, so we'll just be together forever and ever."

Since Rose Lee's death, Walter had more or less withdrawn into solitude, and he had hesitated entering his old world with a new young wife. But word of his marriage had got out, and some old friends called and said they had not wished to intrude during his grief, but now that his life had taken a happy turn, he shouldn't deprive them of seeing him and his new bride. He knew they'd want to meet her, and that was fine with him. He and Lucy couldn't hide forever. Still, he felt uneasy. He told an old friend, Mercer Huddleson, that what he'd done, marrying a woman young enough to be his granddaughter, might not be much appreciated by his old circle.

"Walter, don't you worry about that," Mercer said. "Times are changing. Why the Yankee judge on the Supreme Court married a young one, too. If you're happy, we're happy."

Walter spoke to Lucy about meeting his old friends. It was good for their marriage, he said, to live a normal life. It was time to reach out and enter society.

A party was given in their honor. His old friends were glad to see him. The women fussed over Lucy, tried to make her feel welcome. Mary Arden who had known Walter for forty years took Lucy aside. "So you are from Roanoke. Well, you just tell me about yourself. I bet you know the Woehmers down there. Wonderful people." Lucy did not know them, and she did not wish to discuss her life in Roanoke.

"I have been away from Roanoke for some time. I have lived in New York and Richmond in recent years."

"Well, isn't that nice?" Mary Arden said. "You have seen something of the world. But tell me, just how did you meet Walter, the dearest of men?"

When Lucy told her, Mary laughed and clapped her hands.

"A flat tire brought you together? That is the most wonderful thing I ever heard." And she told others, and they found it charming and fateful.

"The Good Lord is looking out for you, Walter," Arthur Laidlaw said.

"I believe so, Arthur."

The party was a huge success.

There were other occasions where they entertained and were entertained by others. But Lucy did not feel comfortable with Walter's friends.

"They are nice to my face, but I sense their condescension and disapproval. I don't like being under scrutiny, Walter. They are measuring me. At every social gathering, I feel the presence of your former wife. They are comparing, comparing. I know what they're thinking. That you married for sex and nothing more, that you have lost your mind to get tied up with me when you could have married someone like Rose Lee."

"Why, honey, you are imagining things. They like you, they all told me so, they are not comparing you to anyone."

"You always think the best of people, you are naïve that way, and I love that about you. But I can't fit in with them, and I never will. I wish we could leave here. Couldn't we live in Washington for a time? You said we might. Remember?"

He did not give up his old house in Virginia, but agreed to live in Washington. He wanted her to be happy. Any sadness on her part would upset him until her mood brightened again.

They bought a house in Cleveland Park, with a garden in the back. It was the garden she fell in love with.

"I love planting things. I start digging with my trowel, and I forget the world. I want you to know I won't be just planting flowers but vegetables, too. I'm just going to keep you so healthy you'll live forever."

She took him shopping, and urged him to buy a pair of loafers with tassels and some colorful shirts and ties. "I'm going to brighten you up, Walter. You're too long a study in Confederate gray."

He was happy and glad that she was happy. Each time she smiled was a victory for him.

He doted on her, and tried not to dote too much, fearing to appear foolish in her eyes. But, then, he knew he was foolish out of love and saw no reason to change.

Walter bought her a little red sports car. When she had first seen it in the show room, she had laughed with pleasure. "Oh, I just love it, and I love the color."

Her response so pleased him that he surprised her one day with a silk bathrobe of nearly the same shade of red.

"Walter, I adore this robe. I'll always think of you when I wear it."

On some mornings, they'd make love, and then have breakfast on the back porch overlooking the garden. Later they'd walk through the neighborhood and admire the old houses along Newark Street; and they liked Macomb Street nearly as well.

They explored Washington. One clear day, they went to the top of the Washington Monument and saw the city spread out below.

"It's so beautiful, Walter. You have made me so happy."

He loved to show her new places and talk of the past.

Some days they crossed the Potomac into Virginia. They

toured the nearby plantations. One morning, they went to Alexandria and saw Robert E. Lee's boyhood home, then walked to Christ Church where Washington and Jefferson had worshiped. Walter had seen all this before with his parents and brother when he was a boy, and had returned as a man. Rose Lee would never go with him. It was a point of contention. He so glorified Virginia, she said, that he had brushed over its slave-holding past. "Rose Lee, you misjudge me," he'd said. "Yes, I'm interested in the history. It's what I came out of. It doesn't mean that I can't change. Why, I have changed already."

"You can never change, Walter, because you have been so poisoned by your mother's notions of Southern glory that you are lost, lost, lost." But it was the past, he said, that gave meaning to his life; it did not altogether dictate his response to the present or damage his ability to think. She'd laughed at him. "You are sick, Walter, and you don't even know it. I swear you don't know which end is up. And it's all your mother's fault."

He loved the outings with Lucy. She enjoyed hearing him speak of former times. She told him that she had not been well educated in that regard. "I don't know my history, Walter, but I'm glad you're here to explain things."

In September, they drove into Maryland. He wanted to show her the battlefield of Antietam, or Sharpsburg as the Confederates called it. It was in September that the battle was fought, about a hundred years before.

"It was in 1862. Lee brought the Army of Northern Virginia into Maryland hoping to get that state into the Confederacy. There was a lot of sympathy in Maryland for the Confederate cause," Walter said. "My great uncle Albert Desmond was here with Lee and Jackson and Longstreet and both Hills, A.P. and D.H. Albert survived the battle but later died at Cold Harbor near the end of the war." He pointed out South Mountain to the west. He told her about the gaps in the mountain, Turner's Gap and Crampton's Gap, through which the Union troops came. "Albert was up the mountain with D.H. Hill's division, and they had to retreat before McClellan's superior force, but they'd held out long enough for the different parts of Lee's army to unite, and the army retreated to a valley near the town of Sharpsburg along Antietam Creek. Lee was quite surprised by McClellan's rapid advance, for he knew McClellan to be the soul of caution, but what Lee didn't know was that a Federal soldier had picked up a packet of cigars lying in the street and on the cigar wrapping was a headquarters copy of Lee's plan of action, Special Order 191. It covered the movement of his army, showing his whole battle plan, so McClellan moved fast for a change, as he knew exactly where Lee was. Can you imagine such a thing, Lucy?"

"No, Walter, I can't," she said.

"Lee was fortunate to save his army for another day."

"Well, it didn't help him. He lost in the end. "

"Yes, through no fault of his own. It was a war of attrition, and the South could not resupply. We were woefully short on manpower and material. We were an agrarian society, while the North had great wealth and industry. We had only one major armament factory, and that was in Richmond. And when Richmond fell, it was all over. But really, Lucy, it was over before that."

She did not say anything. She seemed to withdraw. He wondered if he'd talked too much, had bored her with matters about which she cared little. He was afraid that he'd displeased her.

They drove to various points along the road through the battlefield, and stopped occasionally and walked over the ground. They walked along the sunken road, passed Dunkard Church and the West Woods, and stood by the cornfield.

Walter nodded. "It looks the same as it did then. In that cornfield took place one of the greatest slaughters in the war."

She shook her head and sighed.

"War is awful. I don't know how you keep living through it time and again. It's all just so sad and gruesome and hopeless."

She said that she did not really care to see any more battlefields.

"I understand your interest, Walter, but maybe the next time you'll have to go alone."

"Honey, I'm sorry if it depressed you."

"Walter, you don't need to apologize, you've done nothing wrong."

He said that he'd not come to re-live the slaughter and agony of those times but to honor the Lost Cause and other things that he had not the eloquence to explain. "When I walk the battle-fields, I feel I'm on sacred ground," he said.

"Well, I see it all as useless," she said.

Looking back on it, Walter felt that things had changed after Antietam. For one thing, his role as her mentor had ended.

She was still a caring wife. She still prepared meals that she considered good for him. They still took their walks in the morn-ing, sat together in the garden, still made love, though less fre-quently than before and, he thought, with a more dutiful feel-ing on her part. It seemed to him that she was making an effort not to appear displeased with her life; it saddened him that effort was now required.

After a month in Washington, their excursions were less fre-quent, then stopped altogether.

She said that she needed space, more time to herself. She joined an exercise club, took an advanced painting class at the Corcoran Gallery, and shopped at Woodward and Lothrop.

Walter stayed at home. He read, he sat in the garden, he thought of how things had changed. He tried not to feel sad. Maybe, it was good for her to spread her wings. Freedom was good for marriage. He could not be her warden.

One morning when she was away, he went down to the mall. The expanse of ground between the Capitol and the Washington Monument, with its serene proportions, gave him a sense of philosophic calm.

He sat on a bench at the reflecting pool, watching children sail their boats; and he thought as the small boats were cast adrift that you could not hold on to things; that you had to let go without grievance or despair of those matters which you could not control, for change was the essence of life.

He later wrote in his journal. 'The enlarged perspective I feel at such times does not last when we're together. I feel a growing anguish. I cannot bear the thought of losing her.'

In the late fall, they went back down to Walter's home in Virginia.

It rained the entire weekend. She seemed depressed, at loose ends. He invited her to play cards, a game of rummy, which she'd once enjoyed. "No, I'd rather not," she said. "I have a headache. I don't feel well."

She sat on the porch. He sat down beside her and took her hand.

"What's wrong, honey?" he said.

She told him that she did not like the country anymore, and could not live there, even for a short time. "Not even for a day, not even for an hour." He could come down alone, if he wanted, but she would not come with him. "I just want to go back to Washington. And I want to go now. I can't wait another day."

"But we are invited out to the Ardens' this evening."

"Well, I'm not going. You can call and make some excuse. Say I'm unwell."

"Well, if you feel so strongly—."

"I do, Walter. I don't like it here. I'm sorry, but I don't. But you can stay if you want. I'll take a bus back."

"Lucy, I'll call and decline. We'll go back together in the car."

"No, I need some time alone."

"Well, then you take the car, and I'll ride the bus up in a day or two."

"Yes, I'd like that."

He went to the cemetery and spoke to the dead. It was not going well, his young wife was upset from morning to night, and he did not know what to do. "You would hardly know me now," he said. "I'm not the old Walter. I do not know who I am anymore. I've lost my self-possession."

He stopped talking and waited, then heard his father's voice.

"Walter, you can't tell about women. Don't try to understand them. You never will. You'd best be patient and wait for her to come right again."

He waited but she did not come right again.

When she walked in the house late one night, having been away since morning, he asked her to please sit down, he wished to talk to her.

She sat down with irritation.

"All right, what is it?"

"Lucy, if I've wronged you, I wish to make amends. If I've hurt you, if I've offended you in any way —"

"Stop it. You are offending me now, if you must know. Can't you leave anything alone?"

"I'm sorry you're upset."

"You upset me, Walter. You just harp on things."

"We have a problem, and I feel we should discuss it."

"You know what the problem is? You're self-centered. You think everything has to do with you."

"If I'm not the cause of your distress, then please tell me what is. It must be something."

"Will you leave me alone?"

"I love you, Lucy."

"What am I supposed to say, I love you, too?"

"Only if you mean it."

"Oh, good. Well, I don't right now, you're not being lovable."

"What have I done? I just want you to be happy."

"Oh, good. Well, I have sat long enough. I have things to do."

It went on like this into winter. She avoided him. He had not shared her bed for some time. His snoring, she said, kept her awake, she'd been deprived too long of her rest. She moved him to the guest room.

She no longer made him breakfast or lunch or any other meal. She was too busy; she was sure that he could do for himself.

He did not know what to do. It seemed that she tried to provoke him with cruelty, wished to hurt him for no reason. And why that was, he couldn't say. He'd been good to her, she'd once loved him for it, he'd done nothing wrong that he could tell. He thought maybe it was something physical, some ailment had altered her mood, some complaint peculiar to women. At the right time, he'd suggest that she see a doctor.

But then it could be there was no reason for it, or none that he could ever know.

As his father had said, "Women had their moods, and you had to honor them. A woman by her nature is more sensitive, more unstable than a man. They are constructed differently and require special handling. A woman is a mystery that no man can fathom."

One evening as he sat reading, she entered his room; he was startled by her appearance. She was smiling, with an air of apology.

"Walter, I know I've been awful. I've not felt well. I've been horrid and unkind. Can you ever forgive me?"

He was surprised and moved by her apology; he took her hand.

"Honey, I don't need to forgive you. I knew you were going though something."

"Yes, something terrible, Walter. I've been upset for so long. I only understand it now for the first time."

"What do you understand?"

"The nature of my frustration. My creativity needs release. Gardening and painting are no longer enough for me. But I know now what I need."

"And what is that?"

"I need to act, Walter. It may surprise you, but that's exactly what I need."

"You want to be on the stage?"

"Not as a career, but I want to go to acting school. I heard about an acting group in New York that starts up in the spring. I do love acting so. I can play a part, I can be somebody else. I'd tap into my own life to bring truth to the role I'd play. And I'd learn about myself. Do you understand what I'm saying?"

He did not exactly understand, or his understanding of it was not like her own. He felt suddenly let down.

"I want to do this, Walter. I'd go to New York and stay overnight. There'd be a class on the evening of the day I arrived and another the following morning."

He could hardly conceal his disappointment. But he uttered no word of protest, for he could see that her mind was made up.

"It's good for marriage to have separations," she said. "Don't you agree?"

"If that's what you require, then I agree. Though I will surely miss you while you're gone."

"I need space, Walter. I need some time of my own, and then I can come back and be married again."

"I've always tried to give you space, Lucy. I never wanted marriage to be a prison for you."

"Well, fine. I'm glad. And, Walter, I'll pay for it out of money I saved before we married."

"You don't have to. I'll pay for it, gladly."

"No, thank you. An old friend has already paid. And I'm going to pay her back."

She seemed her old self, friendly and pleasant; they took some meals together, they took walks; but he remained in the guest room, and their sex life did not resume. She hoped he'd be patient.

"I am exhausted, Walter, in body and soul. I can't deal with making love. I have been through an ordeal."

He did not wish to know more. In the best of marriages, he knew there were times so bad that you wished only to forget them.

He did not feel well. It seemed to him that his powers were failing. His memory was not what it had been. Thinking of the Battle of Gettysburg, he could not remember whether Pickett's division was in Longstreet's corps or attached to A. P. Hill's. He had angina pain that travelled down his arm, and on occasion he experienced shortness of breath, and he was bothered by vertigo.

He thought of life before Lucy, how he'd tried to keep the peace between his mother and Rose Lee, whom his mother called the arch betrayer. "You are disloyal, Rose Lee, a traitor to the memory of those who died for the Confederacy. I will never forgive you for your apostasy." "Mother Desmond, I say to you most sincerely that you are a lunatic." And Rose Lee would say to him later, "Can you believe her? Can you believe what your poor demented mother has the audacity to profess almost a hundred years after the Civil War?" Walter told Rose Lee that she might show more compassion and mercy toward someone who did not share her views. He told his mother the same. But his mother did not want to hear of compassion. "Your wife is a walking declaration of war. And I will fight her, Walter, I'll fight that turncoat till my last breath. Yes, she is your wife, but she is the enemy of all that I hold dear." He loved them both, and felt torn by their enmity, which ended only in death.

Spring came around, and the time came for Lucy to leave for New York. It was cloudy, after a night's rain. She stood in the living room holding a small suitcase. Walter tried to appear cheerful.

"Honey, let me drive you to the station," he said.

"There's no point, Walter. I'm running late, and you don't know the city. I've called a cab."

The cab arrived. He felt quite moved. It was their first real separation. Leaning inside the cab, he whispered that he loved her more each passing day.

"My goodness! You're so ardent, Walter!"

As the cab pulled away, he waved. But she was speaking to the driver and did not look back.

When she returned from New York she was sullen, nervous, easily upset; she was not glad to see him. As he tried to embrace her, she jerked away.

"You're hurting my shoulder."

"I'm so sorry," he said.

"It's very sore, and you just grabbed me, Walter. I don't like to be grabbed like that."

She unpacked and remained in her room for hours. When she came out, she hardly spoke, did not mention the acting school, or say a word about her trip.

He finally asked her how it went.

"It went fine."

"It's a good school?"

"Yes. Now I'm tired, and I need to rest."

He was disappointed. He'd looked forward to talking to her about acting, a matter that had great interest for him.

In his perplexity, he did not know what to think, he did not know what to do. He'd given her space and time to herself, he had sent her to New York with his blessing.

But the trip had not improved things, had not brought clarity to their marriage. He understood her no better, she still eluded him, he was always a step behind. In mind and body, he'd become tentative, a man who could not get his bearings.

One evening he said to her, "Honey, I never see you reading plays or books on drama. How do you prepare?"

She exploded in fury.

"What? You are questioning me? Am I on the witness stand? Well, if you must know, Mr. Lawyer, I think of my past, that's how. I think of misery I've known. I get in touch with sorrow and joy and other human emotions. I don't need to read books or plays. We conjure from the past, we create scenes of our own devising. But what could you know about actor's truth? Nothing, I'd say. God, you're so stodgy, Walter—and so ungenerous. And I don't need you cross-examining me!"

Later, he wondered if it was her painful past that had so upset her, that it had not to do with him at all. The thought gave him a fragile hope. Maybe what she needed was more time to get the misery out; she was only half-free from its effects.

One night after he'd been asleep in the guest room, the telephone rang, and he woke to hear her talking, and he heard her say, "I told you not to call me here, Trevor. I told you clearly." And she hung up. As he drifted back to sleep, he wondered who Trevor was, and why does he call so late, and why does she not want him to call her at home. In the morning he hoped he might have dreamt it, he was vulnerable to dreams and imaginings of all kinds, but he knew it was real, and he could not ignore it.

Frank Hartley nodded.

"Mr. Desmond, we can check all this out. Just give us certain information, like the train she takes to New York, and we'll need a recent photo. Do you know where she stays?"

"At the Plaza Hotel. That's where Rose Lee and I used to stay when we went up there. I have such fond memories of the place. You know, I just love New York. New Yorkers are unusual. I admire their single-minded devotion to whatever they're about. They are so alive to their purposes, big or small. Well, how'd I get off on that? You just go on up there, Mr. Hartley. I pray you bring me good news, or at least something definite that I can rely on."

Hartley had unexpected problems. He never got to the Plaza. His car broke down on the New Jersey Turnpike. It was the alternator, he said.

"Of course, I expect no payment for the time I put in. But I'll go up next week when she's there," he said.

"No, Mr. Hartley, I don't think that will be necessary. I don't think I need your services now. I thank you for your efforts, and I insist on paying you for your time."

Hartley's failure reminded him of J.E.B. Stuart. As Lee's cavalry commander, Stuart scouted the Union armies and reported their progress. When Lee had moved north up the Shenandoah Valley in 1863, Stuart remained on the eastern side of the Blue Ridge to keep an eye on Meade's army. But Stuart could not report on his movement, for he could not pass through Meade's lines to reach Lee in the Valley. Lee remained in the dark about Meade's position, and this contributed to his defeat at Gettysburg.

Lee needed Stuart but Walter did not need Hartley. He could not trust him on so delicate a mission. He could not trust another man's judgments on the matter of his wife's fidelity. Walter knew his wife, knew her nature, Hartley did not. He might see things that weren't there, could make the wrong interpretation or leave things in a state of ambiguity. No, he should have known from the start that he could not trust Hartley. He'd go himself to New York with no plan or method but his own intuition.

Walter bought a raincoat, a fedora, and a pair of dark glasses. He hid the purchases in the trunk of his car. It did not feel right. He'd always been open, disliked being devious. Though it might be all right in war, it's not what a gentleman would do in relations with his wife.

That evening, as he sat alone in the garden, he said to the flowers, "I grieve for what I'm doing. I've sunk to a low place, but I've been placed there by events not of my own making, and I have no choice but to spy on my own dear wife. May God forgive me. But I can't live with this uncertainty."

On the day she took the train to New York, he flew there.

Though it was sunny and warm all along the Atlantic seaboard, he wore his raincoat.

About five o' clock, he went to the Plaza Hotel, hoping to arrive before her.

Wearing dark glasses, his hat tipped slightly forward, he stood not far from the front desk, near a bank of elevators. He held a newspaper before his face. As he peered between the top edge of the paper and the brim of his hat, he felt absurd, like the worst kind of fool. He hated his disguise, felt disreputable and dishonest, thought at any moment he'd be asked to leave the hotel.

Sweating under his raincoat, he moved to a place at the edge of the Palm Court, where he could view the entrance, while remaining concealed.

An hour passed. He wondered if she'd stopped off someplace or gone to another hotel altogether.

He was surprised to see someone he knew sitting alone at a table in the Palm Court. It was Irma Braverson, Rose Lee's old classmate at Wellesley College. She looked thin and drawn. He was startled by how she'd aged since he'd last seen her at Rose Lee's funeral a few years before; he wondered if she'd been ill, or suffered a loss over which she was still in grief. He'd always liked Irma, and he wished he could have renewed their old acquaintance. Years before, Rose Lee had invited Irma down to Virginia for a visit, and he remembered how kind and pleasant she had been. After she'd gone back to New York, his mother and Rose Lee had gotten into an argument.

"Why must you generalize so about Yankees?" Rose Lee had said. "The truth is that intelligent Northerners are far more realistic and moral and balanced as a general rule than the white people of the South. So don't you dare try to make a demon out of Irma."

"I do no such thing, Rose Lee. I concede that she is a young woman of refinement and good family, but she is misinformed and ignorant of our history. Why, she knew nothing at all about the atrocity of Reconstruction after the War Between the States. She knew nothing of the vengeful treatment we received at the hands of the Yankees. It is no wonder that the South went slightly mad and did some regrettable things. But you have to see the provocation to understand that, and I'm afraid where she's from they don't teach the true history, and it's no wonder she has a biased view. She's a product of her distorted education."

"I can always count on you, Mother Desmond, to twist things around to suit yourself."

"As always, it is you who do the twisting, Rose Lee."

He watched Irma rise from her table and walk through the lobby and leave the hotel through a revolving door, and then with surprise Walter saw the same door bring in Lucy and a male companion. The man, ruddy and slight, appeared to be in his forties. He carried her suitcase.

They entered the Palm Court and sat down at a table near where Irma had been. The man, self-assured and relaxed, had the sort of easy charm that Walter feared was particularly appealing to women. He wondered if this was Trevor.

After the waiter took their order, the man began talking. He spoke for some time with eloquent gestures and changes of expression. Whatever he was saying seemed to make a great impression on Lucy. Her eyes shining, she nodded, shook her head, smiled with amazement, or looked grave. Walter noted with anguish that she gave the man the sort of rapt and adoring attention that she'd once given to him. He felt old and graceless and dull by comparison. It would be natural if she preferred this younger man; they were perfectly suited for one another. But he fought his jealous impression. He knew her, understood her nature. She was simply the ideal listener; it's what he'd first loved about her, it was a gift that she had; and he tried not to make more of it than was there. The man was no doubt an aspiring actor. He'd moved her by his performance, it went no deeper.

But when Lucy took his hand and kissed it, and touched his face with a caress, Walter felt a jealousy and anger so fierce that he wanted to run in and kick over their table and smash their cups and saucers, to grab them and shout, "How dare you both!" but fearing public embarrassment, he clutched the lapels of his raincoat to steady himself.

When they left the Palm Court, Walter followed them.

They went to the front desk. Lucy registered. He heard the clerk say, "Madame, you're in 812."

Walter watched them get on the elevator. He felt a huge weight bearing down on his head and shoulders, his hands were trembling; he pulled a handkerchief from his pocket and squeezed it to stop the trembling, then wiped the perspiration from his face.

He went to the Oak Bar. He needed to sit down and quiet his nerves and consider what he then must do. Feeling a tightness in his chest, he had a shot of bourbon; and the tightness eased. He tried to understand what he'd witnessed. But then it did not require much thought, he understood already. It was clear, it was obvious. How could he ever explain it away? She'd kissed his hand, touched his face with great tenderness. They'd gone up to her room. What more did he require? He'd seen enough, he'd suffered enough, he could leave and go home, but then he thought, 'Walter, you could be wrong, if you leave now you'll never know for certain, there is still room for doubt, a kiss or touch in itself cannot be considered final proof of anything, life is full of strangeness, friendship has many guises, the man might have seen her to her room as a courtesy, carried her suitcase to relieve her of a burden, or perhaps, and this was not farfetched at all, they'd need her room to prepare a scene in private, a scene of their own devising, before leaving for their acting class; they could not do this in a public place.'

He had another drink. It began to take hold. He closed his eyes, and in a drowsy half-dream state, he saw himself as a boy running down a deserted road with his brother, Weber. The sun was shining, and they were laughing, but there were storm clouds over the Blue Ridge. And Weber said, "Walter, we better get on home before the lightning strikes."

He placed the cold glass against his forehead, and took a deep breath and wondered what he should do now. He didn't know one thing for certain. He'd come all this way with nothing to show for his trouble. Sick at heart, humiliated by his own indecision, he thought, 'I must take some bolder action. I've got to face it, whatever it is.'

And then Walter formed the only plan that made sense to him. He'd stand outside the door of her room. Behind that door was the truth that would end all speculation and doubt. 'If I stood there, just looking at the door, something would happen, it would all come clear,' he thought.

He got on the elevator and went up to the eighth floor.

Faint with exhaustion, having not eaten since early morning, still affected by the bourbon, he stood outside the door to her room and listened. He hoped to hear some harmless talk with no hint of passion. But there was no sound from the room.

And he thought, 'Walter, what is now appropriate?' And he could not think of anything civil. He could pound the door, demand entry, and shout bloody murder. But it was alien to his gentle nature, to his sense of dignity, and even if he could do such a thing, he thought, 'What if I'm wrong? I'd ruin everything, there'd be no hope for us, not ever again. And maybe they're just talking, but in these old hotels, the rooms had good thick walls, ordinary conversation would not carry.'

Then he thought, it was possible that the man was not there at all. He could have seen her to her room and then left. He could have come down while he was still seated in the bar. Or while he came up in the elevator, the man could have been going down.

He should have not let them out of his sight. He'd blundered, he thought, as he'd blundered in so many ways. And he knew why: he'd lost his moral compass, did the wrong thing as naturally as breathing, sought error as the moth sought the lamp.

To ease the humiliation of lurking like some madman in a hotel hallway, to make less painful the sorrowful possibility of losing her, he tried to enlarge his perspective, to see himself as part of the vast community of human suffering. What was happening to him happened to everyone. It was the common experience of mankind to suffer. And he was no exception. It was all vanity.

But hard as he tried to see his predicament in a new light, he could only think, 'Is the man in there with Lucy, and what are they doing? And how in God's name have I sunk so low?'

He heard the clatter of a room service cart.

Stepping away from the door, he saw a waiter moving in his direction.

Walter walked toward him, passed the cart, saw champagne in an ice bucket, glasses, and some covered dishes.

When he heard the cart stop, he looked back and saw the waiter outside Lucy's room. He pushed the buzzer by her door.

"What is it?" a male voice said.

"Room service."

"Leave it outside."

"Yes, sir."

As the waiter passed by him on his way to the elevator, Walter stood facing the door of a nearby room. He pretended to look for his key.

Then alone in the hall again, less than twenty feet from her door, he stood with his back against the wall and waited.

When the door opened, he heard her voice for the first time.

"Oh, darling, come here," she said.

A man's bare arm reached out. On top of his arm was Lucy's arm, in the sleeve of her red silk bathrobe.

"Champagne. Oh, good," she said, as the cart was pulled in and the door closed.

Walter was too weary and shattered and heartsick to do anything more than just stand there a few moments before walking slowly to the elevator. What he felt most was not injured pride or rage but disillusionment with another person, and for that there was no remedy.

What had happened did not seem possible when he married her. This Lucy who'd once loved him, been so concerned for his health that she'd read books on coronary disease, who'd made sure he took no foolish risks, she'd done this. But he should have known that nothing lasts, that everything changes.

Walter waited in the lobby.

When they came out of the elevator, he watched them go into the Oak Bar. After they were seated, he waited a few minutes, then took off his raincoat, removed his hat and dark glasses, and entered the bar.

They were at a small table.

She saw him. She brought her hand to her throat and made an effort to smile.

"Why, Walter. What a surprise. You just came to New York, did you? Trevor, this is my husband, Walter."

Trevor stood up, saw it all at once.

"Sorry. Must leave. I'm late for something."

He smiled, nodded, then walked away.

Walter watched him leave, then sat down. He regarded the tabletop, took a deep breath, then looked up at her.

"I can see why he left so abruptly. He could not feign to be comfortable with me. Don't deny it, Lucy. I know he's your lover."

"Why, Walter, that's not—"

"Don't say anything. Not a word. I was outside your room when the waiter came. I heard you speak. I caught a glimpse of your bathrobe when your lover opened the door."

She began to cry.

"You are a fine little actress," he said. "I think you have found your true calling." Then regretting his sarcasm as something unworthy and unkind, he waved his hand to disclaim it. "Well, I'm leaving. You can stay at the house in Washington. I'm going down to the country. We'll work it out with lawyers."

He walked out and did not look back. He'd not been so purposeful since before he'd met her.

He called his lawyer to prepare a settlement. He wished no delay, sought no reconciliation. He wanted to live in peace in the time he had left.

Lucy did not stay in the house in Washington but returned to Roanoke, where she lived with an elderly aunt.

After more than a month had passed, she wrote to him.

She'd lied about everything. She'd never gone to acting school. It was a lie from beginning to end.

Nothing could excuse what she'd done, but she'd been suffering from depression, thinking of death, of how life was short. She'd lost her father, her mother had died of cancer, and she was afraid he'd die on her, too, and then she'd met Trevor at this low point in her life.

"It was an accidental meeting, much like ours had been. It was in the fall. He was an actor, appearing in a play at the National, and one afternoon he showed up at the Corcoran. I was there looking at paintings, and he just came up beside me and began to speak about art. He was so easy and engaging, Walter. He asked me to have tea, and it all seemed so innocent. We became friends, and in time lovers. But when his play closed, he went back to New York. I missed him. No, I longed for him. I couldn't seem to do without him. And so I made up the story about acting school. I know it was a mean deception. I was awful to you. Believe me when I say I loathed myself. And I loathed you as well for your patience and long-suffering, which made me loathe myself even more. Yes, I despised myself. But I want you to know, Walter, however strange this might sound, that I truly longed to be a good wife. And I thought I could be and have Trevor, too. But I was sorely mistaken. I could not give myself happily to two men.

"I don't ask for forgiveness. I don't deserve it.

"I'm sorry to have hurt you. You are good and deserve only good from others.

"I ask for nothing. I don't want a dollar or a dime."

Walter did not reply, but through his lawyer gave her a generous settlement.

He felt responsible, he'd caused the misery, it was his fault. He should have known better than to have married her; but he'd denied his own perceptions and the experience of a lifetime. And therein lay the tragedy.

He sold the house in Washington and moved back to the country.

He lived a quiet life, not straying far from home. He went to town for supplies, read the novels of Thomas Hardy and works on the Civil War. He sat on his porch.

Most days he walked to the cemetery.

On occasion, he saw old friends, and they talked of former times.

He lived mostly in the past.

Rose Lee was often on his mind. Their differences seemed nostalgic now and sadly humorous. He felt affection for her memory, enjoyed thinking of her manner and her turn of phrase. 'Walter, do not walk backwards into the modern age' and 'What a poor old relic you are!'

He loved her as he loved a story in a book which he could read and ponder at his pleasure.

He thought of his mother and father, of his brother, Weber, of friends and family, of the living and the dead, but mainly the dead.

When he thought of Lucy, he felt a confusion of feelings.

Along with grief and remorse, he felt the anguish from not only what she'd done to him but what he'd done to himself. He had pursued a happiness that any clear-eyed man could see was hopeless and tragic. She might have betrayed him but he'd also betrayed himself. He'd not soon forget the events in New York. The memories of his disguise, of his furtiveness, were among the most painful of his life. He had demeaned himself. He tried to remember where he had precisely crossed into error and made the fatal misjudgment to marry. But he could not remember. He could only rue that it had ever happened.

But there were mornings he'd look down to where her car had pulled over and remember when they were in love, walked arm in arm, and she hoped he'd live forever.

On a fall day, the sky like slate, he nearly fainted while walking through the woods. He knelt down to steady himself. Listening to the wind in the trees, he thought he might die; and it surprised him that he felt no fear of death, that he was ready to go at any time.

But his head cleared, and he rose up and walked home, and went about his life as before.

Winter came.

On a cold, clear morning, with no mist or fog on the Blue Ridge, Walter died suddenly.

His heart failed at the family cemetery while speaking to the dead.

"Mama, I read something that might amuse you," he said, then collapsed among the gravestones.

He was found by a man walking on the road adjacent.

The day before, he'd written in his journal. 'Looking back on my life, I see that error was no stranger to me. I have been foolish, I have made mistakes, I have acted against my better judgment, I have caused harm. I have gone wrong any number of times. But what truly matters is to admit one's wrongs and make amends, and to suffer with grace the sorrows in one's life.

'I can truly say that I'm at peace tonight. And I look forward to the morrow.'

The day of his death, a letter arrived from New Mexico. Lucy wrote that she'd joined an art community in Taos. Art was the one thing that made her happy for it came from inside her and did not depend on others. She wrote that it was all over with Trevor. She had enclosed a small Indian carving. "I think it's Zuni. I hope it brings you luck." She asked him to please take care of himself. "Walter, you were the best friend I ever had."